It's high summer in Oxford. The university vacation has just begun. The eight governors of the Moneybuckle Endowment (an architectural library) are assembling at All Saints College for the annual dinner before their meeting under chairman Mark Treasure, merchant banker. The talk at table is of some pricey sketches said to be by Constable, and on offer from a dealer in the town. Only the talk turns to shock when murder's done in Walton Street with the sketches as clear motive. The police are quick to make an arrest, but Treasure is sure they've got the wrong suspect – even though all other likely culprits are Moneybuckle governors, or Moneybuckle's Custodian himself.

So what links a fire in Peking with a yellow bicycle? Or a professor's fetish and a family Bible? Or a pair of silver handcuffs with a young woman's love-life?

Treasure fans expect a puzzle literately and lyrically presented, and they won't be disappointed. The characters are finely drawn and juxtapositioned, the place endearingly described, and the fulcrum of the plot (this time John Constable and his single Oxford visit) is, as always, well researched and digestibly interwoven with the mystery.

Reviewing David Williams' last book, *Divided Treasure*, John Coleman in *The Sunday Times* wrote: 'Complex plot, dovetailed with commendable, dependable wit' – the same tale that William Weaver in *The Financial Times* summed up as 'completely convincing. Tasty fare'. Here's more from the same pot.

by the same author

UNHOLY WRIT
TREASURE BY DEGREES
TREASURE UP IN SMOKE
MURDER FOR TREASURE
COPPER, GOLD & TREASURE
TREASURE PRESERVED
ADVERTISE FOR TREASURE
WEDDING TREASURE
MURDER IN ADVENT
TREASURE IN ROUBLES
DIVIDED TREASURE

:

TREASURE
IN OXFORD

David Williams

M
**MACMILLAN
LONDON**

First published in 1988 by
MACMILLAN LONDON LIMITED
4 Little Essex Street London WC2R 3LF
and Basingstoke

Associated companies in Auckland, Delhi, Dublin,
Gaborone, Hamburg, Harare, Hong Kong, Johannesburg,
Kuala Lumpur, Lagos, Manzini, Melbourne, Mexico City,
Nairobi, New York, Singapore and Tokyo.

British Library Cataloguing in Publication Data

Williams, David, 1926–
    Treasure in Oxford.
    I. Title
    823'.914[F]

    ISBN 0–333–47597–6

Typeset by Matrix, London WC2

Printed and bound in England by
Richard Clay Ltd, Chichester, Sussex.

This one for
Bob and Joyce Haslam

Chapter One

'Move yourself, Marilyn, we're late this morning,' said Decimus Radout, giving the object of his address a friendly nudge on the bottom.

Marilyn shot an archly appreciative glance backward, before tripping lightly through the opened front door, down the two steps and into the small and scruffy front garden of 16 Arcady Road in North Oxford. After a brief and customary enquiry into alternative spots, more a gesture to enduring instinct than to demonstrate any serious intent to change the habit of a lifetime, she then settled beside a long-suffering but surprisingly resilient rhododendron bush, sighed, and piddled all over the root.

Dr Radout stayed framed in the doorway, but now averted his gaze from the indelicately placed Norwich terrier – in response to her reproachful stare.

A good deal of the doctor's slight, five foot eight inches was shrouded in a sombre, ancient Jaeger dressing gown, tied about the waist by a shredding cord that had once had tassles. High summer was an unsuitable time of year for so warm a garment, except it did for all seasons and more than satisfied the proprieties. The touch of cotton primrose pyjama showing at the neck and below – crinkled above one ankle but not evident at all above the other – was more appropriate to the season, as well as the wearer's disposition and present air of light contentment.

It is the end of June – the time when Oxford takes a short breather, when students and their instructors are

7

for the most part pleased to quit the place and each other, when the colleges empty before the summer schools begin, when the university dourly contemplates and the city hopefully estimates the size of the tourist hordes shortly to descend upon both. But for now the bicycles have departed, while the motor coaches have scarcely arrived in strength. Blackwell's and the other Broad Street bookshops have already increased the displays of guide books. The Commemoration Ball tents have been put away. The sound of pop music, live and recorded, will pierce the night air now with less frequency, and in less strident competition than during the recent term-end.

But the sun stays high at noonday, and the evenings remain balmy. It seldom rains – more often of course than it did fifty years ago when the summers were hotter and drier, as those old enough to remember are always eager to attest. Even so, the walks in the college groves, through the meadows, along the river banks, across the parks, are decked in green, and full of blooms and rich with scents, and the drones of bees and the songs of birds – an idyllic prospect with people hardly intruding at all to spoil things: well, *other* people, that is.

The peace that has descended has nowhere landed more softly than in Arcady Road. It is one of the succession of quiet, short, crossing avenues which, like ascending treads to a ladder, link the Banbury and the Woodstock Roads on their nearly parallel northern progresses, from their beginnings at wide St Giles above the city centre. Shaded Arcady is solid late Victorian, all red brick, dressed stone, and low street walls with copings un-skimped if sometimes a bit loose in places. It is also overgrown with mature ash and limes whose exposed roots make giant intaglio designs with irrupted paving stones under humpily parked motor-cars.

Number 16 had been the home of Decimus Radout (Doctor of Fine Art, not Medicine) for longer than the recollections of any of his neighbours. When the Radout children had been growing up, the family had occupied

8

the whole house. Decimus and his wife had later had the place converted into three flats, keeping the lower one for themselves. Now seventy-six years old, a widower for the last five, the doctor had stayed on here out of choice after retiring from his Fellowship of All Saints College. He still had his writing, still needed the museums and the libraries for his research – and he still loved Oxford more than any other place on earth. Nowadays, he loved it even more during this summer time of quietude when half the residents of Arcady Road were away.

It was not that the doctor courted solitude – only that he enjoyed change in human contact, and the next two days were to provide plenty of that. Tonight there was the Moneybuckle Dinner, followed tomorrow afternoon by the meeting of the Moneybuckle governors. Although he had been divested of all other official college and university appointments, Dr Radout was still the college's nominated Moneybuckle governor, from which there was no retirement age. Although being one of the eight governors was an unpaid appointment, and one requiring little involvement, it was still a formal function that he cherished, and not because it was the only one he had left.

Marilyn made a token effort at covering her traces with a brisk scrape of her back paws at the bare, baked earth, then tripped importantly up the steps and into the hall, glancing up at her master through eyes coyly fringed with the fairest of hairs – a beguiling feature of her breed.

'Good girl.' He was closing the street door, then stiffened as he caught sight of the crouched figure moving suddenly and quickly from behind a tree in the street.

Head well down, the man rushed the open double gateway to Number 16, tripped on the central iron gate-stop, staggered toward the door, and righted himself in time to take the steps and push past the doctor into the outer hall.

'Don't think anyone saw me, Doctor.' The tone was deep and Oxfordshire-accented.

'At seven-fifteen one wouldn't expect. Does it matter? Good morning, Mr Cormit.'

If it had been a fellow academic, junior to the speaker – and almost everyone was nowadays – the appendage of 'Mr' would have been omitted. Since it was Ernest Cormit, retired staff sergeant in the regular Royal Air Force and sensitive about his social standing, Radout eschewed what the other might regard as a demeaning mode of address.

'G'morning, Doctor. Didn't want you coming to the shop, see? In case.' He tapped at the large envelope in his hand, and nodded like a conspirator. 'In case of being overheard,' he shouted, debiting the doctor's earlier blank look to deafness, not incomprehension – something Cormit did regularly. This usually irritated Radout. He was quite deaf, without being that deaf.

Cormit kept a second-hand bookshop in a terraced house in Walton Street. He was in his mid-fifties, divorced, and lived above the shop – nominally alone, but the neighbours would have reported differently. Of medium height, with a sallow complexion, sharp features, and dark pomaded hair, he was wearing a brown seersucker suit, an RAF tie – and a handle-bar moustache meant to indicate that he had been an aviator, not a groundling member of the supply branch.

'Marilyn takes in more than you'd guess, but she's very circumspect,' said Radout gravely, a twinkle in the lowered grey eyes. He shut the door, absently running one hand across his temple and above it, through the unparted shock of soft white hair.

At the sound of her name, Marilyn wiggled her rear-end impatiently: breakfast was now overdue.

Cormit gave a half-smile to the rejoinder about the animal, in case the old boy meant it: you couldn't always tell with the professor sort, not at that age. 'I was careful because we don't want the collectors queueing up, do we, Doctor?' he offered, still too loudly.

'I sometimes think you do my reputation too much honour, Mr Cormit. And possibly even your own,' the

10

other added dryly. 'First edition, is it?' He eyed the brown envelope speculatively. He was a distinguished art historian, but his late collecting passion was for rare books – still a much cheaper indulgence than investing in pictures.

'It's not a book, Doctor.'

Radout's face evinced a lowered expectancy. 'Why don't you join me for a cup of coffee?' He led the way through the open doorway to the lower flat, closed it behind them, then followed Marilyn down the passage and the stairs to the kitchen in the half-basement.

'It's your opinion I'm after, Doctor,' Cormit continued when they were both seated at the table with mugs of coffee, while Marilyn scoffed cereal in milk from a bowl in the corner. 'Your opinion on some pictures. Whether I should let them go for what I've been offered.' He gave an embarrassed cough. 'I'd expect to pay, of course. To pay,' he repeated loudly, with accentuated lip movement.

'No need to shout, I'm not deaf.' Radout paused, then shrugged. 'Well let's see what you've got.' The tone was noncommittal.

He rarely authenticated works of art for commercial purposes. For someone of his standing to attribute a picture to a noted artist could multiply its value a thousand times or more. For a museum curator he was usually prepared to offer an objective opinion without reward, but he generally avoided providing attributions for dealers. Doing so for a fee put a price on his reputation; doing so for no fee did the same in a negative sense.

The doctor took a pair of gold-rimmed half-spectacles from a case he had fished from his dressing-gown pocket. He doubted that whatever Cormit had come upon was likely to make or break reputations. Second-hand book dealers were not a normal source of lost old masters: this one was not even a very respected member of that trade, though one Radout had charitably tried to help in the past.

11

Cormit had withdrawn three small folders from the envelope, opened each in turn and placed it on the table before his host.

There were two sketches in pencil and one in oils. The pencil items were the same size – about four-and-a-half by seven inches, the viewer judged. The paper they were on was yellowed. The oil sketch was on card and an inch or so larger all round than the others. It was also mounted – narrowly on thick paper. It depicted the same easily iden-tifiable subject as one of the pencil drawings – a bridge with a tower beyond. But for fear anyone should be in doubt, the artist, or someone, had scribbled 'Oxford Bridge, June 10. 1821' in the top left-hand corner of the pencilled ver-sion. On the second pencil drawing – of a different and wider landscape – in the same corner, the same hand had inscribed 'Christ Church, Oxford, June 9. 1821'.

Radout's eyebrows had lifted slightly at first sight of the exhibits, but he made no comment, only grunted from time to time while he slowly examined all three. Then he turned them over to look at the backs.

'There's handwriting on the back of all of them,' Cormit put in, nervously breaking the silence. His mouth gave an involuntary twitch.

'Yes, I see that,' replied Radout, studying the reverse of the oil sketch. The mount had in turn been pasted over with a sheet of light-grey paper. 'This study of Oxford Bridge – it's Magdalen Bridge of course – it has, "To David Lucas. Believe this better. Compare", followed by what looks like . . . ' He stopped, squinting at the faded surface and moving it to catch a different aspect of the light.

'"October 20. 1830,"' blurted Cormit, clearly unable to contain himself. 'The pencil drawing of the bridge says, "Sent to David Lucas, August 5. 1830." That's nearly three months before.'

Radout looked up at the speaker impassively to indi-cate he found that deduction less than astonishing, then returned his gaze to the picture.

12

'The writing's a bit faded,' Cormit offered, massaging his hands anxiously.

'Hmm. As you'd expect.' Radout paused, then picked up the other pencil drawing. 'This is a long view of Christ Church Cathedral across the Meadows. Much more characteristic,' he added, almost to himself. Then he held it up to the light, as he had with the other, looking for a watermark in the paper.

'How d'you mean, Doctor?'

'He didn't much care for drawing buildings in close-up,' the other replied absently.

'Who didn't, Doctor?'

There being no immediate response to this eager question, Cormit then volunteered. 'On the back of the Christ Church drawing it says— '

'"Walked here early with John Fisher,"' Radout provided. 'Very early. Yes.' Now he spread the three sketches in front of him, facing upwards. 'They're very beautiful, Mr Cormit.' He smiled.

'But are they by ... by John Constable? The dates fit.'

'By John Constable, you say?' The doctor affected half surprise.

'Wasn't that who you meant? Just now?'

'Perhaps. I forget. You know Constable's currently considered the most seminal English landscape painter of all?' The comment was almost reproachful. 'Fashion could change that, of course.' He punctuated with a short grunt. 'Well now, one is tempted to ask, does it matter if they're by Constable? Will they give us more aesthetic pleasure if they are, d'you suppose?' He was amused at the growing look of consternation on his visitor's face. 'But of course it matters to you, my dear Mr Cormit. If you own these beautiful studies. So. I should say I think they could be by Constable. Obviously we're intended to think they are. There again ... ' Now he was staring at the oil sketch, shaking his head.

13

'Constable was in Oxford in June eighteen twenty-one,' Cormit broke in. 'After he'd done a tour of the Berkshire archdeaconary. With his friend Archdeacon Fisher. John Fisher. It was Constable's only visit here. Ever,' he said, almost in one breath.

'Obviously you've read it up more recently than I have. In Leslie's *Life of Constable*, perhaps?' The doctor frowned. 'As I recall, the only known artistic product of the visit is a pencilled sketch of University College.'

'That's right, Doctor. That's in London. In the British Museum. I've been to see it. It's dated on the front as well. June 9. 1821. The day he did the drawing in Christ Church Meadows. The day before the other two.'

'The day before the pencil drawing of Magdalen Bridge was done, certainly,' Radout corrected. 'The oil sketch of the bridge may have been painted on a different day. A succeeding day probably. Say June the eleventh? Assuming it was done from life.' At the end, he seemed to be debating with himself.

'I don't understand,' said Cormit warily. Nor did he understand: there had been no advance briefing on the point.

'As I recall, there's nothing in his letters to show he stayed on in Oxford after June the ninth?'

'That's right, Doctor. And nothing to show he didn't either.' He changed to a questioning expression. 'Why couldn't he have done the oil of the bridge on the tenth? The same day as the pencil drawing?'

Radout was comparing the two treatments of the same subject as he replied, 'Because of his utter artistic integrity, Mr Cormit. His commitment to reflect the perfections of nature. The effects of natural light as he saw them, when he saw them.'

'So they couldn't have been done the same day?'

'Unlikely. Because they were quite evidently not done at quite the same *time* of day. The oil was made at early light, but in the way of things he would have done the

14

pencil sketch first, then the oil, because he'd warmed to the subject. More coffee?'

'No thanks, Doctor. There's plenty of references in his letters to an Oxford Sketchbook. It was a small book. And the cover had a drawing on it. Of Oxford Bridge. It was lent to the Archdeacon later, then returned, but there's nothing about it after that.'

'Because it's most likely to have been broken up?'

'There've been no separate sketches either, Doctor. Not till now. Not that anyone knows about. Except the one at the British Museum, and that's probably from a different book. It's bigger than these.'

'Because Constable called it his Oxford Sketchbook doesn't mean it had nothing but sketches of Oxford in it. Except, I suppose, it suggests there'd be more than one.' Radout poured himself more coffee from the electric percolator on the table. 'If one knew how long he was here, one would have some guide to the extent of the work.'

'But there are still the references to one sketch of Oxford Bridge, Doctor. And I've got two. I've only got to prove they were done by Constable.'

'The painting will be easier to authenticate than the drawings. Certainly in terms of date,' Radout offered carefully. 'It would have been easier still if it had been painted on canvas. Paper is the very Devil to date.' He frowned. 'Do you want to tell me how you came by these sketches?'

'A house clearance, Doctor. Semi-detached cottage off Iffley Road. After a death. I nearly didn't bother. Except the bloke who got the clearance job from the estate agent, he usually offers me first choice of any books. He said there was a few good-looking old volumes. More than you'd expect from a hard-up spinster. Ninety-two she was. So I went and had a look. Took away a case of books. Paid cash. On the spot. The sketches were in the back of the family Bible. Tucked in, like. I always take a family Bible where offered. This time it paid off.'

'You believe you have true ownership of the sketches?'

The other's eyes narrowed. 'No doubt of that, Doctor. I know the law.' But he had hesitated before replying.

'Mm. And the dead spinster was?'

'Selina Mary Smith. Used to be a primary school teacher. Her father was George Wesley Smith. Groom in private service. Born eighteen thirty-eight. In Northampton. Died in London. He married twice. Both times to Northampton girls. They were in domestic service as well. With the same family.'

'You got all this from birth and marriage certificates?'

'More from death certificates.' Cormit corrected with exaggerated solemnity.

'Of course. So you've been busy researching?'

'In a way, Doctor. Really, the best stuff came from that family Bible. From the family history they kept in it. The Bible's over a hundred and fifty years old. There's a blank section between the Old and New Testaments. For filling in by hand. For family events like. You can see from that the Smiths worked for the Lucas family for generations.'

'The Lucases also came from Northampton.' It was a statement not a question.

'You'd know that of course, Doctor.' The speaker beamed.

'They were farming people. But they didn't stay in Northampton or farming.'

'Some of them did, Doctor. Not David Lucas. The one whose name's on the back of those sketches. He went to London. To Chelsea. He was an engraver. Constable's engraver.'

'But I'm afraid that would have been earlier than George Wesley Smith could possibly have gone to London. I'd guess the David Lucas who worked with Constable first went to London soon after eighteen-twenty.'

'It was George Wesley Smith's uncle who went with Lucas. That's what I've worked out.'

'I see. But you believe other Smiths followed?'

'Like I say, they went on serving the Lucas family in London and the country.'

16

'Hm. If you can prove a link that way between your Selina Smith and John Constable, it could possibly help with the provenance of the sketches. Tenuous but, yes, possible.'

'That's what I hoped you'd say, Doctor. So if you think the sketches are by Constable . . . '

'Could be by him,' Radout corrected sharply, but more impressed and excited by what he had seen than he cared to show. 'The technique seems very similar to his.' He looked up over his glasses. 'It happens Julian Barners will be in Oxford tonight. You know who he is?'

'The art expert?'

Radout nodded. 'The Constable expert. I shall be dining with him at All Saints. He's staying at the college.'

'That's to do with the Moneybuckle, Doctor?'

'Yes. Barners' opinion would be better than mine.' And also more commercial in all senses, he thought, wondering what kind of consultation fee might be involved. 'I could mention the sketches to him at dinner, if you like?'

'Please, Doctor. Could I leave them with you to show him?'

'I'd rather you kept them to show him yourself. If he wants to see them. And I certainly don't want you leaving them here. They could be quite valuable. Well, I'm sure you're aware of that.' Radout was putting the sketches back into their folders as he spoke.

'A dealer in Bond Street offered me twenty thousand pounds for the three on Tuesday, Doctor.'

Radout's eyebrows lifted. 'He was taking a risk. But, then, so would you be if you'd accepted. You haven't done so?'

'No, Doctor. If they're genuine, you reckon they're worth more?'

'Good Heavens, yes. If they're Constables. I'd expect the oil sketch alone to fetch many times that at Sotheby's or Christie's.'

The visitor's gasp sounded genuine, but Radout found it incongruous that Cormit should not have known the going price of a good quality Constable oil sketch. He made no more of the point then, when perhaps he should have done. At the time he was needing the rest of his breakfast – and Marilyn was indicating her morning walk was overdue.

Chapter Two

Arthur Midden turned over his newspaper, glanced at the clock, and belched loudly.

'Arthur, really!' exclaimed Val, his wife, more from habit than surprise. 'How the time does fly,' she added, as though underlining the inconsequence of the protest. She went on gathering up the dirty plates from the table.

The Middens had just finished breakfast in the rear extension of the tall, stuccoed terrace house in St John Street. This was half a mile south of Dr Radout's, and close to the centre of Oxford. Most of the upstairs accommodation in the house was let in term time to students – by the room, not the floor.

Val Midden was an Oxford landlady registered by the university, and a well-respected member of that formidable corps. She was a jolly, middle-aged woman, with naturally rosy cheeks, and a comely figure that was only now beginning to run to plumpness.

Her husband was Senior Common Room butler at nearby All Saints College, on the far side of St Giles. When on duty, his short figure invariably dressed in black jacket and striped trousers, Arthur Midden was over-elaborate in speech, pointedly observant, and properly obsequious to the right people. In many respects, he might have been cast for the butler's rôle in a Hollywood film. His round face was pallid and jowled, while his mouth sagged down at the sides – all of which served to cancel out the warmth suggested by the dimples. The few surviving long strands of hair crossing his head accentuated more than disguised the extent of his horse-shoe baldness.

He was smoothing the hairs when he belched again. 'Kippers always bugger up my belly,' he observed: his language was never coarse in college.

'Did you see the bit about Selina Smith in the paper?' Mrs Midden asked as she scraped the fishbones into the bin.

He turned back to the obituary page. It was the evening paper he was reading, appropriated as usual from the SCR late the night before. The Middens got their papers for nothing – late, and second-hand, but still for nothing. Mrs Midden reckoned this was a false economy: she liked to read her horoscope in advance of the day intended. She didn't care so much about the news: they got that mostly from the television.

'Says she was ninety-three. Ninety-two, I thought,' said Midden.

'Didn't matter much at that age, did it? Poor old dear. I could never get over the way she hung on in that cottage.'

Years before, the Middens had lived next door to Selina Smith in South Oxford, beyond Magdalen Bridge. That had been before Arthur Midden had first been employed at All Saints. Val had continued to befriend Selina, taking the bus to see her regularly in the later years. The Middens didn't keep a car.

'Took her to hospital in the end, did you say?'

Mrs Midden sighed at the question from where she was standing over the sink. 'Because she was supposed to have pneumonia. Pneumonia in June. I ask you?' She stacked another rinsed dish to dry in the holder. She could have done with a dishwasher, but her husband failed to see the need, even in term time when she did breakfasts for the students upstairs.

'Those cottages were damp. I always said.'

'She only lasted the two days in hospital. Not from lack of care, I dare say. Just worn out, she was.' Mrs Midden's Oxfordshire rolled 'r' gave the phrasing added poignancy. 'Yes, worn out,' she repeated.

20

'It says here there are no known living relatives.'

'That's right. Won't be many people at the funeral, I don't suppose. It's on Monday. Well, we'll see.' She doubted her husband would see because she doubted he'd be going. 'She was much loved in her time. But most of her friends are dead. And there aren't many of her old pupils still living in Oxford. I expect Ernie will go to the funeral,' she ended pointedly.

Ernest Cormit, second-hand book dealer, was Mrs Midden's half-brother, younger than her by three years.

'Oh yes,' Midden commented guardedly, believing his wife was wrong about Cormit's likely attendance. It would only point to a close connection he knew his brother-in-law would not want advertised.

'Nice lot of books he got. Didn't pay much, I shouldn't think,' said Mrs Midden.

'Fair price, he told me.'

She gave a sharp sniff at this appraisal. 'He offered for some of them back in January. Selina said so. She wasn't interested. I'll bet he paid a lot less now she's dead.'

'There's an executor to see fair play. Her minister, Ernie told me. She left everything to that chapel.'

'They deserve it, too. The chapel kept her going,' said Mrs Midden. 'She didn't have many callers towards the end, except for the minister and his wife.'

'What about you?'

'I didn't go that often. Fair play, Ernie went quite a few times. Good of him, really.'

'There's good in everybody,' Midden offered sanctimoniously, but without consciously intending to ascribe virtue to Ernest Cormit.

'It was since the time I told him Selina's family came from Northampton. He was interested in that,' mused Mrs Midden who, in turn, was only ready to credit her half-brother with an average score for charitableness – and not in every department either. He had shown little kindness to his ex-wife who'd always sworn he was kinky; then there was the way he treated Megan Rees. 'Northampton seemed to count a lot with Ernie. Was he ever stationed there, d'you remember? In the RAF?'

'Don't think so. Suppose I'd better get moving,' he added hurriedly, but only to end the topic: he didn't put down the paper.

'Me as well. I told you I'm doing a day at the Moneybuckle?' Mrs Midden never passed up an opportunity to earn. 'Doing a day' meant a day's cleaning work. She also quite often 'did an evening' in a short-staffed college kitchen, or served at table in a college hall. Most of her extra earnings went into their joint savings.

'They'll be polishing the brass at the Moneybuckle, I dare say,' said Midden, now getting to his feet. He reached for his black jacket which was hanging on the door. The electronic pager was clipped to the outside of his top pocket. The go-ahead college bursar had recently introduced one-way pagers for a few key staff: Midden had been the only college servant to be given one, so he chose to consider it a badge of office. 'Reminds me, I've got to check first thing on the Moneybuckle governors' rooms in college.'

'That's not your responsibility, Arthur?'

'The Moneybuckle governors think it is. All of them. I'm the one who'll get the complaints at dinner tonight if anyone's short on soap. Or a window won't open. Or an undergraduate's gone and left something lying about he shouldn't have. Idle young buggers.' Midden didn't care for undergraduates who, so far as he was concerned, were a source of aggravation and no income.

'You'd think they'd be given better than students' rooms. Fellows' rooms.'

'Some will be. There aren't enough Fellows' sets empty for all of them. Too early in the vacation. Anyway, all the Moneybuckle governors are Oxford graduates, including the two women.' He glowered at the last fact before continuing. 'They mostly don't mind getting students' rooms.

Brings back memories. All the rooms in New Quad are posh enough in any case. And they don't have to pay for anything,' he ended darkly.

'Somebody must do.'

'The Moneybuckle does.' He didn't trouble to add that most of the male governors tipped well – some of them extremely well, which is why he made it his business to figure as their universal provider for the whole time they were in college.

A minute later Midden's short legs were hurrying him along sun-bathed St John Street, although he had time in hand before he needed to be at the college. He didn't turn right into Pusey Street which would have taken him up to St Giles. Instead he carried on across Wellington Square, then turned left at Barclays Bank into Little Clarendon Street. He was on his way to Walton Street for a quick chat with Ernie Cormit: he needed to know the latest.

'Valuable items have been destroyed in the fire,' announced the BBC radio news-reader, with only middling graveness, that being the least unnerving part of the day's bad tidings. 'Many of the exhibits were on loan from American and British cultural institutions, including the Morgan Library in New York, the Sir John Soane Museum in London, and the Moneybuckle Endowment in Oxford. Meeting in Zurich today, members of the nuclear disarmament teams from— '

'Is that a disaster? For the Moneybuckle?' asked Clair Witherton, stretching to switch to a music programme. She was lying on the carpeted floor clad only in a figure-hugging, low-necked leotard. When she found some music she returned to her exercises.

'Not a disaster. Shouldn't think so. Bound to be insured. Whatever they sent. Probably architects' drawings,' replied Steven Bickworthy, then added, 'Somehow you'd think modern exhibition halls in Peking would be made of concrete not wood.' He had just come back from showering, and was pulling on his clothes. The two were in his centre-landing room in All Saints, on one of the staircases in New Quad.

All Saints is a small college. Its narrow frontage onto St Giles squeezed between neighbouring St John's College and the yard of the Lamb and Flag.

New Quad had nearly doubled the college's residential accommodation when it had been built – of stone and concrete, with large windows – over part of the college gardens in the mid-sixties. The style was modern but not uncompromising. It harmonised well enough with the rest of the buildings, most of which had been there since the late seventeenth century. New Quad comprised twelve independent staircases of three storeys over connecting basements – in the traditional manner. But while there were four bed-sitting rooms on every landing, each grouping of rooms was clustered around a shower room, lavatory, and a small kitchen, built into the centre core – which provided a considerable improvement on tradition.

'Don't you find this diverting?' Clair's bare legs were making energetic cycling motions in the air. They were well-shaped legs, like the rest of her body. She was a big girl and well proportioned. She wore her auburn hair long, usually pulled back in a pony-tail as it was now, away from her well-nourished, pretty face. Her mouth was generous; the eyes were large, brown and mischievous.

'If you mean do I find it sexy, yes I do. And only a bit lewd,' Steven answered from the alcove at the back of the room where there was hanging space for clothes.

'Pig.' But the word came out as a near endearment. 'And nobody can see me, in case you're bothered.'

'So all the people I sold the tickets to will want their money back? Shame.'

The long windows in New Quad made the ground- and first-floor windows easy to see into from the quadrangle. Clair's own room was on the top landing of the same staircase. It had a similar aspect but a longer view over rooftops.

Like Steven, Clair had just finished her second year at the university. She was studying English, not very successfully; Steven was expected to get a first-class degree in Law. She came from a Home Counties, monied background, and private schooling; he had been to a comprehensive school in West Yorkshire.

Steven was tall and fair, a bit skinny, with a strong chin and a studious expression.

The two, both twenty, believed they were very much in love. They had long-term plans to marry — despite being politically incompatible: Steven was a Tory.

'Don't you think these are good, child-bearing loins?' Clair was now strenuously lifting and lowering her pelvis, bent legs wide apart: she was breathing hard from the effort.

'I don't know. Anatomy specimens are usually ungirded.'

'Want to do something about that?'

'Not now. You going to do any work today?' he asked pointedly while vigorously brushing his very straight hair.

'Of course.'

Clair had been directed by her tutor to stay an extra month in college to revise the work she had skimped in the previous year. The instruction had suited her because Steven was just beginning a six-week job helping to computer-index the possessions of the Theodore P Moneybuckle Architectural Endowment – otherwise known as the Moneybuckle – which was housed directly opposite All Saints on the west side of St Giles. As well as his salary, the Moneybuckle was paying for the vacation use of Steven's college room. He was far from informed about the Moneybuckle's treasures, but he happened to be adept at cross-referencing by computer.

The pay from the work meant Steven could join Clair later on a trip to Turkey: she was well enough off to pay both their expenses – but she knew better than even to suggest that she should.

'It's the start of the two-day event at the Moneybuckle. The governors' annual knees up,' said Steven, coming into the centre of the room just as a glowing Clair had got to her feet. They kissed, but only in passing – she was pulling on a short bathrobe at the time.

'Did you bring in the coffee? Oh goody.' She poured some for herself, then curled up with it on the narrow bed. 'And will you have all the governors peering over your shoulder, to see you're doing the job right?'

'Shouldn't think so.' He went to the small desk to sort some books. 'Most of them won't know a personal computer from a pig's cranium.'

'So did you get the inside dirt on the Moneybuckle? About the grasping founder?'

'I knew that already. I told you, Moneybuckle was a nineteenth-century banker and philanthropist.'

'Yes, American.'

'But an Anglophile who spent a lot of time in England.'

'Salving his conscience and improving his image by giving away the profits of usury. Or some of them.' Clair claimed to be a socialist, much to the irritation of an enduringly indulgent, wealthy father.

'He gave away quite a lot, actually. Housed the poor. Built churches, hospitals and schools. Here and in the States. He was a devout Episcopalian.'

'And a regular little one man welfare state.'

'He believed in self-help and private benevolence for the helpless. Just like today's Tory Party.' Steven swung back on his chair, smirking ahead of the expected scandalised reaction.

'A do-gooder. A creepy paternalist who probably used charity for tax avoidance. Well the Oxford needy couldn't have got much nourishment from the Architectural Endowment. It's a terrible building too.'

'The Endowment was different from everything else. Moneybuckle used a lot of architects to design his churches and other buildings. When some of them moaned to him

26

that there wasn't an Oxford Chair in Architecture he offered to fund one. The university authorities weren't keen— '

'The subject being too plebeian for Oxford. Typical,' Clair interrupted.

'I expect that's about true. But remember this was around eighteen-sixty.'

'So instead of the Theodore P Moneybuckle Professorship in Architecture— ?'

'Oxford got a gothic building, not to your taste. Also a magnificent architectural library, archive and collection of drawings to go in the building. A lesser collection of pictures. Oh, and enough money to pay the upkeep for ever. That included a Custodian and staff.'

'But it's still not part of the university?'

'That's right. It's independent, but open to all accredited students from recognised places of learning. It does have special relations with All Saints College. According to the Moneybuckle's constitution, one of the governors has to be a senior member of the college. And once a year the college lays on a dinner for the governors, on the night before their annual meeting. That's tonight. The Moneybuckle foots the bill, of course, and the cost of putting up the governors in college overnight.'

'Because they're too drunk to go anywhere else?'

'Not all of them stay in college. Some live in Oxford anyway.'

'So how d'you get to be a governor?' Clair drained her coffee mug after she spoke, and shifted her position on the bed.

'The board of governors is self-perpetuating. When one dies the rest elect a replacement.'

'For life? Are they paid?'

'I think quite a lot retire, and they're unpaid. They have to be British or American, members of the Anglican Communion, and one has to be a clergyman. They all have to be graduates of Oxford or Harvard.'

'Theodore P Moneybuckle being a well-born graduate of both, of course?'

'Of neither originally. He was self-made. Didn't go to a university, but he was given honorary degrees by Oxford and Harvard late in life.'

Clair frowned at the inconvenient news of the mountebank Moneybuckle's humble origins. 'So what do the governors do?'

'They meet once a year to hear from the Moneybuckle's Custodian. He reports on the finances, any fresh acquisitions, anything they've loaned out in the year.'

'Like the drawing that went to Peking and got burned yesterday?'

'Suppose so. The governors also have to decide on making grants out of surplus funds to other learned bodies.'

'Like?'

'Well there are four other collections of architectural drawings in Oxford alone. And a lot more across the country. The owners aren't usually as well off as the Moneybuckle.'

'And who told you all this?'

'The lovely Edith Norn, over a sandwich lunch yesterday. She's the Assistant Custodian.'

'Is she really lovely?'

'Depends on your tastes.'

'I was thinking more of yours.'

'She's short, dark, and quite pretty. Also very intelligent, and very underpaid.'

'What about her boss? Moneybuckle's Custodian?'

'Mr Westerly? I met him when they hired me. He's not pretty.'

'Very funny.' She hurled a cushion at him, which he caught and nursed in his lap. 'Is he underpaid as well?'

'I've no idea. Very possibly. Edith says both jobs were meant to be sinecures. For architectural historians who need a basic income to cover them while they're writing books.'

'And is that what they both do?'

'It's what Mr Westerly seems to do. That's according to Edith Norn. She says she's too busy running the place. But she does have a doctor's thesis on the go.' He paused before adding diffidently, 'She was on the phone in the afternoon to a boyfriend. I heard them.'

'You listened in? For shame.'

'Couldn't help it. I'm in the next room to her. I think she'd forgotten I was there. She has a right penetrating voice.'

'So, was there a lot of heavy breathing?'

'I didn't hear any. It was someone she called darling a lot. And he's got a wife.'

'Who doesn't understand him?'

'I don't know.' Steven paused. 'I think he may be one of the Moneybuckle governors though.'

'Not the clergyman? Imagine what Theodore P Moneybuckle would have said?'

Chapter Three

'Ah, well met,' called Miss Arabella Chance to the tall, distinguished-looking man in the subdued grey check suit. The man, bronzed and in his early forties, had just extricated himself from a tightly-parked, blue Rolls-Royce. 'Well met, Mr Treasure,' she repeated, still hugging the shade as she paused from pushing a venerable, yellow-painted bicycle along the single, close rank of cars.

It was mid-afternoon, and very hot.

'Hello, Miss Chance,' Treasure answered, engaged as always by the singularity of the name when applied to so determined a woman. 'Are you well?'

'*Quite* well, thank you.' The emphasis indicated that question and reply had been treated as more than a polite exchange. Short, wiry and sixty-two, Miss Chance was dressed in a sleeveless, flowered blouse, a gusseted green skirt, white ankle socks, and no-nonsense, lace-up shoes. She pulled off a silk headscarf – a bold souvenir commemorating the Montreal Olympics – before fluffing up her short grey hair. 'That's a very banker kind of car,' she offered, it seemed with approval.

'I am a banker,' responded the smiling Chief Executive of Grenwood, Phipps, merchant bankers in the City of London.

'I know that, Mr Treasure. Very appropriate. Will the car be all right there?' She looked about jerkily, as though expecting to light upon predators unawares.

'I hope so. Anyway, it's the only car park All Saints

30

offers.' He fell in beside her. 'Quite full already, too. I did reserve space in advance, otherwise they wouldn't have let me in.'

The area in question was a long narrow strip starting from the college vehicle gate onto St Giles. The iron gate itself was kept open in the daytime, allowing access for pedestrians and cyclists; cars were allowed through only after the lifting of an electrically-operated boom set inwards of the gate. The boom was remotely controlled from the porter's lodge in the main college entrance along St Giles, in the centre of the college façade. The duty porter there kept observation on the vehicle gate via closed-circuit television – another of the bursar's novelties.

The parking strip ran up between the north back of Old Quad and the high stone boundary wall to Lamb and Flag Yard. It ended at the wide paved beginning of New Quad, where, on the right, an archway tunnelled through the building into Old Quad.

Miss Chance glanced back at St Giles. 'I've never understood how the porters can devote all their time to watching what's happening at that gate.'

'On the closed-circuit system, you mean? They don't,' supplied Treasure. 'There's an entry-phone arrangement in the old gatepost. You announce your arrival that way. I just did. The TV picture simply confirms your identity.'

'Still very Orwellian. One has no complications with a bike,' Miss Chance observed in her quick-fire way, and a touch primly. Vigorously she humped her machine into the cycle rack they had just reached, near the archway. 'There we are, then,' she said, pulling a bulging leather briefcase from the still over-full wicker basket attached to the handle-bars.

'And you leave your scarf and those other things in the basket?'

'My threadbare gaberdine cloak, and my box of glucose sweets? Only required when on the move,' Miss Chance

31

observed with an indulgent smile. 'The cloak is unfashionable, but invaluable against the cool of the night. And glucose for energy, you know. Before cycling uphill. You could call it a quick fix.' The analogy was followed by a loud intake of breath signifying mirth. 'I recommend it. Would you care for a tablet?'

'A fix? No thanks. I'm not planning anything too energetic.'

'Quite so.'

'And you don't lock your bike either?' Treasure gave a backward glance as they started in the direction of the archway.

'Its great age and distinctive colour have militated against illegal appropriation. So far,' Miss Chance snapped back with great good humour. 'As I recall, All Saints is not your old college, Mr Treasure. But you'll be staying the night here, I expect?'

'Yes. That's why I'm going this way. I have to get a room number and key from the porter. I hope they've put me in New Quad. You'll be coming for the governors' dinner, of course. And how have things been going at St Agnes in the past year?'

'Settling splendidly.' The response was confident. 'No known pregnancies nor reported orgies,' was next added in a distinctly triumphal tone.

Miss Chance was a Fellow of St Agnes College in North Oxford, in another of those crossing avenues between the Banbury and the Woodstock Roads – two above Arcady Road. Previously a women's college, it had only recently offered places to male undergraduates. Miss Chance, who taught philosophy, had been the leading protagonist for the cause of admitting men into residence, and despite the dire forebodings of some of her colleagues. She was also a governor of the Moneybuckle where her great-grandfather had been the first Curator.

'Now which staircase do I want?' Miss Chance demanded loudly of herself, frowning as they emerged into the ancient dignity of Old Quad – all mature stone, battlemented parapets, and cobbles underfoot. 'I'm here for tea with the chaplain. He needs help and attention urgently, poor misguided man,' she said, giving the clear if disquieting impression that the succour she was here to provide was of a moral not physical nature. 'Another one hung-up over women, you know,' she added darkly in a sharp whisper, and seeming to confirm the worst foreboding.

Treasure had no intention of risking involvement with either the chaplain's moral suspension or his tea-party. 'D'you know anything about that fire in Peking?' he put in, purposely changing the subject before his companion could continue. 'It was on the radio this morning. Something on loan from the Moneybuckle was burned.'

Miss Chance, effectively diverted by competing outrage, gave a disparaging snort. 'Would you believe, it was a drawing by Nicholas Hawksmoor of a John Vanbrugh design? Dated seventeen-four. For something at Blenheim Palace. Better than any of the Blenheim drawings at the Bodleian. We really shouldn't lend things to careless people. I have no other details.'

Which seemed to make the condemnation a bit premature. 'Any idea of the value?'

'Priceless I imagine, Mr Treasure.'

'Indeed? Well, I shall hear the dread details shortly. I'm due across at the Moneybuckle in ten minutes. To go over the agenda for tomorrow. It's why I came down early.'

'The Custodian tells me you're proving to be a most conscientious chairman.'

'Hardly that, since I'm so rarely in Oxford. But one tries.' He had been elected chairman of the governors a year before, on the death of the previous incumbent.

'Then I shall see you at dinner, Mr Treasure. Farewell till then.' Miss Chance ducked into a staircase doorway. She was wearing an expression appropriate to a dedicated moral crusader about to grapple with a back-sliding college chaplain.

'We have to view the Chinese Cultural Ministry as a very serious set-up. Very er . . . serious.' But Moneybuckle's Custodian, smiling broadly after he had spoken, seemed more cheerful than resolved – until Treasure recalled the man smiled as a sort of punctuation after every utterance. 'Everybody lends the Chinese things, nowadays. They have so much to offer in return, you see? It's been most . . . unfortunate. This fire in Peking,' Westerly ended uncertainly. He cleared his throat, stroked his full beard, then beamed at the wall just over Treasure's shoulder.

The shirt-sleeved Norman Westerly was a big man, and around Treasure's own age. He was an architectural historian, but with little published work to his credit. Treasure, while not disliking him, sometimes wondered whether he was academically too lightweight for the job. The appointment had been made a year before the banker had become a governor. It seemed to Treasure that Westerly brought neither scholarly distinction nor special organising skill to the Moneybuckle – and that he should have brought one or the other. He considered the man again: the heavy features, the immense amount of untamed black hair on face and head, plus the perpetually misdirected smile all suggested a benign Mephistopheles.

'And the value of the drawing?'

The other swallowed. 'The true value? Very difficult to judge,' he offered, but with finality not uncertainty; he was searching his beard now as if something was lost in it.

The two were seated in Westerly's book-lined room in the Moneybuckle – an over-adorned gothic revival building of modest size, fronting onto St Giles. It was immediately opposite All Saints, on the northern corner of Pusey Street.

Outside, the two-layered central porch with pointed

doorway was flanked by oblong bays rising through both main storeys – mullioned, ballustraded, and gargoyled under high-pitched twin gables.

The Moneybuckle interior was equally Victorian and predictable.

Treasure had earlier been admitted by Edith Norn. She had since returned to the only apparent major concession to changing times – one of a pair of glass-fronted, partitioned offices. These were on the right after a visitor emerged into the main area, through swing doors from the panelled vestibule. Together the two offices were less than half the size of the Custodian's domain, which was directly above them on the upper floor.

The Assistant Custodian had introduced the banker to Steven Bickworthy, closeted with a desk computer in the smaller office next to hers – a place normally used by a part-time secretary-cum-library clerk who was at present on holiday.

The remainder of the ground floor was as Theodore P Moneybuckle had ordained – a library and reading room with small tables in arched alcoves, and books on open shelves. More books were stored in the basement. The ponderously balustraded stairs to all floors were set in the centre, across from the swing doors.

The main upper floor (there was also an attic) housed the collection of architectural drawings in wide wooden chests with banks of slim drawers, or else in bound folios in locked oak book-cases which were pointed and romantically embellished. Special exhibits were displayed in secure, glass-topped cabinets. The better pictures from the not very distinguished art collection hung on the walls here.

An oblong oak table, normally used for the study of cumbersome items, had already been arranged outside the Custodian's room with enough chairs to accommodate the next day's formal meeting of governors.

On his way to join the Custodian, Treasure had come upon several cleaners – Mrs Midden amongst them –

busy burnishing the fitments, but reverently like acolytes in premises only nominally more hallowed.

'But the drawing was insured?' the banker now continued, in a pressing tone.

'Of course. But, as you know, most of our items are nearly impossible to value.' Westerly leaned forward, bringing bare, hairy forearms down heavily on the surface of his desk, and directing his gaze more or less at his visitor. 'And they can't be replaced. Any compensation for loss has to be measured in cash not aesthetics. And there's not much real compensation in that. Insurance is very expensive, too. It's not as though the stuff will ever be stolen, you see? Too difficult to dispose of. It's only fire and damage we have to guard against.'

Treasure didn't entirely agree on the last points, but he let them pass. 'So you're saying we under-insure?'

'Oh yes. Measured against any notional sale-room value of our collection. The governors agreed some years ago— '

'That the insurance premium for the contents of this building should be kept to a reasonable minimum. I remember that,' the banker interrupted. 'I don't remember our agreeing that travelling exhibits shouldn't be covered up to the hilt. What's the rule in their case? Is the premium paid by us, or by the institution to whom we're lending?'

'By us, always. But we then send a bill to the borrowers for the same amount, along with other costs like packaging, transportation and any loan fee. That way we can be sure the item is properly covered. So even if it's going abroad, any compensation would be paid in Britain. Not that we've ever actually lost anything before,' the Custodian ended reflectively.

Treasure nodded. 'That sounds fair enough. Provided the valuation is realistic. How much insurance cover did you take on this Hawksmoor drawing?'

'Twelve thousand pounds.'

'That's all it was worth?'

'It's what we have it down for on the master list.'

'When it was sitting here in a drawer, or when it went on its travels?'

Westerly swallowed again. 'I'm afraid there was an error. I discovered it this morning. Our insurance brokers should have been told to cover the drawing for twice the amount on the master list. That's the normal arrangement, agreed with the insurers they use.'

'Who are the insurers?'

'That varies,' the speaker offered uncertainly.

'Was it Edith Norn's mistake?'

'No, I'm afraid it was mine. Entirely mine.'

Although the confession was abject, the cause was still begging. So why wasn't the Assistant Curator in charge of mundane business such as corresponding with brokers?

'I look after all insurance arrangements myself,' came next, before Treasure had the chance to put his question.

And Westerly was parading that tiresome smile again – the banker considered with even less justification than usual.

'I hope you'll be quite comfortable here, Mr Ostracher, sir. That everything will be to your satisfaction. And should it not be, sir, you only have to dial me on that telephone. If I'm not in my pantry, the call switches to my pager automatically, and your number registers on the switchboard in the porter's lodge.' Midden tapped the device on his breast pocket with pride.

'I'm sure I'll be fine, Mr Midden,' the tall, stooping American replied genially, looking out onto New Quad. 'Even more comfortable than last year. These Fellows' rooms are quite excellent.'

'But not by American standards, I dare say, sir. Unfortunately there aren't usually any free this early. Not residential sets. But this year there were two. This one and the one opposite. Two younger college Fellows left earlier than expected. One's lecturing on a cruise ship. The other's taken a post in Australia. The brain drain, I think they

call that, sir. It's an ill wind, of course,' he added philo-
sophically. 'Yes, I've put Mr Treasure in the other set.
Shall I take that case to the bedroom, sir?'

'Thank you Mr Midden. Having a telephone will be a
comfort too. So, house calls I dial direct? And outside
calls go through the porter?'

'That's right, sir. You ask for the number you require.
That's up to eleven o'clock, when the porter plugs in the
night lines. After that people with lines can dial for themselves. You'll have a night line, of course, sir. I've seen to
that. And for Mr Treasure.'

'Thank you for the trouble, Mr Midden.'

'No trouble, sir. Not for important guests. If you could
kindly make a note of your night calls. The numbers and
duration. Then give them to me at breakfast.'

'I'll certainly do that.' Ostracher sat himself on the padded window seat, and glanced about the room approvingly.

'Thank you, sir. And might I ask after Mrs Ostracher,
sir? I hope she's keeping quite well.'

Midden, at his most obsequious, was showing earnest
anticipation of good tidings. He was still holding the bag
but it wasn't heavy.

'Oh, Mrs Ostracher's fine, thank you.'

'I'm very glad to hear it. If you remember, I was privileged to meet madam when she came to collect you last
year, sir. A very handsome lady, if I may make so bold.'

'You certainly may, Mr Midden. I'll tell her you enquired.
She won't be over this summer. Maybe she'll come with me
in the fall. There's a new grandson who's taking all the attention back home at this time.'

'Very gratifying, sir. That's the third as I remember.' Midden kept careful notes of information that had ingratiating
potential.

'That's right, Mr Midden. Three boys, any one of
whom may step into the business just like my eldest
son did. If any of them has a mind to, of course. And
if they shape up to it. No room for passengers these days.

Come to that, there never was in my firm.' Ostracher was chairman of one of the largest independent stockbrokers in New York. He was also the controlling shareholder, a status which would easily have supported an inclination to nepotism.

'I was going to mention I've come on a reliable source of those Victorian silver miniatures madam told me she collected, sir,' Midden said, on his return from the bedroom. 'It's a jewellers in Woodstock. That's not far away, sir.'

'Good of you to think of it, Mr Midden. I know Woodstock. Could you leave me the name?'

'I've already done so, sir. The card is by the telephone. Madam did ask me to look out for a supplier, sir.' He had also arranged a commission with the jeweller. But now there were bigger fish to fry. 'Have you added anything important to your water-colour collection, sir?'

'Why, yes.' Ostracher beamed, running a hand from his brow to the base of his neck, over a noble, wide and hairless dome. 'A small Turner sketch I picked up at auction. In New York, in November. That's J M W Turner, of course. Cost a fortune, but it's very fine. A sound investment.' The last came as self-approbation delivered reflectively. 'It's not only water-colours I collect, of course, Mr Midden.'

The SCR butler had noted that fact several years before, and also that Ostracher was a Constable enthusiast. 'I wondered, sir,' he gave a hesitant cough, 'if you might be interested to see a small oil sketch and two pencil drawings of Oxford, attributed to Constable? John Constable. They've been discovered locally. Not many know about them yet.'

'You don't say?' Ostracher had adopted a poker face. This was serious intelligence.

'They're owned by Mr Ernest Cormit, sir, an antiquarian bookseller in the town.' He had debated whether to disclose the relationship – 'remote kinship' might have fitted, but on balance he had decided kinship with Val would do nothing to improve Ernie's credibility as a dealer in old masters.

'Authenticated Constables are they?' The speaker leaned forward, hands clasped between his knees.

'I believe so, sir. I happen to know Doctor Radout's seen them. He was impressed, so I'm told.'

'That's interesting.'

'If that could be between you and me, sir? In case Doctor Radout thinks I've been speaking out of turn. It could have been the doctor's opinion that made Mr Cormit turn down an offer of twenty thousand pounds. That was from a London dealer. You'll treat all this as confidential, sir?'

'Naturally, Mr Midden. Where can I see the sketches?'

'I could ring Mr Cormit and ask him to bring them up now, if you like. His shop's close by. In Walton Street.'

The American glanced at his watch. 'Let's see. It's not that far from pre-dinner drinks, and I'll need to bath and change. Maybe after dinner? Or first thing in the morning?' In fact there was time in hand now, but his collector's instinct prompted him not to show too much immediate interest.

'What if I leave you Mr Cormit's number, sir? Here it is. I took the liberty of telling him I'd mention the sketches to you. That you were an important gentleman. You can ring him at any time.'

Ostracher took the proffered card, then stood up. 'That's fine, Mr Midden. I'll certainly be in touch.' He paused, then added carefully, 'Tell me, do any of the sketches happen to be of Oxford Bridge?'

'Now you come to mention it, two of them do, sir. Magdalen Bridge, that is.'

Ernie had said that would be the first question – from anyone strong on Constable.

Chapter Four

It was an hour later when Treasure recognised the moving
figure of Edith Norn through the window of his sitting
room. She was hurrying across the quadrangle looking
flushed but pert in a simple white blouse and long red
evening skirt. He had just finished dressing for dinner,
which was to be a black-tie affair. He had tried to call
out to Edith to come in for a drink – the ever-thoughtful
Midden had provided whisky, gin and mixers on a tray.
But the girl had disappeared before he had succeeded in
unfastening the complicated window catch.

He would be seeing Edith at dinner, but he would like
to have had a further private word with her – a tactful
word of enquiry about how the Moneybuckle handled its
insurances, and why it wasn't the Assistant Custodian's job
to do the handling. Earlier, she had left the Moneybuckle
before Treasure had finished his session with Westerly. The
Custodian had remained vague on the insurance point, for
the reason – the banker judged tolerantly – that he was more
an academic than a man of business.

In compensation, Westerly had been well enough informed
when he had given Treasure a review of the Moneybuckle's
cultural programme in the past year.

But it was obvious that the subject of insurance would
need to be tabled formally at the governors' meeting the
following afternoon. Rules needed framing to avoid any
repetition of the Peking episode.

Now Treasure reverted to a previous intention. He

knew Bryan Gavon had arrived – the white Porsche with the distinctive number plate was in the car park. Also he had learned from the porter that Gavon's room was on the top floor of this same staircase, and he now went to invite the occupant down for a whisky. He and Gavon had been contemporaries while students at Oxford, and had kept in touch, if fitfully, over the ensuing years. Gavon had been partly responsible for Treasure becoming a Moneybuckle governor two years before, and had strongly supported his being elected chairman later.

Gavon had made a career in publishing, and now owned his own company – specialising in lavish 'coffee table' books, which were usually price-cut in the stores from the day of their first appearance. Treasure had always assumed that this was part of a profitable selling strategy – although a recent disquieting rumour had indicated that the company might not be doing as well as its owner invariably put out. Certainly Gavon's air of affluence had remained undiminished whenever the two men met.

The internal concrete staircase that Treasure was ascending was narrow and surprisingly ill-lit. There were half-landings on the bends between the floors, and it was just before he reached the topmost of these that he heard a female cry of distress from just ahead of him. A moment later a fleeing, confused Edith Norn came rushing down and cannoned into him.

'So sorry . . . ' the banker began, putting out steadying arms, and before realising who it was. 'Why Edith? I saw you just now, didn't realise you'd . . . '

The young woman's face was deeply anguished and her eyes brimming with tears. She neither spoke nor further checked her flight – just made a gulping sob, shook her head uncomprehendingly at Treasure, then, catching up the long skirt, careered on down the steps before he had finished his sentence.

There followed more hurrying footsteps from above and another familiar voice sounding: 'Edith! Come back!

Come . . . oh . . . oh, hello Mark. Did you see Edith Norn? You must have done. Don't know what came over her. Silly girl. Oh, well.'

The shirt-sleeved Bryan Gavon shrugged in resignation. He was a fraction shorter than Treasure, fleshier too, with crinkly fair hair, kind eyes, a strong chin, and a characteristic expression of benign good humour.

'So how are you, my dear old thing?' he now offered affably, his whole demeanour relaxed.

'I'm well, Bryan,' Treasure replied as the two shook hands warmly. 'On my way to ask you down for a drink. I have a set of Fellows' rooms with all mod cons.' If Gavon chose not to explain Edith's performance that was up to him.

'Have you indeed? So they're showing the deference due to a man of pedigree are they? I've got an undergraduate room, as usual. *And* this is my old college. I shall protest to the admirable Midden.' But he hadn't made the intention sound serious. 'Molly all right?'

'Flourishing, thank you. Working very hard.'

'And keeping them mesmerised with the new play at the National Theatre. Marvellous reviews. We have tickets for next month. What a talent that girl has.'

'Thank you.' Treasure was married to Molly Forbes, the celebrated actress. He was about to enquire about Gavon's own wife when the other broke in again.

'Well I'm delighted to accept that drink. Soon as I've finished dressing.' He looked more than usually debonair, the dress shirt not yet completely buttoned above the cummerbund: a heavy gold neck-chain and medallion glinted against a well tanned, hairy chest.

'Am I invited too, Mark? I hope so.'

In contrast to the just flown, unsophisticated Edith Norn, the striking ash-blonde who had now appeared from the top of the steps exuded cool self-possession, something that melded easily with the low, sensuous voice. She was a little older than the dark-haired Edith – and her wide-eyed, confident expression suggested she was a great deal more worldly wise.

'Of course you remember Charlotte Lundle, Mark? We drove up together.'

'Our newest governor? How could I forget? Glad to see you again, Charlotte. And naturally you're invited. Is your room up there too?'

'No. On the floor below.' She smiled disarmingly, looked straight into his eyes, but made no effort to explain why she had been on the top floor. The white bathrobe she was wearing, and the towel over her arm, were left to suggest a reason – or an excuse: but there were two shower rooms on her own landing.

'Then I'll expect you both shortly. Door Two. Ground floor.' Treasure turned about, quite sure, even in the poor light, that the pale smudge on Gavon's mouth had been lipstick – only he wondered whose.

'Gin and tonic with ice, no lemon.' The banker handed Charlotte Lundle her drink. She had arrived shortly after Bryan Gavon who was already established with a whisky and soda. It had been barely ten minutes since the three had met on the stairs.

'Mm, just what I needed. I like your rooms. Make me feel positively under-privileged,' quipped the young woman.

'That'll be the day,' Gavon murmured from where he was standing near the window.

Treasure regarded the now elegantly dressed Charlotte with open appreciation, mixed with disguised speculation – and there was justification for both kinds of assessment.

Charlotte Lundle was a celebrity as well as a beauty. A year or so before this she had given up an academic career here in Oxford to become editor of the *Bloomsbury Review*, a weekly magazine devoted to the arts: its circulation had since quadrupled. Since moving to London, she was also making a name for herself on television, with a short, experimental television series of her own scheduled for the autumn.

But there was no gainsaying that these events were deeply coloured by another. For some time there had been a story circulating that Miss Lundle was amorously involved with a prominent member of the Royal family. Although there was no real substance to the tale, it had endured, mostly because of foreign press reports. It had served to inject a spicy interest into all aspects of the lady's life: some cynics said it had also been a marvellous boost to her career.

'D'you enjoy coming to Oxford?' Treasure asked her.

'Not especially. I find it unsettling.' But she looked perfectly poised as she smoothed one padded shoulder of the V-necked, peacock-green silk blouson she was wearing – over an ankle-length, black slit skirt.

'The lady's too young yet to succumb to nostalgia's deadening embrace,' said Gavon.

'Not that either.' She smiled, sitting on the arm of a chair. 'I'm still never sure whether I should have left the place. University life is so gloriously protected. And that's not nostalgia. Just natural inertia.'

'Nonsense. It's not in your nature to be cosseted,' Gavon insisted, moving closer to her.

'I wish that were true. Anyway, I'm glad to be a Moneybuckle governor.' She had been elected the year before, but this was to be her first meeting.

'A link with the university that's not too arduous to maintain?' offered Treasure. 'I feel the same way. Though I'm beginning to think the governing body needs to be more involved, more often. To bring the place up to date.'

'That sounds ominous.' Charlotte looked sharply from one to the other, which incidentally made her square bobbed hair swing quite gracefully.

'We did authorise computer-indexing last year. That was fairly forward looking,' Gavon put in lightly. 'I mean, for a library and art collection that probably hadn't been freshly indexed since eighteen sixty-one.'

'That's just my point.' Treasure frowned. 'That job isn't done yet. The computer wasn't even ordered till May. There's been a lot of cogitation over which software programme to use, and the work was being handled entirely by Edith Norn. She's now got a temporary assistant. An undergraduate. I hope he's competent. He looks it.'

'You think they should have brought in consultants? A professional team to do the work?' asked Charlotte.

'Edith is properly qualified, of course,' said Gavon, but without answering the question.

'I suppose outsiders would have meant a lot of extra expense?' mused Charlotte.

'Expense, yes,' Treasure answered. 'But unlike almost every other educational establishment in this city, the Moneybuckle isn't short of operating funds.'

'Because your bank looks after its investments?' Gavon observed with a chuckle.

'Grenwood, Phipps are the trustees, certainly. And I think we manage the portfolio competently. Since well before my time, incidentally. But tomorrow the governors' big job, as always, will be giving away money to similar but impoverished museums. The ones who've applied to us for help in the last year. The costs of running the Moneybuckle itself have hardly increased at all. Relative to income, that is. There's quite a hefty surplus.'

'So we could easily have paid outsiders to do the indexing. I understand,' said Charlotte. 'Incidentally, I heard about this Peking fire. Were we covered by insurance?'

'Yes, but only for half the value of the item. There was a . . . clerical error,' Treasure replied.

'I see.' Charlotte paused. 'Do you know why Edith Norn is so stingy? She's the one in charge of the operational budgets isn't she?'

'In theory, yes. But I'm beginning to think Norman Westerly interferes a good deal more than anyone imagines.'

Gavon came in vigorously at this. 'I'm sure that's right.

Traditionally, the Assistant is supposed to relieve the Custodian of business chores, so he can get on with producing enduring literature. But dear Westerly hasn't published anything in the four years he's been with us. Claims he's working primarily on a magnum opus on Inigo Jones, except lesser writing keeps getting in the way.'

'Lesser writing being learned commentaries on items at the Moneybuckle?' questioned Charlotte.

'Again in theory,' Gavon answered. 'Though I happen to know at the moment he has absolutely nothing of that sort in preparation. I believe he tries to make up for lack of academic output by seeing the Moneybuckle runs on a shoestring.'

'Do you know that for sure, Bryan?' Treasure asked.

'Yes. I'm in Oxford a good deal, one way and another. I usually pop into the Moneybuckle. I've even been doing a bit of reference work there since November. Did I tell you, Mark, I'm co-authoring a book we're publishing on British canals?'

'No, but I promise to buy a copy. Canals are fascinating, and very much back in fashion. Edith did mention this afternoon that you dropped in quite often, also— '

'When I was here in April, I got an earful from her about the way Westerly holds back on buying things,' the other man had interrupted. 'For instance, it was he who held up the buying of that computer. That's held the whole programme back, of course.'

Treasure made a pained expression. 'I gather you know Edith's found a lot of items that aren't listed on the old indexes at all?' he said. 'Mostly drawings. Not valuable probably, but still Moneybuckle property.'

'Architectural drawings?' asked Charlotte.

'No. Mostly fine art,' Gavon explained. 'There's a sort of sub-collection in the basement that no one's looked at in years. Hundreds of drawings of no especial merit. Edith wants them indexed too, but they can't be till she's catalogued them properly.'

'That could be very time consuming,' said Charlotte. 'Still, I suppose it's what she's paid for. And really, it does sound a bit lax to have original drawings she's never even seen. What if some of them turn out to be important?'

'I don't think there's much chance of that,' Treasure answered. 'But in principle you're right, of course.'

'Except the poor girl does have her work cut out keeping up with everyday work.' This was Gavon. 'She's only been with us a bit over a year. And it's not entirely true that she's paid for what she's doing. The Assistant Custodian is also supposed to have time for original research. You know she's going for a doctorate eventually?'

'So why doesn't she have an assistant? She does have a secretary,' said Charlotte.

'Part time only, and shared with the Custodian,' Treasure corrected. 'There really is a strong case for increasing the staff. And improving the quality.'

'Does that include the Custodian and the Assistant Custodian?' Charlotte enquired. 'I don't want to be unkind, but they neither of them seem to be exactly whizz at their work, do they?'

The banker shook his head. 'Westerly has three more years tenure of office. That's according to the agreement on his appointment.'

'So we couldn't get him out before then anyway?'

'Not except for gross misbehaviour,' said Gavon with a grin. 'And grossness in any context hardly seems to be our Custodian's forte. Edith's on a term's notice only, and I'd say quite close to giving it. She seems a bit mixed up at the moment.'

'Highly strung, d'you suppose?' asked Treasure pointedly, recalling the incident on the stairs.

'Problems with her private life, I think,' was all Gavon chose to volunteer.

'Well I'd be sorry if we lost her,' the banker said. 'Also, I doubt we'd get better candidates for either job. Not for the money we pay at the moment.'

'So we should pay more,' said Charlotte.

'We can't,' Gavon supplied flatly. 'We've been down that road before. I quote from the Founder's Articles, "The Custodian's reward to be the same as that of the Hawkley Fellow at All Saints College, and the Assistant Custodian's reward to be half the same sum".'

'Who's the Hawkley Fellow?'

'It's a research fellowship of this college, of almost primaeval origin,' Treasure answered. 'The stipend of that's increased from time to time, but not by very much. It's supposed to provide the holder with just enough to live off while working toward higher academic goals. Obviously Theodore P Moneybuckle had the same idea in mind.'

'So did our previous chairman, and most of the older governors,' said Gavon. 'It's why our new blood was carefully chosen,' he concluded, with a smile at the new chairman and the newest governor.

'Yes. I'm sure we have to find ways of bending the constitution,' Treasure observed quietly. 'We just need to protect our charitable status, that's all. For tax reasons.'

'This is all very dreary,' Gavon complained dismissively. 'Wouldn't you rather hear about Charlotte's new TV extravaganza, Mark?'

'It's nothing of the sort, I'm afraid,' the young woman protested modestly. 'A series of six programmes only. A design and architectural magazine on Monday afternoons. With me chatting-up the luminaries.'

'Pre-digested for housewife viewing?'

'Quite the opposite, Mark,' Charlotte responded, this time sharply in defence of her sex. 'And there's a late-night repeat on Thursdays.'

'Armin Ostracher tells me he's arranging for tapes of the programmes to be sent to him in New York,' said Treasure, who was pouring fresh drinks for everyone.

'How flattering,' said Charlotte.

49

Treasure handed her back her glass. 'He was in here earlier. Then went off to find Julian Barners. Needed his opinion on something.'

'Is he about to buy a work of art?' Gavon asked.

'He didn't say so, so perhaps he is,' quipped Treasure, though his thoughts had reverted to something else.

The banker was impressed that Gavon had earlier not stressed the amount of help he had been giving Edith Norn on his recent visits to the Moneybuckle. According to the over-worked Edith, Gavon had several times dropped what he had come to do, and instead spent the time with her getting those tiresome drawings documented and into manageable order. Treasure felt all this to be much to his publisher friend's credit.

Chapter Five

'I can give you a verdict on the oil sketch without equivocation,' announced Julian Barners in a piercing stentorian
voice. 'Without equivocation,' he repeated, savouring the
phrase and airily making circular gesticulations with an
immaculately white-gloved hand. Then with no warning
he stepped off the pavement, provoking near seizures in
three motorists as well as in the entrails of their motors.

After a momentary hesitation, and with a show of embar-
rassment proper in a law-abiding foreign visitor, Armin
Ostracher elected to follow his singular, lanky companion
who consistently halted traffic against nature, in the style
of Moses parting water.

'Now you've seen all three sketches, on the evidence,
do you believe they're by Constable?' the American pressed
when they were both on the other side of Walton Street.
They had just left the premises of Ernest Cormit, second-
hand bookseller.

Barners stalked leftwards into Little Clarendon Street.
The usually extended chin sank sharply, while its owner
sought to lift a glance of tolerant compassion at the speaker,
over an elegant pair of pince-nez. Since Ostracher was the
same height as Barners, the intended diminishing effect was
marred, the gaze levelling somewhat below the American's
black bow-tie.

Both men were in dinner jackets, the hatless and glove-
less Ostracher in a conservative version. In comparison, the
exquisite Barners affected the appearance of a slimmed and

elongated Oscar Wilde. He was wearing a flowing velvet bow, a tight, four-buttoned, double-breasted jacket with embroidered, high lapels, and a dramatic black hat with a lyrically swooping brim.

'My dear Armin, what you term *evidenc:* is of small account.' Barners vouchsafed a regal nod on a pair of tight-lipped elderly women who had stood out of his way, not in deference but to avoid being stepped on. 'In the end,' he pontified, 'divination of a picture's authorship is a gift of nature, not something injected into the unelected as a reward for grubbing *evidence*.' He permitted a moment for the digesting of this before he continued. 'Bernard Berenson learned that too from Giovanni Morelli. It was the making of him.' The upraised hand made another expansive gesture that narrowly missed clipping a passing cyclist.

'I'm sure.' Ostracher had fallen slightly behind in what inwardly he acknowledged was an unworthy attempt to avoid attracting an equal share of the irritation or hilarity that accompanied Barners' public progress. It had been the same on the way down – in a city well used to eccentrics. 'You wouldn't say Berenson's reputation as an art connoisseur has been a mite flawed since— '

'No I would not. And anyone who subscribes to that view does so at his peril. Bernard had many detractors but few equals.'

'I'm sorry. Certainly the oil sketch seemed to me to have distinct similarities— '

Barners stopped suddenly, placed a hand heavily on the other's shoulder, and drew him into intimate proximity before interrupting with a hissed: 'So you saw that? Isn't Constable's *impasto* unmistakable? You should have asked Seurat or Pissarro that question. Hah!' The pince-nez fell off his nose to be saved dramatically by the black silk cord attached to it.

'The . . . the Neo-Impressionists owed Constable a great deal,' the American agreed, leaning back as much as he could while unable to alter his stance without risking offence. 'The oil sketch— ' he tried again.

' —Must have been done from nature. He was meticulous in such matters.' Barners grasped his companion's arm and now began propelling him swiftly past a dress shop, as though the window display would otherwise corrupt him. 'You will never understand Constable unless you believe in the pain he took over the natural effect. The chiaroscuro of nature, he called it.'

'The light and shade?' Ostracher wished he could be treated less like an ignorant colonial.

'Yes,' Barners frowned, balked by the comprehension. 'The light and shade that he insisted never stood still. He was simply not understood, of course. Never properly recognised in his lifetime. He belonged neither with the Romantics nor the Neo-Classicists. He was unique. Only the French— '

'You were saying the oil sketch was done— '

'From nature. Indisputably. Yet the light— '

'And the shadows, yes?'

'The light source was different in the pencil sketch of the same subject. The bridge. The sun was not in the same place for the two studies. Thus one is not a copy of the other. They are both originals, and can hardly have been executed on the same day. Not from life.' Barners paused, then uttered shrilly, 'There was undoubtedly a second coming at Magdalen Bridge.'

The Messianic pronouncement prompted a passing priest to look back uncertainly and trip on his cassock.

Everything Barners was offering seemed to Ostracher devilishly close to being evidence – the sort that Giovanni Morelli had said should be despised, whoever Morelli might have been, and the American had made a mental note to find out later. But it was still evidence that he enjoyed hearing about, since he was on the brink of buying works of art of uncertain attribution.

He cleared his throat. 'You say there are no records,

no letters of Constable's, for several days after June the ninth, eighteen twenty-one? The day he did the sketch of University College. The one in the British Museum. And presumably also the one we've just seen of Christ Church?' It was clear to him that Barners had the minutiae of Constable's life at his fingertips.

'He did the Christ Church much earlier on the same day. They're both very detailed drawings. The shadows in the University College sketch indicate midday, or thereabouts. I know the work well.'

'The pencil sketch of the bridge has June the tenth written on it.'

'And was also done quite early in the day.'

'The oil sketch of the bridge?'

'Would have been the second study of the subject, made even earlier on a succeeding day. The lighting confirms as much. Unquestionably the pencil sketch would have been done first. Then, when he'd slept on it, he did the oil because the concept was growing on him.' In this Barners had unknowingly confirmed Dr Radout's conclusion.

'You suggest he'd have been planning a major painting then?'

'I suggest only that it was something formulating in his mind.' Barners was now using the silk cord to swing the pince-nez about like a censer – and quite dangerously. 'But such a painting never materialised. Nor even a full-size oil sketch. If either had existed I would surely know of it.'

'So if he did the oil the day after the pencil sketch, he must still have been in Oxford on the eleventh.'

'That usually follows the tenth, yes,' Barners replied with a lift of an eyebrow.

'I meant. . . . Well, of course it does.' Ostracher abandoned the excuse for his advertised inanity. It was simply that he found Barners' company induced confusion at times. They had come to the top of the street now,

54

and had turned right into St Giles. The American was relieved that his companion chose to ease the pace slightly. 'The handwritten instructions to Lucas . . . ?' he began again.

'This man Cormit is right on that. Lucas was the artist-engraver who did Constable's five volumes of mezzotint engravings. Between eighteen-thirty and eighteen thirty-two.'

'The five volumes called *English Landscape*?'

'Yes. There were four prints to a volume. Now *they* were a deserved success. Oh yes.'

'And around that time Constable would have been sending sketches to Lucas in Chelsea? For Lucas to copy as engravings?'

'Pencil or oil sketches. Or water-colours.' The last was for some reason delivered like an order and frightened a small dog away from a nearby lamp-post.

'Which would explain why Constable wrote "To David Lucas. Believe this better. Compare,"' said Ostracher. 'That was on the back of the oil sketch. With the date. Compare what?'

Barners shrugged. 'With the proof from an engraved plate already made of the subject, or the pencil sketch sent earlier.'

'But you told me there was no engraving of any Oxford Bridge in the four volumes, or anywhere else?'

'None that we know of. But Constable set Lucas to attempt many more than the twenty original prints they eventually produced. Constable rejected far more than ever he approved.'

'He was a perfectionist?'

'By nature.' He looked at the other man to be sure the apposition had registered. 'Constable's relations with Lucas were often severely strained because Constable destroyed or mutilated many of the finished plates. They say it was Constable who drove Lucas to drink. That's calumny, of course. Or else drink agreed with Lucas. He lived to be seventy-nine. He died in eighteen eighty-one.'

'And you think it possible that of the lesser works Constable sent to Lucas, some never went back to— ?'

'To Constable in Charlotte Street? It's not merely possible, it's highly probable. Constable was a prolific producer. Especially of sketches. He'd put them aside carefully enough, but didn't especially value them after he'd fetched them out for the purpose for which he'd made them. Of course, that might have been years later.'

'He'd make small sketches as detail input for bigger works?'

'When he was making the full-scale sketch for a major picture.'

'D'you suppose Lucas would have kept back original work on purpose?'

'Purloined it, you mean? No. But he was a busy young man, and later very celebrated. He worked with many artists. His studio and workshop would have been crammed with other people's pictures. Some of the lesser ones could easily have been mislaid.'

'And eventually ended up the property of a servant to the Lucas family?'

'And a forebear of the late Selina Smith of Iffley Road? Quite possibly. When Constable died in eighteen thirty-seven such bits of his work as we've just looked at would have been regarded as mere remembrances, of infinitesimal value. Shortly after his funeral, bundles of his sketches were sold at auction for a few shillings. Bundles of them!' Barners halted suddenly, either by way of emphasising an outrage or merely in preparation for crossing the road. It happened the pair had just drawn level with the Moneybuckle.

'It's a shame Mr Moneybuckle didn't buy some of those bundles,' mused Ostracher.

'He may not have been a serious collector early enough,' Barners replied absently, his attention now on a different

56

subject. 'Good evening, Professor Bodd,' he exclaimed, raising and replacing the hat in a courtly gesture. 'I trust we find you well, and, like us, returning to All Saints for the governors' dinner?'

The clergyman thus addressed had just rounded the corner from Pusey Street and, despite his ample size, clearly had been contriving to pass the others unobserved.

'Hello, Barners. Hello Ostracher,' he uttered cautiously. The guilty expression was replaced by a brief half-smile. Then a look of the deepest melancholy suffused the moon face. The sad eyes were enlarged by the lenses of oversized, square-framed spectacles. 'Yes, I shall be dining,' he offered next, as if announcing a visit to the dentist. 'I haven't changed yet. Didn't see either of you earlier. I arrived a bit late.' Throughout he had been preoccupied with an unsuccessful attempt to hide a small oblong box held awkwardly with one hand behind his ample back. 'You've been for a walk, I expect?'

'We've been to look at some important sketches at an antiquarian's in Walton Street,' Barners replied portentiously, to indicate the other's expectancy had been very wide of the mark. 'Quite probably Constable sketches. Come to think of it, you were a Suffolk man. From the Constable country,' he added, almost too promptly for it to have been a genuine after-thought.

Bodd nodded, moving from one foot to the other. 'From the Colne Valley, west of Colchester, yes. There are a lot of Constable forgeries around at the moment,' he completed gratuitously, in the manner of one who had bought some and found out later.

'One is aware of that. You've been shopping?' Barners changed the subject, focusing on Bodd's discomfort, and conscious that Ostracher was looking alarmed. 'Ah, the moment to cross, I believe,' he then declared loudly, grabbing the American's arm and urging him into wide and still busy St Giles. He finessed their moves with balletic and necessary precision during the ensuing fifty yard *pas de deux*, enacted before braking buses, swerving cars and terrorised cyclists.

'Strange fellow Bertram Bodd,' Barners commented coolly when they reached the other side. He pointed back across the road. 'Still standing where we left him, d'you see? I fear that's the story of his life.'

'Isn't he a Doctor of Divinity,' asked Ostracher, a respecter both of caution and of academic achievement. 'And a Professor of Theology?'

'At a minor university somewhere in the north where the subject is rarely studied and, they say, is likely to be dropped in the next round of faculty cuts.' After delivering this surprisingly current piece of intelligence about a still-unidentified campus, Barners took the other's arm again, directing him toward the main entrance to the college, while continuing, 'He's also a deeply boring man. Spits when he speaks. Did you notice? He corners one with the sorry story of his unsuccessful life. He's done it to me twice.' All of which seemed a less than charitable assessment of someone he had greeted with a cordiality bordering on deference not three minutes before.

'But he looks only fifty or so, time enough— '

'And about the same around the waist, wouldn't you say? He has six children with whom he finds it difficult to communicate. And despite a lack of musicality in himself, he married a woman who plays the violin, not well, but persistently. She's driving him mad. He'll tell you, given the chance.'

'Why was he made a Moneybuckle governor, d'you suppose?'

'The reasons are obscure. Of course, there has to be one clergyman. I believe Bodd once held an Oxford Fellowship. Very briefly.'

'He never seems to miss a meeting.'

'I imagine Professor Bodd never misses an opportunity to escape the responsibilities of job and family. He finds both daunting, and the cause of his profound insecurity.

His opinions are most unreliable, by the way.'

'Weren't you going to ask him something about Constable?'

'Certainly not,' lied Barners haughtily and with utter conviction.

'I'll have to go quite soon, Rebecca.' Norman Westerly moved across the bedroom toward his angry wife who had entered moments before. She was standing just inside the doorway. 'Quite soon,' he repeated, while calculating the real time he had available. She was easily excited when she was riled.

'More money, Norman,' she said again. 'You can't manage otherwise. You can't even afford this house any more. If it weren't for me. And it's not fair.'

It was quite a small house, at the top of the Banbury Road, close to the Ring Road.

Rebecca was very dark and slender – an almost unflawed beauty with immense animal attraction. He was her second husband. She had married him on an impulse, at the end of the affair that had followed her divorce. Now it was Westerly's turn to try keeping her.

He moved directly in front of her. 'I'll ask. Tomorrow at the meeting. Not tonight.'

'You should have asked Mark Treasure this afternoon. He wouldn't have eaten you.' She flung the long straight hair back off her face, then folded her arms under the slight pout of the half-unbuttoned shirt that hung loosely over a ruffed gypsy skirt. Her supple figure was more like a young girl's than a thirty-four-year-old woman's.

'I've told you, the problem's the link with the Hawkley Fellowship.'

'Screw the Hawkley Fellowship,' she snapped.

Her bare brown legs were set apart, there were no shoes on her feet. An artist, she had just come from the studio at the top of the house: she smelled of turpentine mingled with the heavy musk scent she always wore.

Her paintings didn't sell – not yet. What she got from her advertising work was compensation for her lack of celebrity from the other, and substantial in money terms. She still resented having to do the commercial stuff, persuading herself it was denying her progress as a real painter.

'I'll do my best,' he said automatically, putting his arms around her, trying to pull her close.

'I wish you'd sound as if you meant it. And you'll have to do more than your best,' she said petulantly, resisting him. 'Tell them your salary's out of touch with reality. You're a Custodian, not a bloody caretaker.'

'I'll find a way.' He ran his hand under the shirt, then along her bare back, kneading the tight flesh.

'I think you'd better.' But her mood was softening. Soon she was responding compulsively, her arms reaching up to him, her nails searching the back of his neck, her body moving hard against his.

She hadn't wanted to succumb, especially not tonight. But even after four years together the sensual attraction was still as potent as ever for her – inexplicably generated by this bovine, otherwise colourless man whose body aroused hers at will. At the time of their marriage she had suppressed the idea he would satisfy only one of her needs – the need she was indulging now as she allowed him to press her back onto the bed.

'You said you had to go,' she murmured. 'And you're in a bow-tie already, for God's sake. Why didn't you think of this before?' Her voice trailed off as his hands began caressing her more intimately. She pulled his shirt apart and began biting his bare flesh. Soon she was moaning and writhing beneath him.

Once more he had turned her anger into a different sort of passion.

Possessing Rebecca had become Norman Westerly's whole reason for being: keeping her had justified everything.

When they had first met she had been impressed at his being Moneybuckle Custodian. That was before she knew it carried more status than reward, and not too much of either.

Later he had tried for better jobs, but he seldom got an interview, and was never short-listed. He had been lucky to have the Moneybuckle.

Even now, Westerly couldn't bring himself wholly to regret what he'd done. It was galling, though, that they were back again relying on her earnings. It wasn't that he was proud, only scared that she resented the situation quite so much.

And he was even more scared that increasingly her work was taking her to London, into the company of men she clearly found stimulating, despite her disdain for commerce.

Of course, the risks he had been taking had bought him time with Rebecca. Up to today he had relied on their continuing to do so. But this morning everything had started going wrong for him.

'That was so good,' she sighed when they finished making love, and she was lying dishevelled and exhausted beside him. 'The spontaneous times have been the best, you know? The times to remember.'

'Always,' he agreed, unalerted by the terminal hint in her words.

He had been fired enough by their coupling, but now the thought of the reckoning he was facing had come back to him.

It was clear already that the fast trip to Reading in the day had solved very little. He had to dispose of everything tonight. And even that would only allow him a little extra time to find what was still an impossibly large sum of money.

But he was a realist enough to know the alternative would be quite a long jail sentence.

Chapter Six

'I suppose I should take the pole,' Steven Bickworthy resolved aloud, but with a serious lack of conviction. He suffered the same hang-up each time they came on the river, which wasn't often. Now he was balancing unsteadily in the centre of the punt. A non-swimmer, he was never at ease on water.

'Because you're male? Bit of phallic symbolism, that is. Part of ancient river seduction rites, d'you think?' Clair Witherton answered breezily, standing on the landing stage of the Bardwell Road boat-house from where she was busy passing him essential supplies. 'No. I'll do the work. You save your energy, then you can have your way with me when I'm too exhausted to resist. I'll look forward to that. But do sit down, Steven. You're rocking the boat.'

He did, on the big cushions, facing sternwards, after stowing the bags of food and drink behind the seat-back.

Clair stepped aboard well aft, behind the other seat, kicked off her shoes, then over-confidently moved further along the up-sloping, slatted bottom. Her boisterous movements brought some water lapping in over the side. 'Sorry!' she cried, anticipating Steven's apprehension. 'They punt from the other end in Cambridge. Must make it even more difficult to get your balance at the start. Whoops!' she finished, nearly losing hers again.

'That would make their decked-over end the stern, and the bit you're on the bow. Except the punts are identical. So the difference is one of usage not fact.'

Steven, the law student, frowned judiciously – glad to have something other than the possibility of falling in the River Cherwell to occupy his mind. 'Could produce a nice problem in maritime law. Case of irreconcilable definitions. In a collision. If one punter claimed he was going astern, and was therefore being carelessly overtaken by the other,' he added, warming to the subject with his eyes closed.

'Shipwrecked punts? Don't be daft.'

The elderly boatman on the landing stage was also unmoved at the prospect of litigious punting disasters between here and the River Cam. He had been waiting for some time to pass Clair a metal punt-pole. 'Mind you're back by ten at the latest, Miss. We close at ten tonight,' he cautioned. It was already six-thirty.

'Before then if the bugs are biting. Thanks.' Clair gave him an expansive smile as he shoved them away. She found bottom with the pole and kept the momentum going – her smooth, strong thighs straining against the confines of the white tennis shorts she was wearing.

'You look very Betjemanesque.' Steven was covertly enjoying the rhythmic performance of that nicely turned body slaving away for his benefit – covertly because his Yorkshire upbringing dictated the roles ought to be reversed.

'Betjeman girls were always strong, weren't they? Like Joan Hunter Dunn?'

'And Myfanwy. "Strong and willowy, strong to pillow me, Gold Myfanwy, kisses and art," he recited, but not at all loudly, while wondering if the late Poet Laureate had let his Myfanwy do the punting.

'I'm not gold, I'm auburn.' But Clair wasn't displeased either. 'Did you have a hard day at the Moneybuckle?' They had met only minutes earlier at the boat-house: Clair had been playing tennis nearby for the previous hour.

'Quite hard.' He reclined more comfortably on the cushions: after all, Clair hadn't been gainfully employed all day. 'Yes, got a lot done.' He reached in the cooling

63

bag for a bottle of German wine and a corkscrew.

'With Edith Norn?'

'Some of the time. She went early. About half-three. I think she was seeing one of the governors. Oh, and I met the chairman. Mark Treasure. He's head of Grenwood, Phipps, the merchant bankers. He came in to see Mr Westerly. He had a word with Edith and me on the way.'

'Did you start lining up a job for yourself in his bank?'

'Of course not.' But he reflected on whether he should have done as he drew the cork from the bottle.

'But it's what you want to be. A banker.'

'Well you can hardly— '

'But isn't that what the Oxford old-boy network is all about? Despicable as it may be to those excluded.' She gave an extra hard thrust on the pole to register the disdain of the unemployed – while privately deeming the Treasure acquaintance as fortuitous and worth developing.

'I'll be seeing him again tomorrow, I expect.'

'Or even tonight,' Clair supplied knowingly. 'He's got one of the Fellows' sets at the bottom of our staircase. I checked in the lodge. After I saw a few well heeled elderly gents trooping in from the quad. Thought they might be after me. They weren't.' She gave a self-deprecating sniff. 'They were all Moneybuckle governors. Some on our staircase. One or two next door.'

'Mr Treasure isn't at all elderly. About forty I'd say.'

'The American in the rooms opposite his is much older than that. I did see him. Must be important as well. He's got a Fellows' set too.'

'His name's Ostracher. New York stockbroker.'

'You've boned up the list?'

'Only to check on the ones you think should employ me,' he commented dryly.

'Very funny. So you know they're not all men.'

'There are two women. Miss Chance. I know her. She's a don at St Agnes. She won't be staying in college. The other one's— '

'The celebrated Charlotte Lundle,' Clair interrupted. 'She's on our middle landing.'

'Really? Have you seen her yet?'

'No. There was a woman who called on someone called Gavon just before I left. He's on the top landing next to me. I just caught sight of him. He's young too. And dishy.'

'He's a publisher. And the woman couldn't have been Charlotte Lundle?'

'No. I know what she looks like. Well, everyone does.' Clair was trailing the pole in the water, steering them toward a tree-hung section of river-bank where they could moor. They hadn't come very far, but the river was fairly empty and she was out for a romantic supper, not for exercise. 'Is Edith Norn short, with dark frizzy hair?'

'Yes. And a bit toothy.'

'Wearing a pink dress this afternoon?'

'Er . . . yes, I think so.'

'That was her then. Mind your head.' Clair crouched too, ready to avoid the leafy willow branches that were just brushing over Steven as the punt came to rest in the short reeds against the bank. She shoved the pole hard down against the outside gunwale and into the muddy bottom, where it would stop them from drifting. Then she stepped over to sit close beside Steven who was pouring them wine.

'Edith was much better turned out today than yesterday,' he said, giving Clair a gentle kiss on the lips before passing her a glass. 'The whole place was being smartened up for the governors. Tomorrow I think I'd better wear a tie.'

'She's got something very heavy going with Mr Gavon, the publisher,' put in Clair flatly, looking unusually pensive as she took a deep draught of still cool, low price Piesporter.

'Edith has? I think she was probably seeing him on business.'

'Her place of business is the Moneybuckle, not the next room to mine. Not at half-past three on a Friday afternoon. Remember the phone call you overheard?'

'I think he's married:' a circumstance which still to Steven's way of thinking should on the whole have militated against sexual promiscuity by Moneybuckle governors.

'All the more reason I suppose for going to bed at half-past three on— '

'How d'you know they did?'

'They started by making noisy love with the window open. They probably thought they had the floor to themselves.'

'So you tactfully switched your radio on?'

'A tape actually. That cut down the volume of the ardour. And they shut the window. But I went to make tea in the kitchen later.' She didn't need to explain the point further because they both understood it.

The ventilator shafts from the central service areas on New Quad staircases had an unintended function. They transmitted and amplified sound from the student rooms into the little kitchens – and on a quite spectacular scale. No one understood why this was so, why the amplification didn't work the other way around, and why nothing had ever been done about it. The students knew the problem, of course, and the more careful ones remembered always to keep their voices low at appropriate times.

'You shut your ears, of course,' said Steven, but anticipating that further revelation was on the way.

'I wonder if governors' mistresses have to be Church of England too?' Clair mused without replying directly. She continued to regard a well stuffed ham vol-au-vent while deciding on which side to bite it.

'I don't think the Church membership part is applied all that carefully. Not any more,' answered Steven with unnecessary gravity. He was watching a mother duck approach the punt with a lone baby duck paddling hard behind; both were searching for food. 'Anyway, I don't really believe Edith and Mr Gavon can be that much involved. I mean the governors only meet once a year,' he ended, again ingenuously.

'Maybe they're on a sub-committee that gets together more often. Maybe they *are* a sub-committee.' Clair answered with her mouth full. Her gaze was also following the baby duck: she threw it a piece of pastry which the mother duck promptly snatched and consumed.

'That was infant preservation, not parent greed,' Steven pronounced with the conviction of a townsman who picked up rural lore from articles in other people's copies of *Country Life*. 'In case the food was dangerous.' He paused. 'Did you actually hear Edith say she and Gavon had other meetings?'

'Not directly. She didn't need to.' Clair swallowed some more wine. 'I mean, they must have met at least once around May. She said she thought she was pregnant. Then she went on quite a bit about what you'd call infant preservation.' Clair gave a pained look. 'Your Mr Gavon seemed keener on abortion.'

'Both of 'em came?' exclaimed Arthur Midden, scratching his bottom, a note of triumph discernible in the muted voice.

He was speaking into the pay-phone in his own front hall. Some years before he had found it cheaper to have a pay-phone installed than to go on allowing undergraduate lodgers to make calls on a rarely honoured 'cash-in-the-box' arrangement. It also discouraged his wife from using the telephone. The frugal Midden had accepted the personal inconvenience – which included not having a telephone in the private part of the house. His employers didn't know he had a telephone since he'd told them the old one had been disconnected: pay-phones are not listed. This used to save him from being summoned at inconvenient times by members of the SCR, an advantage cancelled when the pagers were introduced, with beams that reached well beyond St John Street.

'Did B make that suggestion? Like I said he would?' he went on, in a muffled tone, because he didn't want his wife to overhear. His face suffused with satisfaction as he listened to the answer. 'Told you so,' he put in knowingly, then listened again, but this time with impatience. 'Never mind he didn't say how much . . . All right, didn't name the percentage. You said he didn't have the chance . . . He'll tell you soon enough when he comes back, or rings you, more like. More important, he's committed.' The person he was speaking to explained something complicated before Midden broke in again. 'If he asks for twenty-five, offer him twenty. If he sticks, give him the twenty-five. It'll be worth it.' But what the SCR butler got by way of answer to that injunction didn't please him as much as what had gone before. 'So with my cut you'll be thirty per cent light altogether on the whole deal . . . Call that ruinous do you? I call it fantastic. Bloody marvellous. You want jam on it, you do . . . No, I'm not going halves on any extras. No way . . . I'm not even discussing it. Listen, I've got to get back. We'll talk again after, OK? But a deal's a deal.'

Midden put down the receiver with a scowl, picking up the extra coins he hadn't needed to use. At least the last action gave him some small satisfaction.

'Was that Ernie you were calling?' Val Midden enquired as her husband came back into the kitchen where she was ironing.

'It might have been.'

'Which means it was. I could tell by your tone of voice. It shows with you, if you don't like someone. Beats me why you have anything to do with Ernie, seeing you don't like him. All said and done, he's my brother, not yours. Half-brother,' she added for accuracy.

'You heard what we were talking about?'

'No. And if it's secret, I don't want to know either.'

Well that was a double blessing he thought, before saying, 'Ernie's all right, I suppose. We've got a bit of business on, that's all. Matter of fact, I'm doing him a good turn. It's just . . . Well he ought to be more grateful.'

'Ernie was never grateful. Even as a child. Not in his nature.'

'Well so long as he remembers his obligations. Any tea left in that pot?'

'Just a drop. I can top it up if you want? Or make fresh?' She put down the iron.

'No. Don't think I've got time now.'

She glanced at the clock, then got up quickly. 'Yes you have. Just.'

During term time he went back to the Senior Common Room pantry at five-thirty for the evening, after a break from three o'clock. In the vacations, if there were important (meaning high-tipping) visitors using the SCR, he worked through the afternoon and came down here later for an hour, returning around six-thirty, and it was after that already. Still, sherry wasn't being served to the Moneybuckle governors until seven-thirty.

He watched while his wife re-boiled the water left in the electric kettle. 'That dopey-looking girl Ernie's got in the shop. What's her name?' he asked.

'Megan. Megan Rees.'

'Is she all right in the head?'

'Of course she is. She's Welsh.' Val looked round at her husband to see whether he'd accepted Celtic origin as any proof of sanity: he hadn't. 'Her father's a preacher,' she went on. 'She's been to university somewhere. She told me. Dropped out though. Through illness. Then other things. It's a sad story,' she ended darkly.

He let a brief silence indicate that, sad or not, what she had related hadn't answered his question. Then he said, 'But she still can't do any better than work for Ernie?'

'She writes poetry.'

He gave an impatient sigh. 'Sleeps with him too, does she?'

'I'm sure I wouldn't know,' she answered stiffly, while refilling the teapot. 'Anyway, that's their business.'

'He wouldn't be going to marry her, you think?'

'Go on, she's half his age.'

'All the more reason.' He sometimes thought his wife lived in a different world from everyone else.

'Well, I've told you, I don't know. Here's your tea.' She passed him the cup, then went back to the ironing-board. 'This good turn you're doing Ernie. Is he paying for it?'

'In a way.' He sat down at the table, and began slurping the hot tea.

'Got it in writing, have you?'

He didn't answer, but she could tell from the expression he hadn't. Well, serve him right if Ernie didn't cough up.

'The Moneybuckle governors settled in all right, I expect?' she said, shaking out a pillowslip and changing the subject.

He looked up sharply over his cup, eyes narrowing in suspicion. 'Yes. Any reason why they shouldn't?'

'Not that I know of. I was only asking.' She wondered why he was being so touchy. 'That Mr Treasure's a real gentleman. He was in this afternoon, seeing Mr Westerly. Always has a word in passing, he does. It was the same last year. Knows a lot about the things they've got on show, too. Like what was in the glass case I was polishing when he came by me. Ever so interesting he was about it.'

'He's a banker, not an expert on books,' her husband commented dismissively.

'Well he talks like an expert. Better than Mr Westerly, if you ask me. In the clouds he is, and never a word with the likes of me. Anyway, it wasn't books in the showcase I was cleaning. It was drawings.'

'What sort of drawings?'

'Drawings of buildings and that. Architect's drawings, Mr Treasure said.'

'Oh yes, they're different.' He finished the tea and got up to leave. He didn't trouble explaining what exactly architectural drawings were different from. He was asking himself whether he could have charged Ernie more if he'd contracted to recruit the unknowing assistance of yet another expert.

Chapter Seven

'If the sketches are by Constable, perhaps we should buy them. For the Moneybuckle, I mean,' the Reverend Professor Bodd put in haltingly during a lull in the conversation, and in the nervous manner of someone made uneasy by lulls in conversations. He was holding his port glass between two hands, like a chalice, and had been studying its just replenished contents with a lowered expression, as though he felt guilty at having twice drained the glass already.

'Why buy them for the Moneybuckle?' demanded Bryan Gavon, touching his mouth with his napkin. He was sitting across from Bodd at the large round table, between Charlotte Lundle and Julian Barners. There had been ten present at the dinner just ending.

Ostracher said nothing, but gave a noncommittal cough: this was his way of registering displeasure, though only one or two of the others knew him well enough to appreciate the fact.

To the American's way of thinking there had been no need to discuss the sketches at all – *his* sketches, as he already thought of them. But the subject had been introduced first by Bodd who had chosen to ask Julian Barners about the origin of the works. Dr Radout had then admitted that he had seen all three sketches: the interest of the others had stemmed from there.

Perhaps there had been some justification for Bodd's first question, Ostracher persuaded himself. It was Barners who in all conscience should really have known better when he told the professor about the sketches in that quite gratuitous way outside the Moneybuckle. The American had been uncomfortable about it at the time, even though he hadn't said as much. He assumed Bodd was not affluent enough to be in the market himself for expensive works of art: he also took it that Barners' question to Bodd about his Suffolk origins had had some useful objective behind it – even though Barners had whisked Ostracher out of Bodd's presence pretty promptly, following the undermining comment about fakes.

Ostracher had still not expected Bodd to make commonplace conversation about the sketches again later. There were others present probably quite able to find the price of such works, whatever that price might be. It would all have been different if Barners had advised him to buy already, instead of equivocating.

Oblivious to all this, the emboldened Bodd said, 'A few Constables could only enhance the Moneybuckle fine-art collection.' He then applied himself to relighting the cigar he had abandoned more often than he had refilled his port glass.

'Wouldn't the sketches be beyond our means, Mr Westerly?' asked Charlotte Lundle.

'That would be up to the governors to decide,' the Custodian answered carefully, stroking his beard. He directed a wan smile toward the painting hanging behind Barners who was placed nearly opposite him.

'There being mays and means . . . ' Arabella Chance began, paused, frowned, stared erratically around the table, then attempted a correction with a carefully articulated, '*Ways* and weans,' which though again not right, seemed, by her following grimace, to satisfy her hugely.

Miss Chance was wearing an ancient blue satin dress and a long rope of pink beads which, in the middle of dinner, she had been given to grasping and swinging about with some abandon. It had been the first indication that she was not entirely herself. She was seated to the right of Dr Radout who, as Moneybuckle governor at All Saints College, was nominal host for the evening.

The group was gathered not in the main Senior Common Room but in the more intimate, single-cube anteroom. This was panelled and shuttered in dark oak, with an exquisitely carved fireplace and overmantel reputed to be by Grinling Gibbons. An equally notable crystal chandelier graced the centre of the ceiling, beneath a delicately fashioned moulding. The gilt-framed pictures on the walls were late seventeenth or eighteenth-century paintings of college notables. The polished mahogany table and chairs were by Chippendale. The sparkling glasses, the rare Georgian silver, and the precious bone china added more lustre. The setting of the Moneybuckle dinner was never less than elegant.

'You think we could justify dipping into the capital fund for a Constable or two, Miss Chance?' enquired Treasure, who was directly opposite Radout, with Edith Norn to his right and Ostracher on his other side.

'Surely not simply on the basis that they happened to have turned up on our doorstep, as it were?' Gavon half-protested.

'The terms of the Endowment certainly wouldn't preclude our buying genuine Constable sketches,' offered Radout, swinging away from Miss Chance energetically, like the arm of a metronome, and precipitating his whole trunk toward Charlotte on his other side. He had been repeating this manoeuvre throughout dinner in a cunning ploy aimed at his seeing further down the front of the younger woman's V-neck – each time with increasing abandon and improving success. Radout was having a most enjoyable evening.

'More decaffeinated coffee, Mr Ostracher, sir?' Midden enquired with extra solicitude from behind the American's chair.

'Get them cheap . . . the sketches, could we?' asked

Miss Chance, stifling a violent hiccough in the middle, and confirming beyond lingering, charitable doubt that she had drunk too much. She fixed a beady eye on the heavy port decanter which had just appeared on her right, before propelling it on its coaster with reckless speed to her other side, without sampling its contents. Her disarming, self-approving expression was meant to qualify such evident restraint. This would have convinced better if she had not just directed Midden to recharge her brandy glass. 'Buy them for a song if we ponce now?' she continued. 'Ponce?' she repeated questioningly and, staring hard at Barners, much to his irritation. 'Pounce, I mean,' she corrected, giving Westerly a conspiratorial dig with her elbow.

'Good pictures never come cheap. Not unless the dealer's a fool. Or a rogue selling fakes,' said Bodd, turning slowly toward Ostracher on his right.

The American responded with a pained look, though this was largely on account of the dandruff he had observed accumulating all evening on Bodd's shoulders – a condition Ostracher had been led to believe was probably infectious. 'Do you know Mr Cormit?' he enquired.

'Positively not,' Bodd replied promptly, this time adding to his neighbour's disquiet by firing saliva at his lapel, which the other was too well mannered to remove immediately. 'Positively not,' Bodd repeated, doing it again, and meaning to emphasise that such lack of familiarity could hardly work to Cormit's advantage.

'In my view Cormit is neither a fool nor a rogue,' said Barners, commanding everyone's instant attention. The well-manicured long fingers of both hands joined in a suppliant manner before him, and pointed, like his gaze, in the direction of the chandelier. 'He's not a dealer in the strict sense, of course. Not a fine-art dealer,' the expert elucidated further. 'Just someone weighed down by the fortune on his back, and obliged to swim in water already beyond his depth.'

No one observed the startled expression that passed across the face of the normally imperturbable Midden in the wake of the last remark. He was at the serving table, facing the wall.

'And have you advised Ostracher to take advantage of the situation?' asked Gavon, waving the smoke of his own cigar away from Charlotte Lundle and in the direction of Barners on his other side. 'You evidently believe the sketches are genuine.' But there was more than a touch of enquiry in the last statement.

'Not to take advantage,' Barners replied weightily, and without denying the contention. He leaned back slightly. 'It's not uncommon for art finds of this kind to change hands for the first time at a disproportionately lower price than they fetch at subsequent resales. Even quite soon after the first sale. The reason for that is obvious.'

'Very nicely put,' said Gavon. 'Meaning the first seller's usually too timid. Or doesn't take the best advice. Or any advice. Makes me feel I should offer for these sketches myself.'

Ostracher winced.

'The reason for the low price at the first sale being primarily the lack of a reliable provenance? But the next part doesn't always follow, surely?' Treasure was challenging Barners. 'I mean, because a work changes hands several times doesn't make it any more genuine.'

'Logic would suggest as much, certainly,' replied Barners. 'Human nature often defies logic, however.' He shrugged. 'Every sale lengthens the back list of known owners.'

'Without always improving it?' Treasure offered cynically.

'Quite so,' replied Barners. 'Of course, if the first sale is at auction, the price may still be high.'

'Because with a lot of knowledgeable people bidding, the genuineness is hyped from the start, and the price with it,' said Charlotte.

'Still confirms the good sense of asking the advice of an

expert like Julian Barners. Making a private killing where opportunity presents,' Gavon insisted lightly.

'You're convinced they're missing Constables, Julian?' Treasure asked, aware like the others that Gavon's similar question had been ignored.

Barners hesitated before replying. 'One can but offer an opinion.'

'In your case a very expert opinion,' urged Charlotte. 'Is there anyone who knows as much about Constable as you, Mr Barners?'

'Oh, numbers of people. Doctor Radout amongst others,' the subject offered, but with conviction clearly tempered by modesty.

'Nonsense. Not at all my speciality. You're being much too humble, Julian.' This was Radout, with a sentiment which most of the others found privately hilarious.

'Did someone say Constable only came to Oxford once?' enquired Charlotte.

'I may have,' said Miss Chance suddenly. She blinked several times, as though she had just been asleep – or possibly because she was trying hard to stay awake.

'It's true, so far as anyone knows,' Radout supplied. 'He and his friend Archdeacon John Fisher of Salisbury had been touring the Berkshire archdeaconry.'

'Which was then part of the Salisbury diocese,' supplied Bodd.

Radout nodded. 'Fisher called on parish clergy while Constable sketched. After they finished the official tour in Abingdon, it seems they went sightseeing. To Woodstock and Oxford. Fisher was a keen amateur artist. He enjoyed sketching with Constable along as his tutor. Who wouldn't have done?'

'How well informed you are on the detail,' said Charlotte.

Heady with the compliment, Radout again swung toward her, so close this time as to make it necessary to clasp her hand to prevent himself ending on top of her. 'I confess I

76

looked it all up this morning. After Cormit had been to see me,' he offered bashfully, and pretending he'd forgotten he was still holding her hand.

'I believe the arsh . . . archdeacon eventually became Bishop of Sal . . . Sal . . . ' Miss Chance elected to start again. 'Was he later Bishop of . . . Salisbury?' She almost shouted the last word. It was at that point also that the bent elbow she had placed on the table suddenly fell off it.

'No. The Bishop was his uncle,' supplied Bodd quickly, before Radout could do so. 'Also called John Fisher, and also a patron of Constable's. He met Constable after the future Bishop married Dorothea Scrivenor. She was a Suffolk Scrivenor. She brought him sixteen hundred pounds a year.' The speaker's eyes enlarged at the contemplation of such riches. 'The Bishop was later known as the King's Fisher. A great favourite of George the Third. *Unsoiled by courts and unseduced by zeal, Fisher endangers not the common weal.* That was how Samuel Parr described him.'

After the murmur of general approval that follows apposite declamation of remembered verse, even in cultured circles, Treasure asked, 'Constable did a sketch of University College. Were the Fishers members of the college?'

'Neither was. They were both Cambridge men.' This was Bodd again. 'The archdeacon's father, Philip Fisher, was at Oxford. First as an undergraduate. He later became a tutor at University College. It's assumed Constable did the sketch for his benefit, though I don't believe he ever possessed it.'

'It seems we're awash with Constable experts,' said Gavon.

'My knowledge was almost inborn, I'm afraid. I was brought up in Constable country,' Bodd admitted.

'Have you seen the sketches, Professor?' asked Charlotte.

'No, but I should dearly like to. To see any of Constable's work is a privilege. To own any must be a satisfying experience. That's something that has always been well beyond my aspirations, I fear.' Bodd's last words were ruminative, and he had turned on Ostracher who drew back in time to avoid being showered by the aspirates.

The American was, even so, relieved that at least one member of the company was admitting he wasn't in the market.

'Will they be so expensive, Mr Barners?' This was Charlotte again.

'That depends on the seller.'

'Can't you be more specific?'

'I fear not.'

Charlotte grinned, leaning forward. 'What about you, Doctor Radout?' Her movement coincided with his swing toward her, so that at last it was revealed to him that she was wearing nothing beneath the silk top.

Radout gulped in appreciation – and, heady with the glimpse of bare breast, he declared rashly, 'If the sketches are genuine, the pencil works should fetch twenty thousand pounds apiece.'

'And the oil?' Edith Norn enquired quietly, and to the surprise of those near her. Despite Treasure's efforts at conversation, she had hardly uttered during dinner.

'For the oil sketch, I should say up to a quarter of a million,' pronounced Radout expansively. 'That's only my far-from-expert view, of course.' He looked at Barners, who declined to be drawn.

Midden, still at the serving table, had caught his breath when the last sum was mentioned.

'That's if they're all proved to be genuine,' put in Bodd.

'Naturally. But I'm sure our Mr Cormit could do even better than that eventually,' added Radout. 'If he's prepared to collect opinions. To pay for scientific tests, and all the modern mumbo-jumbo.'

'And risk the stuff being proved fake by the same process?' questioned Treasure.

'Always possible,' Radout agreed. 'He did tell me he's already been offered twenty thousand in Bond Street.'

'That's a bit of a come-down,' said Charlotte.

'I'd say a try-on. By a dealer who probably wouldn't have risked a thousand pounds on anything he wasn't sure was fairly genuine,' Gavon observed.

'You said they're purported to have come from the family of David Lucas the engraver,' said Bodd.

'Actually from a family called Smith who were servants to the Lucases,' Radout corrected.

'Are they notched?'

There was a brief uncomfortable silence.

'I noticed that they weren't,' said Radout.

'Any squaring could easily have been excised,' Barners observed unexpectedly.

'Will someone tell me what notching means?' asked Treasure.

'Before they start copying, engravers sometimes mark original drawings with notches at one inch intervals, at the top and bottom,' Radout volunteered. 'They call it squaring.'

'It's the same principle as those painting sets one got as a child. Painting by squares,' said Charlotte.

'Very similar principle, my dear,' Radout agreed, touching her hand approvingly – several times.

Barners frowned. It was difficult to imagine his painting by squares as a child – or for that matter to imagine his ever having been a child at all. 'There is little significance in the absence of notches,' he remarked loftily. 'Not all engravers follow the practice.'

Midden, who had left the room briefly, now returned and deferentially whispered something to Radout who looked toward Ostracher.

'You're wanted on the telephone, Armin,' said Radout. 'From New York. There's an instrument you can use in the next room.'

'Forgive me,' said the American getting up and leaving, but without haste.

'Did you get through before dinner on the phone in my room, Julian?' asked Treasure.

79

'Thank you ... Yes,' Barners replied, but for some reason disturbed at the question. 'I ... I should have reimbursed you for the cost.'

'Please do nothing of the kind. I just wondered if the line was faulty. I couldn't get a connection myself just before you tried.'

'The porters aren't always very prompt in answering. Not in the vacation,' Radout explained. 'Especially in the evening.'

'Is Mr Ostracher going to risk it, and buy the sketches, d'you suppose?' asked Charlotte.

'You must ask him when he comes back,' said Gavon from her left.

'If he trusts to Barners' judgement I believe he will,' Bodd commented.

Barners merely raised an eyebrow.

'Well I'd like to see them before that happens,' said the young woman with enthusiasm.

'You going to offer for them yourself, Charlotte?' asked Treasure.

'No. But I'd like to savour later that I could have if I'd wanted. The situation may be unusual, don't you think?'

'Probably. I'd quite enjoy seeing them too,' said Treasure.

Decimus Radout chuckled. 'I'd like another look. There was something— '

'You may all have to be quick,' Bodd interrupted. 'If you have the least idea of buying. I don't believe Ostracher means to wait about.'

Treasure was about to protest he wasn't a buyer, but gave way to Charlotte who proposed, 'Why don't we descend on Mr Cormit in a body? Right now. If he'll have us. It's not far and the air'll do us good.'

'Splendid idea,' agreed Gavon. 'Should we ring to make sure he's in?'

'I believe I have his telephone number about me,' said Radout producing a pocket diary, and then his spectacles.

'It's in a section at the back.' In the end Charlotte helped him turn the pages which pleased him greatly.

'I think we've exhausted Miss Chance,' said Westerly in a despairing voice. The lady had slipped sideways and had fallen asleep on his chest.

Chapter Eight

'They're quite beautiful. All three of them. You feel almost instinctively they're the real thing,' enthused Charlotte Lundle.

'Julian Barners would definitely approve of that sentiment,' said Treasure who was standing beside her.

'He regards instinct as the only truly reliable method of picture divination,' Gavon agreed.

'Only as applying to himself, surely?' countered Charlotte with a cynical grin.

'But Julian's own instinct is so thoroughly conditioned when it comes to Constable,' said Decimus Radout, on the other side of Charlotte. 'His eye for a Constable comes from having eyed and dissected practically every Constable that ever was.'

'And perhaps several thousands that were only trying to be,' offered Westerly. He was studying the sketches on show more closely than anyone.

'You can perfectly well develop what's called an instinct,' Gavon insisted. 'Which explains why genuine connoisseurs can chance their reputations with an attribution. Often on first sight. Just as Julian has done over these little gems. I mean without benefit of X-rays and carbon tests, and so on.'

'Has Julian quite done that?' asked Radout wrinkling his nose.

'Oh, I think so.'

'I wouldn't be sure,' Treasure put in carefully, surprised

that Gavon had made the admission in front of Cormit. Even if it were accurate, it did nothing to improve the absent Ostracher's bargaining position if he intended to offer for the works.

'Well I dearly wish my instincts were as well educated,' said Charlotte. 'Don't you Edith?'

'I expect some are. On subjects you know about,' Edith Norn answered, in a much less wooden voice than the one that had characterised her few utterances earlier in the evening. She had been looking at Bryan Gavon not Charlotte as she spoke. He had been paying her a significant amount of attention since they had left the college.

'Anyway, I'm sorry my feeling about your Constables is just spontaneous, not tutored, Mr Cormit,' Charlotte continued, turning toward him. 'But I think they're stunning.'

'Thank you, Miss Lundle. Will you have some more tea? No? Then let Megan take your cup. Come on Megan, jump to it.'

The seven visitors were standing around a small table in the centre of the narrow, cluttered bookshop in Walton Street. They had arrived shortly after ten-thirty, having moved down Little Clarendon Street as a slightly self-conscious phalanx.

While Treasure was pleased to have seen the sketches, he had lost some of his enthusiasm for the expedition once it was under way. On reflection, he felt it had made an inappropriate ending to the dinner: to have lingered over another glass of port, or to have strolled in the college gardens would probably have been more agreeable than moving off in a body for a private view in not very salubrious circumstances. He sensed Edith Norn was of the same opinion, but that she, like Westerly, had probably felt a sort of obligation to humour the whim of the majority of the Moneybuckle governors.

Only Ostracher and Barners had declined to come. Arabella Chance, the only other missing member, had been left behind involuntarily. She was asleep in Charlotte's room where she had been taken, without protest, to rest until her 'migraine' improved. She had refused to be sent home in a taxi, sleepily insisting she would shortly be quite able to make the journey on her bicycle.

Doctor Radout had stayed at Charlotte's side and was clearly more intoxicated by her company than he had been by the still quite substantial quantity of wines he had consumed. For her part, she was touched by the court he was paying her, amused by his increasingly overt attempts at flirtation, and impressed by his scholarship.

The street door to the shop had been opened to the party by Megan Rees, a pale, thin young woman who had later brought tea for the visitors. She was tallish, and a little ungainly, with nervous dark eyes and a mop of coarse black hair. Her evident desire to please Cormit struck some present as undeserved in view of his surly attitude toward her.

Cormit had not introduced the girl to anyone, nor explained her function. It was left to the visitors to assume she assisted in the shop, which the owner announced normally stayed open until nine on Fridays – and even later if there were still collectors present: 'collectors' was the word Cormit chose to describe his customers. Even so, from what could be seen of his stock, on the crowded, top-heavy shelves that intruded at various angles, and in the piles of volumes stacked in every available space, it was more the dog-eared commonplace than the pristine rarity that Cormit was offering for sale.

Earlier, Cormit had made a somewhat theatrical entrance down the staircase at the back of the shop, carrying the sketches. Then, officiously, he had ordered Megan to lock the street door before he exposed his three prize possessions to the company.

'Mr Barners noted the watermark you pointed out this morning, Doctor,' said Cormit to Radout in an affected, confidential aside, but loud enough for everyone to hear.

The doctor was holding up the drawing of Christ Church from the Meadows for Charlotte to see, though, for his own part, he seemed to be studying her more closely than the picture.

'There are three incomplete lines of watermarks running to the edge,' said Charlotte. 'One reads "J. What", the next "Turk", and the last the figures "one and eight".'

'Well done.' Radout nodded vigorously as though she had succeeded in translating a particularly difficult passage in faded Sanskrit. 'If we had the full sheet that would certainly have been "J. Whatman, Turkey Mills, eighteen hundred and something". Constable mostly used sketch pads made up of Whatman or John Dickinson paper. So did Turner, as a matter of fact.'

'In this instance eighteen hundred and something being the year the paper was made?'

'It would need to be eighteen twenty-one or earlier to fit the case, of course,' Bodd remarked, peering over Charlotte's shoulder. 'Pity there are no discernible watermarks on either of the other sketches,' he added, though the implication was more one of doubt than sorrow.

'But would a complete watermark be conclusive proof of anything?' asked Treasure.

Radout chuckled. 'Only of the make and year of the paper. Not of anything that had been put on it, I'm afraid.'

'And old paper isn't difficult to come by,' Bodd was quick to offer. He nodded at the bookshelves. 'Pick up any old volume and the chances are you'll come upon blank pages. Endpapers with watermarkings. They're the forger's stock in trade, of course.'

'I see what you mean. About the spare pages,' said Treasure a few moments later. He was turning the blank sheets at the end of a large, dilapidated old tome in thick black covers that he had taken down from the nearest shelf. He held several pages to the light in turn. 'Two of these have watermarks. Not complete, I'm afraid. Oh, this one is.

It reads "Abbey Mills, Greenfield, eighteen sixty-one". Bit too late for Constable, but it'd do for faking say a Frith or a Manet. The paper feels like cartridge too. Very suitable, I'd imagine.'

'Should one assume a watermark increases rather than reduces the possibility of a fake?' asked Westerly who had removed his jacket. He seemed to be more discomforted by the heat in the room than anyone else.

'No, one shouldn't,' Gavon replied. 'You're filling Mr Cormit here with despondency, Professor.'

'Not at all, sir,' said Cormit. 'Mr Barners seemed convinced enough about the drawings being genuine. The doctor hasn't said they're not, and the dealer who offered for them in London felt they were real. I'm certain he did. Except he tried to do me down on the price,' he ended with a glower.

'You still need to exercise a lot of faith where a provenance depends on circumstantial evidence,' said Bodd, in a not very reverent tone.

'Well I think the evidence here is better than circumstantial,' Gavon countered. 'And you say this is the family Bible that contained your Constables, Mr Cormit?' He opened the heavy volume which Cormit had also placed on the table.

'That's the one, sir. It's in fair condition for its age. Hasn't had that much use, not by the looks of it.'

'Not great Bible readers the Smiths, perhaps?' said Treasure. 'Just careful to keep up the entries on the family tree.'

'Neat entries too. They must have been a well-educated lot of servants.' Gavon was flicking over the relevant pages in the centre of the Bible as he spoke.

'But not very bright if they'd ignored three Constable originals all this time,' mused Bodd.

'Well by the look of it, only two or three people at the most would need to have done any ignoring,' said Gavon thoughtfully. 'And their apparent ignorance may have been nothing of the kind. It could quite possibly have been a determined attitude on their part to keep beautiful things in the family. More specifically, under their own personal care. Like the Bible itself.'

'That's quite romantic. Go on,' said Charlotte.

'Well see here,' Gavon continued, turning back some pages. 'All the entries up to eighteen seventy-six are in one hand. Then another single hand does them up to er . . . nineteen twenty-three. And finally someone else takes over and does them to nineteen sixty-one, when the entries stopped.'

'It was usual in the old days for one member of a family to keep entries like that going over long periods, sir,' said Cormit, sounding enough like an expert for the others to pay proper attention. 'Didn't need to have been the head of the family either. More likely a maiden aunt with nothing else to do. She'd act as a sort of post office for family happenings. Recorder of 'em as well.'

'Would the recently deceased Selina Smith fit that role?' asked Charlotte.

'It was she who kept the Bible entries going since nineteen twenty-three, Miss Lundle. She recorded the last death, her widowed married sister, in nineteen sixty-one. Seems that was the end of the family. Except for Selina herself, of course. She lost five brothers in the First World War. Five. Not uncommon that wasn't.' Cormit touched the knot of his RAF tie.

'And you believe she'd have hung onto the sketches?' asked Bodd.

'As very likely did the lady who kept the Bible for nearly fifty years before her, sir. That was Margaret Smith, spinster, in service with David Lucas at the time of his death,' chronicled Cormit. 'It could be she was given the drawings and didn't want to part with them for sentimental reasons.'

'She could also have pinched them, I suppose,' said Treasure irreverently. 'Then found them too hot to get rid of for gain. No, that's uncharitable. It's much more likely they were a gift, as you suggest.'

'It's something that may be hard to find out for sure at this stage, in any case,' said Westerly in a heavily speculative voice.

'Selina was Margaret's niece,' Cormit continued undaunted. 'She was using the drawings as book-marks for the Bible.' He cleared his throat. 'Tell you the truth, I don't think she knew they had any value at all.'

'And the theory is, if they came from David Lucas, they were used by him to copy for engravings,' said Charlotte. 'Which is borne out by the written comments on the backs of two of them.' She put the pencil sketch of Oxford Bridge back on the table. 'You were saying at dinner, Professor, the sketches should have been notched if they were used by an engraver.'

'*Might* have been notched. Julian didn't consider the omission significant.' It was Radout who answered, not Bodd. He had remained at Charlotte's side, and was now examining the back of the oil sketch with her. 'There is something unusual, though. I think I noticed it this morning, without it's registering properly. On this one we're assuming it was Constable who wrote "believe this better" on the back.'

'It's a perfect match for his hand, sir. I've made a lot of comparisons,' said Cormit.

Radout frowned. 'Yet Constable was noted for his poor spelling. You know, I don't remember seeing any piece of his writing where he ever got the "i" and the "e" in the word "believe" the right way around, or, for that matter, in any other word where those letters come in that order. Strange.'

There was an awkward silence before Edith volunteered. 'Don't you think, Doctor, that a serious forger would have known that too?'

'Quite right, my dear. So if these words were written by Constable, it's possible he was steeling himself at the time to improve his spelling. Or got the word "believe" right for once by chance.' Radout beamed.

'Could the Moneybuckle even consider buying the sketches?' Charlotte asked suddenly, turning to Treasure. 'I mean their being fine art, not architectural work.'

'There's at least one gallery here that'd make a more appropriate home for them than the Moneybuckle, of course. The Ashmolean,' said Treasure, without directly answering the question. But even as he spoke he remembered having read somewhere that Oxford's most celebrated museum had only very limited funds available for acquisitions.

'You haven't sold them to Mr Ostracher already, have you?' Bodd enquired, standing near to Cormit.

The bookseller stepped back a fraction, which was commonplace in anyone closely addressed by Bodd. 'Let's say Mr Ostracher has first option on them, sir.'

'Then the Moneybuckle is certainly not aiming to compete with anyone so privileged,' said Treasure, though mostly to head off speculation in Cormit's mind.

'Or anyone so wealthy,' added Bodd earthily.

Treasure looked at the time. 'It really was very good of you to keep open for us like this, Mr Cormit,' he said. 'To treat us to tea and Constables. All very improving. Now I think probably we should be getting back.'

'A great pleasure, Mr Treasure, ladies and gentlemen,' answered Cormit. 'And if I can ever be of service to any of you, you know where to come.' He had already handed them all business cards. 'I wonder would you mind leaving in twos or threes? Calls less attention when there's items of special value on the premises,' he added, implying such occurrences were fairly frequent. 'I'm having a safe put in next week.'

'Mr Cormit is strong on security,' said Radout who privately believed the man was over-concerned with the subject. Next, he grasped Charlotte's arm and started her toward the door. 'We two'll lead the way,' he announced, to deter anyone considering joining them to make a three.

Treasure was the last to leave. He smiled at Megan Rees who was holding the door open for him.

'You ... you know my sister, Mr Treasure. My older sister, Olwyn Rees,' the young woman blurted out, obviously then confused by her action. The voice was husky with a strong Welsh intonation.

'Good Heavens, of course I know Olwyn. How is she?'

There was a nervous half-smile in response. 'She's doing very well. In New York. I think. It was because of you she got the job, wasn't it?'

'I'd be flattered to think so. She's very bright. A quite exceptional corporate finance executive. The bank was sorry to lose her, but since she insisted on marrying an American.' He shrugged to punctuate the point. 'Did I commend her to the bank she joined there? Yes, I believe I did. Anyway, no thanks due, I assure you. They were lucky to get her. Give her my regards when you're next in touch will you?'

'Yes. If I'm in touch. We don't ... ' Her eyes dropped as she left the phrase uncompleted. 'Good night, then.'

'Good night ... Miss Rees.'

'My name's Megan.' The gaze was still fixed on the thin white fingers holding the door latch.

'Megan, then.' He nodded, adding, as she looked up at him shyly, 'I hope we'll meet again.'

The family resemblance was there all right, when you searched for it, the banker thought – as well as the build and the colouring. But Olwyn Rees was engaging and attractive in every way. Her sister was a caricature by comparison, and pathetically subdued where Olwyn had been ebullient.

As he joined Westerly outside in Walton Street he wished he had asked Megan about herself. Too late he had the feeling she had made the embarrassing introduction for a special reason, and that she hadn't had the courage – or the encouragement – to disclose it. Her expression had been almost disturbingly cowed until the end. Then it had been charged briefly with a glimmer of something else – pride perhaps, pride in her sister? Treasure wanted to believe that, except afterwards he was uncomfortably aware that the eyes could have been registering some kind of plea.

Chapter Nine

Half an hour later the last of the long, midsummer twi-light had given way to darkness. There were no clouds in the sky but there was no moon either. Walton Street was largely empty of people and there were few cars on the move. So it was easy for the figure concealed in the alley almost opposite to pick a moment to push across, unobserved, to the sheltered door of Cormit's shop, open it, and slip inside.

The shop was in the centre of a short terrace of what had originally been two-storey, artisans' cottages, built a century and a half before, with stuccoed walls, roofs concealed behind a common parapet, and with an alley to the rear. Each dwelling had at some time been adapted (by opportunist artisans) to accommodate a narrow shop front.

Once inside the bookshop, the gloved intruder paused to get used to the nearly pitch blackness of the hazard-strewn interior. The mumble of voices was coming from the upper floor which Cormit had converted into self-contained living quarters. From outside, light and moving shadows had been showing from behind the bedroom curtains: it was the only upstairs window overlooking the street.

Moving to the back of the ground floor, the figure went up the straight, carpeted stairs on the right, turning round at the top into the narrow corridor.

The corridor was dimly illuminated by a small rear window, and ran past two openings on the right. First came the door to the combined kitchen and living room with a window that looked over the narrow backyard. After that was the bathroom which was windowless. The doors to both rooms were ajar: the one to the bathroom opened outwards into the corridor.

Further along at the end, facing directly down the corridor, was the bedroom door. This was also open.

The light in the bedroom was the only one burning anywhere.

The intruder paused again, this time to listen. The conversation in the bedroom was not easy to pick up.

'Tighter, that's right. Tighter. And the other one. Good. Bloody marvellous,' came breathily from Cormit – the pressing, gravelly tone quite different from his normal voice. He punctuated the words with throaty, satisfied groans.

'In my power now, aren't you? The way you like,' said Megan Rees, who was easier to hear, though her words were a little slurred. 'There's one more drag left in this. Want it?'

After listening to that exchange, the figure in the corridor moved along again, stopped to do something to the bathroom door, then slipped under the arch into the dark alcove opposite. It was a small recess – the width of the staircase immediately under it – and used as an open closet, with a hanging light, shallow cupboards and drawers, and a rack at the back for hanging coats. It also offered a clear sight of what was happening in the bedroom – and a waft of the stale, sweet smell emanating from there.

Cormit was spreadeagled on the bed and had now asked for something in a tone that was too muffled to decipher at all. The intruder had caught only the phrase 'Will you . . . ?'

'Sorry, lover, I forgot. It's still in the bathroom. Won't be a sec,' the young woman answered.

She was kneeling astride him. They were both naked. Curiously, without clothes she looked less scrawny. Her breasts were small but well formed, her skin unusually white, in contrast to the black of her hair.

'Be quick. Be quick.' Cormit was begging, not ordering, the sound of his breathing now noisier than his words.

'All right, Ernie. It's going to be good isn't it? I'll make it the best. Better than Wednesday night. You liked that, didn't you?'

Cormit responded with a repetition of: 'Quick then'.

But the watcher in the alcove gauged the woman's enthusiasm as forced: you could tell she was humouring him. When she moved, the figure drew back deeper into the shadows.

Megan padded to the bathroom opposite the alcove, her movements not quite balanced, like those of someone a fraction the worse for drink. Just after she entered the room, while she was pulling on the light, the intruder stepped softly from hiding, pushed the door closed from the outside, and locked her in.

'Ernie, what you playing at?' She waited for a reply, but getting none she called again. 'Ernie? How d'you do that then? A trick was it? You a Houdini or something? . . . Oh, come on. Stop fooling. I thought you wanted . . . ' She paused again to listen. 'Ernie . . . ? Ernie?' At this stage she wasn't alarmed, only mystified. 'That *is* you, isn't it, lover? Ernie, say something. Say something, for God's sake.' After that she started rattling the door.

'Megan?'

Cormit had only time to speak the name once, turning his head as he did so to see what was happening. His unfocused expression of annoyance changing to one of fearful incredulity as his assailant fell upon him.

In the same moment the plastic shopping bag was forced down over Cormit's head. The thick elastic band followed the bag and was snapped around it – holding it tight to the victim's neck.

Cormit struggled in the blackness, kicking and pulling all he could, fighting to breathe. But he was too well held

94

to effect anything, and his cries were mostly muffled by the bag.

It wasn't long before sounds and movements from Ernie Cormit were sharply curtailed. Then the sounds stopped, and the movements were reduced to a brief series of short, obscene convulsions, before they too died altogether – as Ernie did himself.

The intruder hadn't stood about waiting for the death-throes, being busily employed at other things, and apparently oblivious to the tumult now being set up by the young woman in the bathroom.

Megan stopped rattling the door when she realised the unexplained noises had stopped in the bedroom.

That was when she decided for sure that there was someone else in the house, that something awful was being done to Ernie – when she became dully certain that something worse was about to happen to her.

The sweat on her body turned icy cold at the petrifying, burgeoning gut conviction that she was about to be raped and murdered.

When it came, the squawk of the telephone made her heart leap because, in a reflex way, it spelled help. A split second later, logic cancelled the hope.

The telephone had stopped sounding when she threw herself at the door – beating on it compulsively and screaming for help.

When she heard the key slowly being turned in the lock, she drew away. Her legs weakened under her as she staggered back to the far wall, dropping to huddle against the bath. She was shaking now, uncontrollably.

She had looked for a weapon, but there was nothing – even if there was a chance to defend herself.

The towel she had draped about her was too small to cover her properly: now it made her feel more instead of less vulnerable.

Although she had no window for escape, nor to shout through, she started shouting again hysterically all the same, turning to pound on the wall, beating at it till her fists seared with the pain.

And all this action was out of blind, useless panic. She knew the house on the other side of the wall was empty.

Cormit's murderer knew it too.

But no one came into the bathroom. And after nearly a minute, exhausted, not daring to believe she was out of danger – only sure she was being tricked – Megan stopped the pointless commotion and made herself listen. Hearing nothing, she began edging tentatively, on her knees, along the side of the bath toward the door.

When she was within reach, she pulled herself to her feet, and stretched a trembling hand toward the knob. The movement loosened the towel which fell from her. Grasping at the towel, she turned the knob, then pulled back, cowering against the washbasin, trying to cover herself.

The door had swung open only a fraction.

Everything was silent and still inside the house. The familiar sound of a passing car in the street outside was somehow reassuring – like the footsteps she thought she could hear on the pavement there.

She waited more agonising seconds, then moved back to the door, pushed on it, starting back again because something had definitely stopped its movement.

For a terrifying moment she was certain there was someone waiting behind it.

'Don't hurt me. Please don't hurt me. Please go away,' she uttered, too petrified to be ashamed. Then, weeping, she called, 'Ernie! Ernie!' praying he would answer, willing it to have been all a ghoulish game.

She knew there was nothing that normally stopped the door from opening, but since the eerie silence persisted, still trembling she went to the door again and pushed it much harder.

The door responded to the pressure. When it was open far enough for her to look around the edge, she could see the pile of coats lying behind it. The clothing had been taken from the alcove and dumped to make an obstruction.

Her first instinct when she'd released herself was to rush down the stairs and out of the house – but she stopped at the top step when she thought she could hear movement on the darkened ground floor. The light was still on in the bedroom: she staggered back there instead, scrambling over the coats on the way.

Ernie Cormit was where she had left him on the bed – except his head was covered with a yellow bag and his body was quite still.

Megan slammed the bedroom door behind her, locked it, then rushed to the bed. In a frenzy she tore the bag from Cormit's head. His eyes were open, unblinking and expressionless. Sobbing she held his face in her hands and put her lips over his slack, open mouth, feverishly trying to force air into his lungs, knowing that was what she had to do first – knowing the effort was pointless.

Seconds later, sobbing loudly, she blundered across to the window, leaving the towel where it fell from her. She pulled open the curtains, and threw up the sash.

'Help! Help! Murder!' she screamed, leaning out over Walton Street.

'MURDER!' she screeched again into the still night air, her naked body framed at Cormit's window.

Arabella Chance woke up, blinked several times, and tried to remember where she was and whose bed she was in.

There was no panic attached to her disorientation, only a nice sense of fantasy tinged with nostalgia. She tried to stop the illusion dissolving too quickly, but, in the way of such things, she failed.

If people imagined Miss Chance to be largely beyond any serious expectation of amorous adventure, the lady herself was decidedly not beyond savouring its attraction, nor its possibility. The memories were there too – of other times, when she had come awake, half-clothed as now, in what she dimly discerned to be the room of a male member of the university. And if the earliest of those other occasions had been around forty years before, the latest had been of much more recent date.

For Miss Chance had been something of a raver in her day, and if, for one reason or another, she had been denied marriage, she had denied herself little else in the uninhibited free enjoyment of a stimulating physical as well as intellectual relationship with chosen members of the opposite sex.

Sitting up gave her something else to think about, primarily a stabbing pain in the head. She winced, but at the same time was able to confirm through the open and uncurtained window that she was recovering in a room in the New Quad of All Saints College.

Now she was recalling the whole event with a total and demeaning clarity.

Miss Chance stood up slowly, and straightened with difficulty. Then she smoothed the slip she was wearing, closed the curtains, and put on the light. After more blinking, she looked about for where Charlotte Lundle might have hung the blue satin dress.

In the circumstances, it had been plain stupidity to have drunk as much as she would normally have done – or really to have taken any alcohol at all. Miss Chance was not one who troubled about creating good opinions of herself, but nor did she go out of her way to invent bad ones – except she feared she'd succeeded in doing just that earlier this evening.

Her doctor had specifically advised against alcohol, except in very small quantities. The chemist's label on the new hay-fever treatment the doctor had prescribed had been even sterner, with the typed admonition 'avoid all alcohol'. *And* she had taken an extra capsule that morning when a heavy pollen count had been predicted on the wireless.

So she had only herself to blame. She shuddered at the memory of that insufferable Bertram Bodd pronouncing quite gratuitously that she was undoubtedly suffering from an attack of migraine. And she hadn't denied his sanctimonious euphemising either – even though he had obviously expected it more to compliment his sense of charity than to provide tenable excuse for her parlous condition.

'They all knew you were tight as a tick,' she scolded herself out loud. 'Tight as a tick,' she repeated to show she could. Then she looked at the time. It was twenty-seven minutes past eleven. She must have been asleep for nearly an hour. At least she had made a reasonably quick return to a state of acceptable sobriety.

She found the dress, dropped it over her head, discovered she had it on backwards, wondered if it would matter, decided it probably would, took it off, and put it on again.

Then she sat down for a moment, dizzy with exhaustion.

'Pull yourself together Arabella,' she cautioned loudly, retrieving her long string of beads from where it had become entangled between the inside of the dress and her underwear. 'A quiet and dignified exit is indicated,' she pronounced slowly, still testing for lucidity.

Moving with care, Miss Chance descended the stairs from the middle landing. As she stepped out into the quadrangle, she fleetingly observed Mark Treasure standing with his back to the undraped window of a well lit room on the ground floor. The window was open and there was the murmur of conversation from within. Miss Chance did not consider making her presence and recovery known. Simply, she made off quietly into the enveloping darkness, toward the rack where she had left her bicycle – except, when she got to the spot, the machine was not in evidence.

Miss Chance was sure, or in the circumstances pretty sure, that she had not mistaken the place: she distinctly

99

remembered it had been the same slot in the same rack where she had left the bicycle on her earlier visit to the college that day. There had been no other machines in the rack on either of the two occasions, and there weren't now. Students took their cycles with them for the long vacation, or else stored them somewhere.

It was really very tiresome, coming on top of everything else. Miss Chance supposed she had best return to St Agnes College on foot and come back here to look for her missing machine in the morning – also tiresome because it meant walking home now, or waiting for a bus: she avoided the expense of taking taxis, except in the most dire emergency.

She was confident her property would be returned in course of time: it always was. People only ever 'borrowed' her yellow bicycle, and even that didn't happen often, not without permission. It was far too distinctive a form of transport.

Then it occurred to her that some well-meaning busy-body – possibly Bodd – might have moved the cycle to a place of assumed greater safety in the erroneous belief that she would be spending the night at All Saints. The more she thought about it, the more likely the possibility seemed.

God rot the perpetrator of this disfavour, she thought; though not quite yet, she amended quickly, in case the culprit turned out to be someone she found more tolerable than Bodd.

'I'm so sorry to intrude, Mr Treasure.' She had returned across the quad and knocked on the door of the room, rather than shout through the window.

'My dear Miss Chance, come in. Come in and join us. Are you quite recovered from that migraine?'

'I am recovered as you see, Mr Treasure, but I regret it wasn't a migraine. It was the demon drink.' She gave a wintry smile. 'Not drink taken to excess, I should add. Only incautiously. A matter of incompatibility with a drug I'm taking. I was warned. Happily the effect is quite short-lived. No matter.'

100

'Miss Chance, you're OK?' Charlotte Lundle had joined them at the door. 'You'd have been welcome to stay on in my room, you know?'

'And put you out completely?'

'Oh, someone would have found me a bed somewhere,' the young woman answered, in the confident way of one unlikely ever to encounter a lack of providers in that particular area.

'Anyway, do come in. Would you care for some tea or coffee or . . . er, anything else?' This was Treasure again. 'We're still expecting some of the others. Just ordered fresh supplies from the obliging Midden.'

'Thank you, no. It's rather late for me. I was about to return to St Agnes when I discovered my bicycle had been taken from where I left it. I wonder if some member of our party had perhaps er . . . put it away for me?'

'Not so far as I know,' said Treasure.

'Nor me,' added Charlotte.

Treasure turned to address the other two in the room. 'Either of you young people seen a yellow bicycle this evening? Belongs to Miss Chance here.'

Steven Bickworthy and Clair Witherton were crammed comfortably together on a rather small sofa. They had been invited in by Treasure earlier.

'Yes, I noticed it when we came back at eleven,' said Steven. 'Good evening, Miss Chance.' He stood up, balancing a coffee cup. 'It's in the rack at the bottom of the quad.'

'I fear not. I've looked there.'

'There are two racks. I saw it too.' This was Clair from the sofa.

'Could you have been mistaken, Miss Chance? About the rack?' asked Treasure.

Miss Chance was just about to deny such a possibility, but in view of earlier events that evening decided to play safe. 'It's possible, I suppose,' she declared, but guardedly.

'Let me show you,' offered Steven, putting down his cup, and joining her at the door.

101

'I don't want to be any trouble.'

'It's no trouble, honestly,'

'If you're sure you won't stay,' said Treasure.

'Quite sure. Good night to you all. And thank you.' She turned to Steven. 'Thank you, young man.'

'I'm Steven Bickworthy. I came to your lectures last year. On law and morality.'

'Did you now?'

A few moments later, Miss Chance was being steered by Steven toward the rack she had been to earlier. When she saw where he was taking her she began, 'I'm afraid it isn't . . . '

But it was: the yellow bicycle was exactly where she had first left it – and where Bryan Gavon had been in the act of placing it.

'Ah, Miss Chance. On your way home are you?' Gavon called from where he was standing. 'This is your bike, isn't it? Thought so. It was leaning against the wall outside on the pavement, so I brought it in. Thought you might be staying the night.'

'But it must have been— '

'Can I be of assistance, Miss Chance?' enquired Arthur Midden gravely and looking more than ever like an illustration for a story by P G Wodehouse. He had just emerged from the gateway into Old Quad, bearing a tray laden with pots of tea and coffee, and a plate of assorted biscuits.

'Thank you, no,' replied the mystified lady.

A minute later, Miss Chance was peddling up the Banbury Road, with extra care and determination, sucking hard on a glucose tablet.

She was still wholly unclear how it could have happened that Gavon had used the exact slot where her bicycle had been parked before; that is, if he hadn't been the one who had taken the machine in the first place.

Even so, before reaching St Agnes she had decided to credit the happening to coincidence.

Chapter Ten

At the moment when Miss Chance was being reunited with her bicycle, Norman Westerly was making a furtive entry into the Moneybuckle on the other side of St Giles.

Moneybuckle's Custodian had left Treasure some time before, after the two had walked up from Walton Street together. He had refused the banker's invitation to come back to All Saints for a nightcap.

The already harassed Westerly had been further unnerved by the focus of the conversation with Treasure. So much was this so, that he had now become totally obsessed with completing the rest of his cover-up plan, knowing his future depended on it.

'By the way, about that insurance broker you use.' Treasure had brought up the subject, it seemed quite casually.

'AQC. In Reading,' Westerly had supplied, because he could hardly have done otherwise, and even though the words nearly choked him.

'Yes. You mentioned the address. In Oxford Road, Reading, I think? When I was talking to my secretary, late this afternoon, I asked her to check them out with our insurance people. It seems AQC aren't members of BIBA.'

'Of what?' He had gone quite cold.

'The British Insurance Brokers Association. The professional body. One would have thought AQC— '

'They're . . . they're quite small.'

'They're not even in the telephone directory, apparently.'

'That's because they're new. Only two years old. They just missed the last printing of the Reading directory. They'll be in the next one, I expect.' He had wiped his brow, and hoped his halting delivery hadn't given away that he was inventing the whole thing.

'You haven't been in touch with them yet about the Peking fire?'

Westerly had hesitated again. 'There still hasn't been any point. Not till I have the details confirmed. We know nothing for certain. Only what everybody heard on the radio this morning.'

'I see. I was hoping you'd be able to report formally on the subject at the governors' meeting. Miss Chance is especially concerned. Well, I suppose we all are.'

'Oh, I should have something firm by then. I told you, I called the Chinese Embassy in London several times today.' This at least was true. 'One of the cultural attachés, the one we were dealing with from the start, he's promised information as soon as he gets it. Peking is eight hours ahead of us, of course,' he had ended limply, as though the last fact lent significance.

When they had parted, Westerly had pretended he was heading for the taxi rank opposite the Martyrs' Memorial, further down St Giles. But instead of crossing to the rank, after he'd seen Treasure go over to the college, he had turned right at the Ashmolean, into Beaumont Street, then right again into St John Street.

He had been just as stealthy now on his return. He had come up narrow Pusey Street, and waited for some time in the shadows, at the corner, finally to make sure none of his erstwhile dinner companions was still abroad – or anyone else, such as a patrolling policeman, who would take note of such an unusually late caller at the Moneybuckle.

He went into the building swiftly, head down like some miscreant, and not like the appointed Custodian with every honest reason for being there, whatever the time of day.

104

Once inside, he switched off the burglar alarm, but didn't turn on any lights, again for fear of attracting outside interest.

He knew exactly where the file was kept. Earlier he'd been wishing he'd followed the impulse to destroy it before this. Now, though, he'd concluded that what he'd done with it when he'd left for the day could be turned to advantage.

He had given the file back to Edith on his way out. That had been very late in the afternoon, just after she had returned from taking those extra papers for the meeting to the governors staying at All Saints. That was what she had told him. He remembered she had made rather much of the fact that the papers hadn't been ready to post with the agenda earlier in the week.

It was a pity the young man who was doing the computer work had already left by then, otherwise he could have been a witness to what happened. Edith had been in the smaller office at the time.

Even so, if Westerly came in later than Edith in the morning, and asked for the file, she could hardly deny she had been the last to handle it. Then it would be up to her to account for its whereabouts.

The door to Edith's office wasn't locked.

He knew that a real burglar would have put on gloves. He had gloves available, but he worked out that if there was a police investigation, the absence of his fingerprints here in the Moneybuckle would be more remarkable than their presence.

Of course he was anticipating a police investigation, but not centred here on the premises.

He used his duplicate key to open the main cabinet in Edith's office.

The file wasn't where it should have been. He froze at the discovery. Edith was usually meticulous. His heart-beats began thudding in his ears as he imagined the worst – that he had been exposed already; that the evidence had already been placed in official hands. In a frenzy, he began a futile search through the unlocked cabinets and the desk drawers.

It was ten minutes later before he thought to look in the other office – where Edith had been when he had left her.

The file was there, on the desk, beside the computer. Edith was getting careless, he thought. He hadn't noticed how upset she had been. He was still relieved at finding the file.

Two minutes later Westerly left the building. He thought he had done so unnoticed by anyone. He had put on the old raincoat and tweed cap he kept with other pieces of emergency spare clothing in his own office.

Instead of going for a taxi, he walked the other way to the bus-stop outside the Radcliffe Infirmary and took the next bus up the Woodstock Road. He sat at the back of the nearly empty upper deck. Using this route meant walking across to the Banbury Road when he got off, but it avoided the likelihood of meeting neighbours in the bus, or having the time and destination of his journey logged by a taxi driver who would also remember his face and beard. He had the raincoat buttoned to the neck so that no one would place him later because of the dinner jacket. The file was under the coat, well out of sight.

He met no one he knew on the journey home, no one who might later provoke a question about why it had taken him so long to get there after leaving Treasure.

The whole episode had been as anonymous as his round trip to Reading in the middle of the day. He had taken the five-past twelve train there, and the one twenty-two back: the journey was only thirty minutes each way. He had needed to go in person to get the bank account closed without delay.

The account had been with a big branch of a bank near Reading railway station. He had been there only a few times, making sure on each visit to use different tellers. He was satisfied – unduly satisfied – that no one could ever find out that the account had existed at all.

Westerly's belief in the ingenuousness of the authorities was frightening. But he was a man fixated, his every thought and action dedicated not to plotting his own exoneration, but to a much higher goal – the preservation of his marriage. He had to keep Rebecca.

It was sad that the true hopelessness of that last premise was utterly escaping Moneybuckle's unworthy Custodian.

The tower clock in Carfax, the crossroads at the Oxford city centre, was showing eleven twenty-eight. Professor Bodd passed below it as he went from the bright lights of Cornmarket Street, the shop-lined continuation of St Giles, over to wider, and sightlier St Aldate's.

Anxious as he was to return to the house in close-by St Ebbes on time, there was no obvious haste in Bodd's heavy stride, no cause for remark in the part of town where there had still been plenty of 'Friday nighters' about – drinkers turned out of the pubs at closing time, people window-shopping, queueing for hamburgers, waiting for buses, or just plain reluctant to call it a night. And none paid attention to Bodd. For Oxford is over-used to the sight of clergymen of all weights, shapes, ages and denominations, in cassocks or academic robes, suited or sweatered, dog-collared or necktied with crucifixed lapels, hearty or reverent, militant or fey, sober or not. Bodd, despite his size, was merely part of the scene.

Before he drew level with Christ Church's Tom Tower, he turned right into Pembroke Street. Then, his grip tightening on the small box he was carrying, he went left into Beef Lane, continuing through the same pattern of narrow streets he had followed before dinner.

The expedition earlier had been fruitless. Mrs La Toque had not been at home. When Bodd had talked to her on the telephone during the week, she had promised to be in at six o'clock on Friday evening – unless the traffic delayed

107

her. But she needed to be away again, she had explained, by early Saturday morning.

'My trade's international. Very exclusive, if you follow me, dear? My body has to go where the customers want it, you see? Not the other way round. And they seem to think it's worth it,' Mrs La Toque had expanded, making Bodd feel uncomfortable, as well as apprehensive about prices. Miss Philby, in the same calling, had been much more circumspect. She'd lived in Manchester: he'd visited her twice, and got satisfaction both times, at a very moderate price.

Except Mrs La Toque seemed to be offering something much more rare and exclusive.

'I fear price will have to be the governing factor,' he had cautioned, despite himself.

'You all say that, dear,' Mrs La Toque had answered. 'Let's deal with it when we're together, shall we? When you've seen what I've got for you. I'm not unreasonable, and I'm not one to take advantage of a compulsion.'

'It's not a fetish. Not that at all,' he'd retorted quickly, but knowing perfectly well that it was.

'Of course not dear. Just making conversation, that's all. See you Friday then. And if you'd like any extra professional services, I'll be only too happy to oblige, time allowing. Only that usually means a fixed appointment,' she had ended, with what he took to be importuning.

'No, I shan't want that,' he had answered hurriedly.

'I only mentioned it because it's sometimes convenient, dear. With busy people like you, who come for the other. People who can't always fit things in at the normal times, if you follow me? I'm a slave to my work, you see? And if you can't come early Friday evening, don't worry. I'll be free again after eleven–thirty. At your service,' she had ended jauntily.

He was taking her at her word by arriving so late. It had been too difficult to telephone and check with her from All Saints, and he had an aversion to public phone-boxes:

he felt the same way about them as Ostracher felt about dandruff.

The modest, semi-detached villa, modern and red-brick, was in the new housing development flanked by the St Ebbes shopping precinct, as well as local government offices, court houses and multi-storey car parks. It was an area hugely altered since Bodd's days at Oxford.

The front door of the villa was sheltered under a pointed open porch. Bodd was glad of that – for the privacy it provided. After all, it was the first time he had indulged himself in this way in Oxford, where he was known. He was glad to see there was a light in the hall, reflected through the glass in the top part of the door. There was also light in the curtained bay window on the upper floor.

Bodd pressed the bell, keeping his bulky person close to the door, head bent, his arms hanging downwards, gorilla-like, the small box in his right hand. He hoped Mrs La Toque hadn't gone to bed.

At first there was no response to the bell chimes. They had seemed to peal all around the house, not just inside it. He peered about him through the heavy spectacles. Judging from the darkened houses in the short street, most other residents had retired, and there were no pedestrians in sight.

Then just as Bodd was about to ring again there was a good deal of noise from inside the house – of laughter and loud conversation, of footsteps coming down stairs, of the rattle of a chain before the door was thrown open.

And to Bodd's utter chagrin, facing him framed on the other side of the doorway was a man he had known for more than twenty years. It was one of his early tutors, now a senior and eminent member of the university.

'Why Bodd?' exclaimed the Professor of Moral Philosophy, in a bold and penetrating voice. 'It is Bodd, isn't it? Fancy meeting you here at this time of night.'

'Good evening Doctor— '

'Professor Bodd, is it?' interrupted Mrs La Toque enquiringly, from close behind her other visitor. 'So you two know each other? I should have guessed. Small world isn't it dear? For professors anyway.' She was a vivacious, middle-aged woman, well rounded, with very blonde hair, and wearing a lot of bright red lipstick. The silk housecoat she had on, with dragon designs all over it, was loosely held together by a sash at the waist. On her feet there were open, wooden-soled clogs.

'Well you couldn't be in better hands, Bodd,' offered the other academic, who was slight in build and casually dressed. 'Sets one up splendidly to come here. Puts new spring in one's step.'

'Professor Bodd doesn't come for that,' said the lady, modestly adjusting the cross-over of the coat.

Bodd wanted to protest, but the words wouldn't come.

'Well he ought to,' admonished the older man, tapping his ex-pupil on the chest with an outstretched finger, and showing no disposition to enquire about exactly what Bodd had come for. 'Nothing like it,' the other went on. 'Thank you, Lucille, and good night. Good night Bodd, good to see you again,' he called, moving away briskly in the general direction of St Aldate's. The two men had never been intimates.

'Lovely gentleman. Been coming to me for years. Likes a late appointment,' said Mrs La Toque. She held the door open wider. 'Well come in, dear. Now let me see, you're after Pavlovas, aren't you? And you've brought something for me, I can see.'

Still speechless, Bodd's right arm bent in a reflex action and brought up the small box. The anticipation of pleasure had quite evaporated at the sight of his old tutor.

There were so few really private indulgences left when you had six children, a penetratingly musical wife, and a job that might very well be wound up before you got home.

At the striking of the same half hour, Julian Barners had been standing alone on Magdalen Bridge studying the

110

waters flowing beneath. He was shortly to begin retracing his steps along the High Street, and back in the direction of All Saints.

He was in a contemplative mood, his earlier ebullient state mellowed by his having imbibed just a little too much port, and disturbed only by a sense of self-reproof that he was working to subdue.

It had been a nostalgic walk, the one he often took on overnight visits to the city, and without underlying motive – at least of an admissible sort. He loved Oxford after dark. Of course, there was always the merest possibility of falling in with someone of like propensities to his own, but it hadn't happened tonight: he never knowingly searched for such a companion.

His route seldom took in the garish sections of the city, particularly the Cornmarket and the modern St Ebbes precinct. He found nothing remotely redeemable about the new developments, but it was pleasing that they had not been allowed to encroach on the architectural serenity of the university proper, thanks in part to the vigilance of caring aesthetes like himself.

Barners contributed much in cash, kind and influence to the protection of what was artistically worthy. Without such subscriptions, and being a sensitive man, he would have found it difficult to live in harmony with his accepted image – with his public persona, that is. In the private way, he lived happily enough – in Belgravia, with an exquisite young secretary–valet.

The inward discord that sometimes, as now, taxed Barners stemmed always from his masquerading as an independent connoisseur of fine art when, in fact, he was a secret dealer in it. This is to say that he not only advised private collectors openly for a fee, which is proper, but also contracted with art dealers for undisclosed commissions on resulting sales, which is quite improper.

Even so, while the substantial extra income derived in this way helped pay for Barners' comfortable way of life,

111

it also covered the generous gifts he made toward saving a picture for the nation, or a stately home from demolition, or other similar worthy causes.

Naturally, the sale of a picture involving a secret commission was not an everyday event. Circumstances had to be right, and they too seldom were. It was why Barners had welcomed the opportunity offered by Ostracher and the Constable sketches.

There had been no doubt in Barners' mind that the sketches were genuine – even without the fairly convincing provenance. There was no doubt either that if Ostracher followed the proffered advice, he would be getting a bargain. Barners hadn't asked the American for a fee. He had worked on the assumption that a suitable and confidential arrangement could be made with an easily over-awed Cormit.

Barners remonstrated with himself now for having been too generous to Ostracher, and much too certain over the size of the commission he could extract from Cormit. Otherwise the grave unpleasantness need never have arisen.

Of course, he had seriously underestimated Cormit's strength and obduracy in negotiation – and his knowledge in such matters. It was why Barners had been forced into taking unusual measures.

In aftermath, he regretted the whole pattern of the affair. If he had it over again – knowing as much as he did now – he could have found a way of playing the whole thing differently.

He began the return walk with this last proposition running through his head. Then, almost without being aware of it, when he reached St Giles, instead of returning to All Saints he found himself impelled again in the direction of the little shop in Walton Street.

It was also why, at the first sight of the barriers, the police cars, and the knots of onlookers, with his contemplative mood and steady nerve both shattered, the urbane Barners had turned on his heels and fled.

Chapter Eleven

'This is Detective Inspector Holmes, sir,' Midden announced gravely. With head slightly bowed, he stood against the door he had just opened as the Inspector lumbered past him into Treasure's sitting room.

'How d'you do, Mr Treasure. Sorry to disturb you so late.'

'You haven't disturbed me. I'd not turned in yet. There were some friends here until a few minutes ago,' Treasure observed affably as he came forward to shake hands with the policeman whom he noticed immediately gave off a penetrating whiff of peppermint.

'Ah, Mr Midden said you were still up. Otherwise I could have left it till the morning, I suppose. Better to get things over with though. There's just a few questions. Won't keep you long.'

The speaker was well into middle age, and seemed old for his rank. He was of average height but very heavily built. A strong growth of grey hair, unparted, was brushed straight back from where it started, well forward on the temple. More hairs sprouted liberally from ears and nose. The florid face, the paunch, the bronchitic breathing and the sweaty palm all seemed to witness a fairly dodgy physical condition; so did the rheumy gaze.

'Will there be anything else, Mr Treasure, sir?' asked Midden, still at the door.

'I don't think so. Unless the Inspector would like something? I'm out of hot drinks I'm afraid. There are plenty of cold ones.'

Holmes gave a sidelong, almost shifty glance at Midden. 'Nothing for me, Mr Treasure. Not at the moment.'

'Thank you then, Mr Midden. Time you went home, isn't it? It's gone twelve-thirty. Good night.'

'Good night, sir. Yes, I'd better be getting back. I . . . ' Whatever Midden had intended to say next he now evidently decided to leave unsaid. 'The porter will stay up in the lodge till Inspector Holmes leaves,' he had added before withdrawing, directing the remark at the policeman, not Treasure.

'Do sit down, Inspector,' said Treasure. 'I gather something's happened to Cormit the bookseller.'

'Yes, he's dead.'

'Good Lord.'

'I thought Midden had told you already. Died about eleven-twenty. And if I could change my mind about that drink, sir. It's a hot night.'

'Of course. Something long with ice?'

The Inspector was eyeing the bottles on the tray. 'Just a small drop of whisky would do fine, sir. No ice, makes you more thirsty I always think. No, no water either, thanks very much.' He sat in the armchair Treasure had indicated, rearranged a cushion behind him, and leaned back, while loosening the tie around his damp, unbuttoned collar. As an afterthought, and with something of a struggle, he produced a notebook from the side pocket of his crumpled sports jacket.

'Well this is quite a shock.' Treasure brought over the drinks – a generous neat whisky for his visitor, and a weak one with ice and soda for himself. 'Some of us were with Cormit earlier. Must have left him about quarter to eleven. Presumably you know that or you wouldn't be here. Was it a heart attack?' He arranged a chair opposite Holmes, putting the glasses on a low table between them.

'It was murder.' Leaning on one elbow, the policeman lifted himself slightly in his seat, made a pained face while pulling on an upper part of a trouser leg, then resettled

114

with his knees wider apart, all before reaching for his glass. 'Looks like murder by asphyxiation. A plastic bag was tied over his head,' he said.

'You say it looks like that?'

'That's the medical opinion so far. Cheers, Mr Treasure.' He downed just over half the liquid in the glass, made a satisfied noise from the back of his throat, wiped his lips with his free hand, and the side of a glistening temple with his sleeve. 'Of course, official cause of death will have to come from the post mortem,' he cautioned. 'But you can take it from me, he was suffocated all right. Nasty.' He stifled a belch, not very successfully, then drank most of the remainder of the whisky.

'I see. He couldn't have done himself in? No, I suppose not. Not that way.' Treasure took a draught of his own drink. 'So was there a struggle? And what happened to the girl . . . er, Megan Rees? Was she still there? Is she all right?'

'She'd manacled him to the bed.' Holmes delivered this without emotion, following it with a slow wheezy cough that hadn't quite petered out before he started to add, 'It's an old-fashioned iron bedstead. He was spreadeagled—'

'Manacled him? You serious?'

'She's admitted it. Part of their regular sexual fun and games, see? Service handcuffs they were. He was a bondage freak. Mind if I smoke?'

'Please do. I think there are some cigarettes some-where. Yes, there are. These all right for you?' He offered an unopened pack to the policeman who hadn't so far produced cigarettes of his own.

'Very kind, thanks.'

'Are you saying the girl killed him? She hasn't admitted that?'

'Not yet. And we haven't arrested her. She's at the station being questioned.' Holmes lit a cigarette, and made as though to pocket the pack, but finished up placing it near him on the table instead.

115

'But you sound as if you know the answers to the questions. You think she did it.' The last came as a bald statement.

'She was on a high at the time. Pot. She's admitted that. We could smell it, anyway. Means she may not be held entirely responsible for her actions, I shouldn't wonder.' The Inspector's opinion of this eventuality was clear from the hurt in the tone.

'Meaning a lesser charge than murder? But she hasn't confessed to . . . to tying on the bag?'

'Fixed with an elastic band it was. No. She's only said she took it off.' The Inspector exhaled noisily, then picked up his glass. 'She claims he was murdered by a burglar who locked her in the bathroom.'

'That's different. Was it possible?'

'No sign of forced entry when we got there. Nothing's been taken that she's been able to name, except something we've since found. She alleges a few drawers were open. Some coats dumped on the floor. But the place hadn't been done over. Definitely not.'

'Was she also attacked?'

'No. Nor interfered with. Not in any way.' He drained his glass.

'How did she get out of the bathroom? Did she break the door down? Shout for help through the window?'

'There's no damage to the door, and there isn't a window. It's a converted room in the middle of the upstairs. She said the murderer locked her in, then let her out before leaving. Very convenient of him. She didn't see who it was, of course.' The speaker carefully examined his empty glass for signs of dampness, then looked up. 'When the door was first unlocked, she claims she was too scared to come out straight away. She says she screamed for help when she was first locked in, but no one heard her. Oh, thanks very much, sir. Just a small one, being as I'm on duty.'

Treasure had got up to replenish the Inspector's drink. 'And you think she could be making up the whole thing?

Including untidying the place a bit? That she killed him by mistake, when under the influence of drugs? And during some sadistic love play?'

'It's been known to happen. Cheers then.' He took a long swallow of neat whisky. 'The neighbours on one side say they sounded pretty noisy and violent when they were at it some nights.' But he had avoided giving a direct affirmative to Treasure's last question.

'Did the neighbours hear the screams from the bathroom?'

'They live on the wrong side. The other next-door house is empty.'

'Well, was anyone seen entering or leaving Cormit's place?'

'Not so far as we know. Not yet.'

'And you've questioned all the other neighbours?'

'We're still doing that.'

'Well I appreciate your being so open, Inspector. Do I assume there's a reason?'

Holmes gave a knowing nod and drank some more from the glass. 'Megan Rees says you were the last to leave the shop. Is that right?'

'I believe so. Yes.'

'And you personally saw everyone else in your party leave.'

'Yes.'

The Inspector turned several pages in his notebook, wheezing noisily while squinting through the smoke from the cigarette clamped between his lips. Then he turned the pages back again, scowling at the writing. 'That was four men, and two women. Miss Charlotte Lundle was one of the women. Megan Rees recognised her from the telly. Can you give me the names of the others, please?'

'The second woman was Edith Norn, Assistant Custodian of the Moneybuckle. She left with Bryan Gavon. I think Miss Lundle went out first with Doctor Decimus Radout. Yes, that's right, and Professor Bertram Bodd went after

117

them. Those four are all Moneybuckle governors.' Treasure paused as he watched the other scribble down the names. 'I followed with Norman Westerly, Moneybuckle's Custodian. He and I walked up to St Giles together, behind some of the others.'

'That's double "d" at the end of Bodd?'

'That's right.'

'So far as you know, will all those six be here tomorrow?'

'Yes. They're all involved in a meeting at the Moneybuckle in the afternoon.'

'Good. And after you left Cormit's shop, did you happen to hear the door being locked behind you?'

Treasure thought for a moment. 'I don't believe so.'

'She's saying she forgot to lock the door after you left. Seems Mr Cormit had left that to her. If she'd locked it properly, nobody could have got in without a key. Leastways, not without doing damage. All the downstairs windows are fixed plate glass, except for an awkward little one at the back. Nothing's been disturbed around that.'

'Isn't there a back door?'

'Yes. Yale lock, but bolted as well. Anyway, stands to reason she'd have locked the shop door. Not just left it on the latch. And it hadn't been forced.'

'How's the shop door usually secured?'

'By a Chubb deadlock, separate from the latch. She said she had to unlock it to let you all out.'

'Yes. I remember Cormit telling her to lock the door after we arrived.'

'Well, she says she'd left the key in then, and took it out after you'd gone without turning it. Because Mr Cormit was hurrying her from upstairs to . . . to come to bed.' The Detective Inspector was lighting another cigarette from the burning butt of the old one. 'No way of telling what she really did, of course. The door was unlocked when the first people went in.'

'Were they police?'

'No. Couple of young fellows off the street. They went in when she screamed at them through the bedroom window. In the nude she was.' He shook his head. 'They phoned for us.'

'So it could have been as she said? That she'd forgotten to lock up? That a murderer could have got in?'

'Or that she'd been down and unlocked the door when she was ready.' Absently he had let the cigarette pack drop out of his hand into his pocket while he'd seemed to be preoccupied studying his notes. He looked up blandly. 'Now sir, would you like to tell me the purpose of your visit to Mr Cormit?'

'Our whole party went to see some artist's sketches.'

'Funny time of night to do that?'

'I agree. It was someone's whim at the end of dinner. We all went along with it. It wasn't far, of course.'

'Any particular sketches?'

'They're purported to be by John Constable.'

Holmes made approving noises. 'That confirms what Miss Rees says. Sketches of Oxford. Highly valuable are they?'

'If they're by Constable they will be. It's still a matter of conjecture.'

'But worth the while of an informed burglar to go and nick them, you'd reckon?'

'As a long shot, yes. He'd have to prove their origin, and know how to get rid of them.'

'Yes, a long shot, as you say, sir. Megan Rees would be better placed to try the same thing, would you think?'

'Not necessarily. She'd know about where the sketches came from because we were discussing the point. I've no idea whether she'd know how to dispose of them. What are you getting at, Inspector?'

'Only that there really isn't anything in that shop worth pinching, let alone worth murdering for, except those sketches.' He drew in deeply on the cigarette. 'And the sketches still happen to be there.'

'Megan Rees showed you?'

'The opposite. She described them and said they'd been lifted by the burglar. Well, they hadn't been. My scene of crime officer found them. In the bedroom. That was after she'd been taken down to the station. It was when we were looking for their stash of pot. Found that too, even though she claimed there wasn't one. She now says Cormit must have hidden the sketches in a new place without telling her.'

'Isn't that possible? He was jumpy about security. He mentioned tonight he was having a safe installed next week.'

The policeman again used one hand to ease the tightness in the crutch of his trousers. Then he fixed Treasure with a lowered stare, through smoke-clouded, half-closed eyelids. 'More likely she hid them away herself, expecting to collect them later. After we'd swallowed the cock and bull about the burglar. It's obvious Cormit would have a job hiding them from her in the room where they were sleeping.'

'Where did he normally keep them? Did she tell you?'

'In a locked drawer in an alcove opposite the bathroom. It was one of the drawers we found open.'

'Was the lock forced?'

'No, the key was in it. On a ring she said the burglar took from the bedside table.' Holmes leaned back, picking up his nearly empty glass. 'The sketches were at the bottom of the wardrobe, under a bit of lino Cormit stood his shoes on. Not the kind of hiding place you'd expect him to use.'

'Unless it was temporary.'

The Inspector shook his head after draining the glass. 'More likely the sort of place she'd have used when she moved the sketches from that drawer. When she didn't expect anyone to be looking for them at all. Not after she'd told us where they should have been. And not giving us much credit for intelligence, that wasn't.' He blew his nose loudly on the crumpled handkerchief produced from his top pocket. He was wiping his forehead with the same object as he asked, 'Was there anyone else who knew about these drawings, Mr Treasure?'

'I imagine plenty of people, including all the guests at dinner tonight, for instance.'

'That's involving people you haven't mentioned to me already?'

'Three more, yes. The three who didn't go down to Cormit's shop. Miss Arabella Chance, a Fellow of St Agnes. Mr Armin Ostracher, an American, and Julian Barners, the art expert.' He waited while the other wrote down the names. 'I gather Cormit took the drawings to London earlier this week and showed them to at least one dealer.'

'D'you know the name, sir?'

'No. Cormit may have told Julian Barners.'

'But you said Mr Barners didn't go to the shop?'

'Not after dinner. He and Ostracher were there before dinner.'

'I see. And they'll both be at this Moneybuckle meeting tomorrow?'

'Yes. So will Miss Chance.'

'Well, I shouldn't think we'll need to trouble any of them, Mr Treasure. You mentioned you had people here just before I came. Would they have been members of this Moneybuckle group?'

'Some of them. Miss Lundle and Mr Gavon were here.'

'And were they with you from the time you got back from Mr Cormit's?'

'No. I met Miss Lundle walking in the college garden. She was with Doctor Radout. Professor Bodd was just leaving them. It wasn't long after we all got back.'

'At what time would that have been, sir?'

'When I met them? Oh, about eleven.'

'And they were with you from that time?'

121

'Miss Lundle was. Doctor Radout didn't come in here. He went home. Professor Bodd didn't come in either. I don't know why. Two undergraduates joined us as well.'

'You mentioned Mr Gavon.'

'He dropped in later, around eleven-thirty. I'd been expecting him for a nightcap.'

'Thank you. Oh, Megan Rees claims you know her sister.'

'That's quite right. My company used to employ her. Very bright lady.'

'In a responsible position, was she?'

'Extremely. A corporate finance executive. I gather she's now doing a similar job with a bank in New York.'

'Bit different from her drop-out sister, then?'

The banker gave a disapproving frown. 'I've no idea, Inspector, since I hardly know Megan Rees. And I certainly wouldn't judge her capable of murder, not out of hand.'

'Meaning you think that's what the police are doing? No fear of that, sir. But I tell you, when you've been in this game as long as me, well . . . you learn a thing or two . . . about people.' A sharp cough was followed by a long, painful wheeze. His eyes turned to his empty glass as he said, 'Well, I think that's it, sir.' He made as though to get up as he added casually, 'You didn't know Megan Rees had form?'

'She's been to prison, you mean?'

'Two convictions for shoplifting. The first in Cardiff, then in Bath. She was sent to prison the second time. Only just finished her parole. She lost a hospital kitchen job, here in Oxford, for being late, and for assaulting a supervisor. Lucky not to be in court again over that. She was sleeping rough till Mr Cormit took her in. Act of kindness it seems.'

'But not for entirely unselfish reasons.'

'Very possibly, sir,' the policeman responded as though that detracted little from the philanthropic action of the late kinky, pot-smoking Ernie Cormit.

'Has she got a lawyer?'

'Not yet. She's been told her rights, and signed to say she doesn't want one. That's the law. Seems she doesn't go much on lawyers. Or coppers. Anyway, we haven't charged her with anything yet, sir,' he added pointedly. 'Well, I'd better be off then,' came with evident regret. 'Thank you for your help and the— '

'A small one for the road, Inspector?' Treasure offered, grasping the glass and making for the drinks tray, confident the offer would be accepted. 'Tell me, did you get any kind of address out of Megan Rees?'

'Er, yes. Her parents' home.' Holmes was dragging the notebook out again. 'Not much help to anyone though. Her mother's dead, and she says her father's disowned her. Won't have anything to do with her. He's some kind of free-church minister in mid-Wales. The fire and brimstone sort, by the sound of it. Well, you can't really blame him being fed up with a daughter like that.'

Treasure glanced at the time as he brought back the recharged glass. 'Could you let me have the address anyway? I seem to be the only person who has any family connection with the girl.'

'Yes, don't see why I can't do that, sir.'

The banker had hesitated to add that he seemed also to be the only person remotely concerned for Megan Rees' well being – though, as he was to learn later, this wouldn't have been strictly true.

Chapter Twelve

'I really ought to go to Megan now. Tonight,' said Val Midden uncertainly.

That the proposition lacked total determination owed more to her situation than any weakness in the resolve. She was now fully awake, but distraught, and sitting up in the double bed, her face tear-stained, her head haloed in blue plastic hair rollers.

'No point in that,' replied her husband – gently for him. He was in the act of removing his trousers. 'They wouldn't let you in to see her anyway.' He had been making an effort to be a comfort since waking his wife at one o'clock with the bad news. He had even made her a cup of tea to lessen the shock.

'But she isn't arrested. You said that.'

'May have been by now. Either way they won't let anyone near her.' He had no true knowledge of what happened in such circumstances, but he was firmly against an immediate expedition from St John Street to the police station in St Aldate's, because it would inevitably have to involve him. 'She's done murder,' he said. 'Of your own brother. Half-brother.' He had been astonished at how little his wife had been moved by Ernie's death, and how concerned she was for Megan Rees.

Mrs Midden shook her head. 'I've told you, it's not true. Can't be. She wouldn't hurt a fly, that girl.'

'What makes you so sure?' He buttoned the front of his pyjama top.

'I know, that's all. She's been used. One bad influence

124

after another. And Ernie wasn't much different from the others, not really.' One hand went guiltily to her mouth. 'I suppose I shouldn't have said that. Speaking ill of the dead. Poor Ernie. Expect he meant well, according to his lights.' She gulped back a sob. 'Oh dear, what shall we do about Megan?'

'I know what I'm doing, I'm going to sleep. And you should too.' There was a limit to patient understanding, and he had another heavy day ahead of him. Standing before the dressing-table mirror, he slowly brushed the few long, carefully nurtured side hairs across his otherwise bald scalp – always his last act before turning in. He'd been told that brushing stimulated the roots, especially prior to lying down.

'She talked to me, you know, Arthur? Plenty of times. When I was round there. About things that happened to her before. Terrible things, some of them. Men treated her like dirt. Took advantage.'

'You know she was on drugs?' he asked as he got into bed.

'Who said?'

'That Police Inspector. Nice bloke. He had a drink off me. In my pantry. He'd come looking for Mr Treasure. The duty porter put him on to me first. The police'll want to talk to you tomorrow, most likely.'

'Why?'

'Ernie's only living relative. The Inspector didn't know that till I told him. The girl hadn't said.'

'Too flustered, I expect, poor soul. Well I can't tell the police anything. Ernie and me weren't close. You know that well enough.'

'They'll still want to see you, I should think. Anyway, I said we'd help if we could.'

'Help Ernie? He's dead. It's Megan I'm worried about. He'd have wanted us to look out for her.'

'Not if she did him in, he bloody wouldn't. Come to think, it could have been an accident, I suppose. Dangerous

125

perverts, the two of them, that's all I can say. Did I tell you they were— '

'I don't want to know, thank you, Arthur.' She sniffed, rubbing one eye with a handkerchief.

'All right. Don't blame you. But you're wasting your sympathy on her, I can tell you. She took his life, accident or not.' He checked the alarm setting on the bedside clock.

'And I'm telling you, she didn't. It must have been a burglar, like she said.' She kneaded the handkerchief in her palm. 'The things people do nowadays. It's not as if there was anything worth stealing there either. Lot of old junk mostly.'

'There was something. Some drawings. Famous sketches. It's what she said the burglar was after. Cunning bitch.'

'Arthur!' she remonstrated.

'Well, that's what I think she is. Pretended the drawings was pinched. Except she'd hidden them. Or else he'd hidden them from her, and she suffocated him trying to make him say where. Either way, she was going to keep them for herself. The police found them.'

'Are they that valuable?'

For the first time Midden felt his wife was accepting that there were grounds for a case against Megan Rees.

'They're worth quite a bit,' he said.

'Should we have gone down and locked up the shop?'

'What tonight? There'll be coppers crawling all over it tonight. It won't need locking up.'

'I'll go in the morning then. See what's what. I've got a key.'

'Where?'

'Downstairs. In that box on the sideboard. The wooden one.'

'When did he give you a key then?'

'Ages ago. So I could get in if he was away. In case of emergencies. I thought I'd told you.' Reluctantly she was rearranging her pillows for sleep.

'There'll be the funeral to organise, of course,' he offered in sombre vein. 'Suppose we'll have to do all that. There's a death grant you can get. From the government. You'll have to claim it.'

She sighed. 'I never thought I'd live to bury Ernie. My little brother.'

'He made a will didn't he?'

'He said so once, remember? I think it was Christmas, two years ago. Don't know where it'll be.'

'In his bank I should think.' He scratched his chest while venting a prolonged and noisy yawn. 'I expect he's left you something.'

'He said I'd get everything, I remember that. Don't you? We talked about it after. I didn't take much notice really. Not then. I was sure he'd marry again.' She shook her head. 'So what about the favour you were doing him?'

Midden grunted. 'Nothing'll come of that now.' He yawned again, and moved his legs further down the bed. 'So Ernie may have left you a tidy bit?'

'Well if he has, it can go to put Megan on her feet. When they let her go.'

'That's right,' he agreed, but without in the least meaning it. He was too tired to engage in further argument.

'The handcuffs are probably the same vintage as the bedstead,' Armin Ostracher said with a low chuckle into the telephone. He made approving noises as he listened to the rejoinder from the other end of the line.

He had called the New York number from his rooms three times before this, but without result. It had been one a.m. British time when he had finally got an answer. It had been worth waiting up to recount what had happened. In any case he never tried sleeping before this time of night at the start of a European trip.

'The seller had no up-to-date idea what they should fetch,' he continued, one hand bending the paperclip he had removed from the box on the desk. 'But he didn't pretend to be an expert. Even so, the extent of the ignorance was pretty reprehensible . . . Deserved teaching a lesson? Yes, I thought so,' he had responded to an injected query, then listened to another. 'No, no. There's no question they're genuine. None at all. They're guaranteed by a source you'll consider quite unimpeachable. So do I.' He frowned while listening to the next comment. 'Certainly I could have picked them up this evening, but the morning will do. They're not going anywhere . . . I said they're in a safe place. No one else is going after them tonight.' This time the other speaker's voice crackled shrilly in protest. 'Not a chance. I'm certain. Dead certain,' Ostracher interrupted firmly, almost tartly, snapping the metal clip between his fingers. 'Oh, and I'll probably be bringing back a few surprise items, too . . . No, I'd rather not tell you on the telephone.' Now he smiled as he listened. 'That goes for me too, lover. And stop saying things like that, my wife wouldn't approve,' he added with another chuckle. 'Love you too. Call you tomorrow.'

After putting down the telephone he pulled across the pencil and pad. Dutifully he wrote the time and duration of the call, hesitated, as always, over the number, then wrote that down too after deciding it was necessary. The number was unlisted and he disliked promulgating it in any circumstances. He should have used his credit card for the call, but raising an operator had proved to be too slow compared with direct dialling.

He would remember to give the sheet of paper to Mr Midden in the morning. Armin Ostracher was pedantically honest over all such matters.

Detective Chief Inspector Yolan swirled the dregs of his coffee around the bottom of the plastic cup, decided against drinking them, put the cup back on his desk, looked at the time, and grunted. 'So why not book her for the drugs for now? She's confessed to use and possession.

128

It's in her statement,' he said. 'You're not happy with that, Sherlock?'

'No, I'm not. Not if she goes before the magistrates in the morning, and then gets bail,' Detective Inspector Holmes replied from a seat in front of the desk. 'And what if she's advised to go back on that part of the statement? Before she signs it? When she's got a lawyer?'

There were four policemen present in Yolan's narrow corner office, upstairs in the Oxford police station at the bottom of St Aldate's. The Detective Chief Inspector had been alerted at home about the murder just after it happened. He had come in unexpectedly, after saying he wouldn't, and asked for an up-date meeting at one-thirty in the morning.

Holmes had been addressed as Sherlock by colleagues ever since he had joined the force. Nowadays he sensed it was less a nickname than a snide form of patronising. Yolan, his immediate superior, he considered a thruster. The Detective Chief Inspector was nearly ten years his junior, sometimes over-critical of his work, and had only accepted Holmes as one of the three Detective Inspectors reporting to him because he'd been refused any option. Holmes wasn't supposed to know that, but it hadn't been difficult to work out.

He hadn't wanted a meeting so early on in this case – and he was pretty sure Yolan wouldn't have come in at all if one of the other Detective Inspectors had copped the duty.

'We can oppose bail on the grounds of more serious charges pending, sir,' suggested Detective Sergeant Piper who was propped on the window ledge to the left of Yolan.

Holmes had young Piper pegged as a thruster too, a tall, good-looking, university-graduate-type thruster, single and with a new girl in his bed every night – except the Detective Inspector was wrong on the last point. Piper was attractive to women all right, but he was going steady with a teacher in Cheltenham whom he hoped to marry and to whom he was entirely faithful.

'Oxford magistrates don't like charges pending,' Holmes pronounced firmly, and sure of his ground.

'That's true,' agreed Yolan, clipping the words.

'We could hold her for questioning till the court sits on Monday,' said Holmes, crunching viciously on the two peppermints in his mouth, like a cannibal consuming an enemy's vitals.

'Oxford magistrates don't like the police holding young women longer than necessary either. Not without charging them,' said Yolan. He noted Holmes' undisguised irritation. 'You did tell me it was an open and shut case of domestic murder, Sherlock,' he added accusingly, referring to a telephone conversation between them more than an hour before.

'And that's exactly what it is,' replied Holmes. 'She was never locked in that bathroom by anyone. If she had been, why was she let out?'

'Because otherwise she couldn't have been set up as the killer?' put in Piper.

'So the phantom burglar lets her out, and risks being seen?' Holmes came back fast. 'He'd have been mad.'

'That's always possible, of course,' said Yolan.

Holmes snorted. 'There was no outsider. It was a domestic murder all right. Only it's taken a bit longer than expected for the girl to confess. Just because there's a Saturday Magistrates' Court for once, and— '

'Well it's not only that, is it?' Yolan interrupted. 'So how much pot did you find?'

'Probably too much if she pleads they had it for personal use only,' said Piper. 'And we may find more there yet. We've had a dog in since midnight. It's always possible Cormit was paying the girl in drugs. He took her in six weeks ago. She was an unemployed student drop-out. No skills, a criminal record and nowhere to live.'

'She got a drugs record herself?' asked Yolan.

'As a past user, not a pusher. She says she kicked cocaine after her jail sentence. I don't believe that.' This was Holmes.

'Hm. Well, with her form, she may not get bail anyway.' The Detective Chief Inspector pulled up his chair and riffled through the notes he had been given earlier. 'And you're convinced she's lying about the burglar?'

'Absolutely,' said Holmes, lighting a cigarette. 'And she'll admit it soon.' He hadn't offered Treasure's cigarette packet around.

The Detective Sergeant had raised his eyebrows at Yolan's question, but said nothing. He didn't care to contradict Holmes, his immediate boss – not without substantial reasons, and he didn't have any.

'I got the feeling she was too frightened to be lying, sir.' Detective Constable Kevin O'Donnell broke the brief silence, notebook in hand, from his seat near the door.

The twenty-four-year-old O'Donnell was naturalised British, but originally from Cork. His heavy Irish accent, muscular build, and a rugby scar across his forehead combined to work against his remaining inconspicuous anywhere – but he had a soft voice.

'You interviewed her first, Kevin?' asked Yolan.

'Yes, sir. It was like she couldn't wait to tell her story. It had the ring of truth, if you follow me? I thought the same when DI Holmes talked to her.'

O'Donnell knew that Piper shared his view – and why he wasn't saying so. Piper's silence was in any case making his attitude obvious. And, like a good Irishman, O'Donnell was always ready to support the weakest side of a so far unresolvable argument.

'Were you there later when DS Piper talked to her here in the station?'

'No, sir. DI Holmes and me were at the college then.'

'Interviewing Mark Treasure, the banker?' Yolan picked up one of the papers from the desk.

'Not exactly, sir. I only saw the college porter.' This was accurate and explained the hint of pique in the voice. Unlike O'Donnell's other superiors, Holmes was in the habit of using him as a driver and dog's-body, leaving him out of interviews where statements weren't required. Because of this, the Constable had missed the meetings with Midden and Treasure – and a fair amount of imbibing, judging by the smell on Holmes' breath, and his concentrated way of walking when he had been leaving All Saints. Even so, the Irishman had picked up some worthwhile information from the duty porter.

'Treasure and his party left the shop as a group?' queried Yolan, looking at the report in his hand.

'Yes. He confirmed what the girl said about that.' Holmes, wreathed in smoke, was wiping his forehead and neck as he spoke; he was the only one of the four who hadn't removed his jacket. 'I'll have it checked out tomorrow with some of the others,' he went on. 'Rees said she would normally have locked the door after them. No one else was let in later.'

'Except tonight she forgot the lock?'

'That's what she says,' wheezed the Detective Inspector, without taking the cigarette from his lips.

'In fairness, she wasn't at all certain about that at the start, sir,' O'Donnell volunteered. 'At first she said she'd locked the door. Then she changed her mind. Said she might have taken the key from the lock without turning it. That Mr Cormit was shouting to her to get a move on. Confusing her. Anyway, she wasn't sure.'

'So what? She was saying different to me later,' said Holmes gruffly, half-turning around to give O'Donnell a sour glare through the smoke.

'Because if forgetting to lock was to be an important part of a prepared story, she'd have been certain about it. From the start. Wouldn't you think that, sir,' O'Donnell finished respectfully.

Yolan gave a noncommitting smile.

132

'I don't believe she's absolutely sure on the point even now,' said Piper.

'If she did lock up, did anyone else have a key to the place?' asked Yolan.

'Not that we know of, sir,' the Sergeant answered.

'And what if her story wasn't prepared?' Holmes demanded impatiently. 'What if she did for Cormit when she saw the opportunity, when she knew the value of those sketches, and then fed us the wrong load of cobblers? I mean before she'd worked out there was no way into the place except through the locked shop door?'

'If she did the murder, Sherlock, I think it's the first thing she'd have thought of, not the last,' said Yolan quietly.

'You're not saying we should let her go?' Holmes challenged.

The Detective Chief Inspector considered for a moment. 'I think we should keep her here tonight for more questioning first thing. Charge her in time for court on the drugs count, and for the murder if there's enough evidence. If she still hasn't agreed to have a lawyer, we should get her one anyway.'

'One thing, sir,' O'Donnell spoke up as Yolan was lifting his jacket from the back of his chair. 'The front door of the shop was open when Mr Treasure's group arrived. Someone could have slipped in then and hidden till later. It's all bookcases. Plenty of cover.'

'That's possible,' agreed Piper. 'Like someone who knew about the Constable sketches.'

'At least three other people did,' O'Donnell added. 'A Mr Barners, a Mr Ostracher, and Miss Chance from St Agnes. They were all at the dinner tonight when they talked about the sketches. I got that from the porter.'

'I have those names too,' said Holmes, again impatiently. 'Barners and Ostracher were at Cormit's place earlier in the evening. We haven't got their movements between eleven-ten and eleven-thirty yet, but they sound like sober citizens.' He wished again that Yolan had waited till all the basic evidence had been gathered in the incident room across the corridor and then called the meeting. 'And, let's not forget, anyone from outside who went in to nick those sketches would have taken them away with him,' he continued. 'Only Rees would have left them there, because there was bugger all else she could do. And Midden the butler was at the dinner too, you know?' he concluded, in case one of his subordinates decided to table this too, as another personal if irrelevant exclusive.

'The one whose wife is half-sister to the dead man?' asked Yolan.

'Yes, but he was in the college fetching and carrying after dinner,' Holmes confirmed.

'And his wife?'

'At home all evening according to her husband, sir.' This was Piper. 'I'm seeing her first thing.'

'OK. Let's agree to stick to your basic plan for tonight, Sherlock. And play the court by ear in the morning,' said Yolan. The others noted the authorship accredited by the words. 'But if the girl doesn't cough, we'll need to upgrade the case. All happy? See you in the morning then.' He made to rise from his chair.

Holmes' eyes registered hostility at the last suggestion. Upgrading the case would not only be an indictment of the way he had assessed it in the first place, and handled it subsequently. It also meant that Yolan would take over from his as Senior Investigating Officer.

'There's a funny thing about that Miss Chance,' O'Donnell put in. 'Sure, she went home from the college twice tonight. At eleven–eight and eleven thirty-one. The porter saw her both times on his screen. They have a closed–circuit camera covering the vehicle entrance.

'Forgot her knickers first time, I expect, Kevin,' said Yolan dismissively.

'Ah, it wouldn't be that, sir. A venerable lady she is. Quite old. More likely she went back for a bottle of gin. The porter says she was tipsy earlier on in the evening.'

Chapter Thirteen

'But you aren't being charged with murder,' said Treasure to Megan Rees. 'You're being charged with possessing and supplying cannabis. And before you go to court at ten, Miss Thompson hopes she'll have the supplying charge dropped.'

'Well it was obviously Mr Cormit's cannabis,' said Miss Thompson, a confident, business-like young woman. She had been the local duty solicitor and had made no complaint at being pressed into service on a sunny Saturday morning. A slim, middle-height brunette with a sharp nose and chin, large brown eyes, a generous mouth and brittle diction, she was wearing an unfrilly, sleeveless white blouse and a calf-length, black cotton skirt. Treasure found her appearance pleasing as well as appropriate, and had warmed to her from the start.

'So will I get bail? If I plead guilty?'

'Possibly, Megan, but don't count on it yet. We'll do our best,' the lawyer replied carefully, crossing a pretty pair of legs below but not quite beneath the small oblong table where she was sitting alongside the banker. Megan Rees was opposite.

The three were in a windowless interview room in the basement of the police station. There were two more grey plastic chairs besides the ones at the table, but that completed the moveable furniture in the room. A single, covered strip-light was burning in the ceiling, and a hinged-glass ventilator panel was open above the door. There was a carafe of water on the table, capped by a drinking glass.

It was a few minutes before eight o'clock. Treasure had been up and busy since six-thirty.

After Detective Inspector Holmes had left him the night before, the banker had spoken to Megan's older sister Olwyn in her New York apartment. The telephone number had been provided reluctantly by the girls' father. Fortunately he had remembered who Treasure was, but had shown a staggering indifference to Megan's plight, and to her fate.

Mrs Olwyn Struthers – that was the sister's married name – had promised to fly to London on Saturday night, and to cope with the Megan situation when she arrived. Treasure had volunteered to do what he could meantime – probably rashly he told himself afterwards, but he was fond of Olwyn, and believed Megan's story. He also had a hardening presentiment that if Megan hadn't murdered Cormit, then someone else who had known about the Constable sketches almost must have done – which in turn suggested an uncomfortably narrow field. He was deeply anxious that no one connected with the Moneybuckle should be seen to be implicated, however remotely.

'Where will I go if they let me out? I've got nowhere except the shop. Will they let me back there?'

If Megan Rees had looked drawn and unkempt the last time Treasure had seen her, she looked a good deal worse now. There was a blackness under the eyes in the forlorn, deathly white face, and this had nothing to do with make-up. The voice was dry, and so were the lips. To blink seemed to be an effort, judging by the way the eyelids screwed up every time they were closed. She was sitting slumped in the chair, with her elbows on the table, her head clasped between her hands, her fingers pushed into the lank and knotted hair. She had on the same stained blue tee-shirt and jeans she had been wearing the previous evening.

It seemed she had had little sleep in the detention room where she had spent the night. The undisturbed time there, followed by breakfast, had done little to re-orient the girl's mind after the frightening experience of the night before. Her reactions so far during the interview had been sometimes aggressive but mostly despairing, with nothing much else in between.

'Mrs Midden is very keen that you go to stay with her,' said Treasure.

Megan's lowered gaze came up briefly. 'In St John Street? Are you sure? She's kind.'

Treasure had learned of the Middens' relationship with Cormit when he had called the police station early and been put on to Detective Sergeant Piper. Along with some other information about the status of Megan Rees, the Sergeant had volunteered that Mrs Midden had already called to ask if the girl was likely to be released, and offering to take her in if she was.

Treasure had stopped at the Middens' house after he had arranged to meet a solicitor at the police station. Mrs Midden had welcomed Treasure inside, and explained that her husband was still asleep. It was evident from the following conversation that Midden would not be in sympathy with his wife's intentions over Megan, but that he wasn't likely to prevent them.

'Arthur doesn't think they'll let her go anyway, Mr Treasure,' the tired Mrs Midden had related sorrowfully. 'He thinks Megan did it, you see?' She bit on her lower lip.

'And you don't?'

'Gentle creature like her? No way. And smoking those drugs doesn't make you violent in any case. Or so they say.'

'I gather the two of them were involved in something of a rave-up, though.'

'That would have been Ernie's doing, not hers. She'd just be going along with his nasty ways, that's all.' Mrs Midden had lowered her voice, though the two had been talking in the front room of the house with the door closed. 'I'm sorry to say that about my half-brother, but it's true. His wife used to complain about him something terrible. What he made her do. In the bedroom. He was real peculiar.' Mrs Midden had gone quite red. 'Came out in the divorce, it did. In the paper and everything. Like it will again now, most likely.' She had concluded with a shamefaced nod.

The conversation at the St John Street house had later been foreshortened in the hallway. Treasure was being shown out when Midden's pager had sounded from the rear of the house. The banker had left Mrs Midden dialling the college porter on the pay-phone to find out who wanted her husband, while complaining, 'It's not fair, Mister Treasure, really it isn't. Arthur's not supposed to be on duty yet. He was working ever so late last night.'

Treasure had left for the police station at least satisfied that Megan Rees had a protector in Mrs Midden.

'Have you been much help to the police, d'you think?' he asked Megan now.

'I'm not helping them. Why should I?' She looked up again between her fingers. 'They're trying to prove I murdered Ernie, aren't they? That's why they'll try to stop me getting bail. I know that. I'm not stupid.' Her suddenly belligerent gaze turned on to the other young woman.

But Miss Thompson was writing something in her note-book. 'That's not what Mr Treasure meant,' she said, without looking up.

'I meant with information about what happened. Anything you've remembered. Anything that could lead them to find out who did break in. And I think they're just as keen to get at the truth as we are, you know?'

The dull, unseeing expression had returned to the eyes: Megan was neither admonished nor enthused by the words. 'I didn't see anything. Whoever it was took the bathroom key and put it on the outside. It was on the inside before. That's all I know.'

'What about noises, Megan?' This was the lawyer.

'I didn't hear anything. Because I was shouting and screaming, I suppose. And banging on the wall.' She swallowed. 'The phone went when I was in there. I told them that.'

'What time was that?'

The girl's face clouded. 'I don't know. It was about eleven-fifteen when I got locked in.'

'It was eleven thirty-one when the police were called,' said Miss Thompson. 'And you said you'd been free for three to four minutes before that.'

'So you were locked in for under fifteen minutes. Was it at the start or the end of that when the phone rang?' asked Treasure.

It was some time before she answered. 'About in the middle, I think. Before the lock was turned. What's it matter?'

'It might. Did it ring for long?'

'Not long. Like it was answered, or whoever it was ringing gave up.'

'You didn't hear the call being answered?'

She shook her head slowly. 'No. It wouldn't have been, would it? Not if the murderer was upstairs. The phone was plugged in downstairs. On the desk in the shop. Ernie hadn't brought it up. It sounds different from the bathroom.'

'So you didn't hear it being answered. You sure it was that phone? It couldn't have been the phone next door for instance?' asked the lawyer.

'Don't think so. It's one of the new ones. Next door's got the old type. You don't hear it from the bathroom anyway.'

Treasure tilted back his chair. 'The police asked you about the sketches,' he said. 'The ones we'd come to see.'

'The Constables? I said Ernie locked them in the top drawer of the chest. In the alcove. The murderer put them in the wardrobe. Moved them.'

139

'Ernie couldn't have moved them?'

'I thought I heard him lock them up. When I was still downstairs. Afterwards we were together all the time.' She was slowly becoming more lucid.

'And you didn't move them?'

'That's what the grey-haired copper thinks.'

'Inspector Holmes? Not the others?'

'I don't know about the others. He's certain though.' Megan took her arms off the table and sank back in the chair. 'I didn't move the sodding things. I thought they'd been pinched. God, why won't they believe me?' Her shoulders started to heave as she attempted to suppress a new bout of sobbing. Then she buried her face in her hands.

'Come on. You're doing so well. Try to keep going. It's hard, I know, but this is important,' said Miss Thompson, leaning over and squeezing Megan's shoulder.

'That's right. And remember we believe what you're saying,' the banker put in, then after pausing briefly he went on, 'Can you tell us, is it possible anyone else knew what was going on in the bedroom? I mean that Ernie would be manacled? That he wouldn't be able to defend himself?'

The hands were lowered slowly from the tear-streaked face. When Megan spoke, the tone was faltering. 'I wouldn't think so. You don't go telling people things like that, do you? He wasn't that kinky. Not really. I know it sounds . . . well, I mean he just liked to be tied up before . . . well, you know.' The last words came almost in a whisper.

'Did the police ask you if you objected to your part in that?' asked Miss Thompson.

'Yes. I said I couldn't care less. It didn't matter to me.' She was silent for several seconds before continuing in a slightly stronger voice, 'He'd been kind. He took me in. I just played along with what he wanted. It was nothing. Nothing really.'

'Did they ask if you'd ever taken hard drugs as well as soft?'

'Yes. I told them. Coke. But not since I was in prison.' She was staring at Miss Thompson now. Before, when she had done that, the look in the eyes had been plainly envious. Now it had changed to sheer hopelessness. 'It'll be in my record anyway, won't it?'

'Afraid so. You were right to admit it though,' the lawyer encouraged. 'Can you tell us, was Ernie a drug pusher? It could be important. For you.'

'I don't think so. He always had enough to make joints for the two of us. That's all I know.'

'So they won't find more than they got at the start?'

'Not so far as I know.'

'You didn't tell the police there were any unused drugs in the place?'

'I was too frightened. I didn't know what I was saying. You don't know what it was like.'

'We're trying to,' said Treasure, smiling gently. 'Ernie told me he was bothered about security. That he was getting a safe installed. Had there been any burglary attempts before last night, do you know?'

'Not when I was there. There was nothing worth taking. Until the Constable sketches.'

'Did anyone else come to see them? Besides my party, and Mr Ostracher and Mr Barners earlier?'

She shook her head. 'Ernie took them for the doctor to see yesterday morning. The one who lives up Banbury Road. He was with you last night.'

'Doctor Radout. Yes, he said he'd seen them. Ernie also took the sketches to London last week.'

The girl hesitated before answering quietly, 'That's only what he said.'

'You mean he didn't take them?' Treasure's eyebrows lifted.

'He went to London last Friday. I don't think he had the sketches with him. They weren't in the case. I saw

141

him open it when he came back. I think they were still locked in that drawer.'

'Did you tell the police this?'

'They didn't ask.'

'But he was supposed to have seen a dealer who made a valuation.'

The girl merely shrugged again in response.

'You mean he could have made that up? About the twenty-thousand-pound offer?' Treasure gave a wry smile. 'He was pretty convincing.'

'He went to London all right. To see someone. And I'm pretty sure it was about the sketches. Did he say he owned them?'

'Yes. Didn't he own them?'

'I'm not sure. I think they may have belonged to someone else.'

'But he found them in a family Bible he'd bought?'

Megan shook her head. 'That's only what he told people. He got them after the Bible.'

'How long after?'

'I can't remember. A few days probably.'

'And who was this someone else?'

'I don't know. Ernie just said to me Wednesday night he wished the drawings were really his. I asked next day what he meant. Who else owned them. But he just told me to forget it. He was angry for saying what he'd said to me.' She looked down at her hands. 'We'd been . . . we'd been smoking a lot that night.' She paused, her face pinched with the effort of concentration. The now closed eyelids gave a twitch as she spoke again. 'I've remembered something. Last night he talked to two people on the phone.'

'At what time?' Treasure asked.

'Both just after Mr Barners had been, with the American. I think it must have been about the sketches both times.'

'You know who the callers were?'

'No. I only heard the end of the first one. He'd sent me out. To the off-licence. For a bottle. He was just finishing talking when I got back. He was angry. I heard him say "twenty-five on top of five is too much". I think it was that.'

'Anything else?'

'That's all I remember. But it fitted with the other call. That was a bit later.'

'They were both incoming calls?' This was Miss Thompson.

'The second was. I don't know about the first.'

'So tell us how did the second fit with the first? You've really no idea about the name of the second caller?' asked Treasure.

'Ernie didn't say. He was cagey about anything to do with the sketches. He took both the calls downstairs in the shop. The second was very short.'

'Where were you?'

'Upstairs in the kitchen. I couldn't hear very well, but I did hear him say twenty-five was too much.'

'Twenty-five what?' Treasure pressed.

'I don't know. But in the end he said he'd think about it. Then he rang off.'

'Well done, Megan. That was a good effort.'

The girl opened her eyes. 'You really think there's a chance I'll get bail?'

'If they don't find more pot,' said Miss Thompson.

'And if they do?'

'We'll still plead not guilty and elect for trial in a higher court. We could still get bail.'

'If they don't charge me with murder as well,' the girl replied quietly.

'All the more reason for ensuring they don't,' put in Treasure cheerfully. 'Tell me, of the people who saw Ernie yesterday about the Constable sketches, how many were existing customers?'

'Collectors, Ernie called them.' Megan gave the ghost of a smile. 'I'm not sure. Doctor Radout is an old customer. He collects first editions.' She thought for a moment, then went on, 'Miss Norn from the Moneybuckle, she's been in before. Oh, and the younger, fair-haired man who came with you. He's a publisher.'

'Bryan Gavon?' Treasure looked surprised. 'He doesn't live in Oxford.'

'He's been in a few times,' said Megan.

'I see. Did any of them ever go upstairs to the flat?'

'Yes. Ernie took special collectors up there. If there was something important to see. Something he was keeping in the alcove. He didn't like bringing down what he called the good stuff.'

'So he took Mr Barners and Mr Ostracher up there yesterday?'

'Yes. To see the sketches.'

'Did Doctor Radout ever go up there?'

'Not yesterday. But another time, I remember. And Mr . . . Mr Gavon as well. He'd have taken your party there, except there were too many of you.'

'So virtually any important customer would know where the valuable things were kept?'

'I suppose so.'

Treasure evinced less reaction to this than he was feeling. 'One other thing. About the key to the Chubb lock. Where was it kept?'

'There are two I know of. One's on Ernie's ring. The other stays in the lock when the shop's open.'

'And when it's shut?'

'There's a hook it hangs on. Under the stairs at the back.'

'So in the daytime, anyone could have taken the key from the lock and put it back later? With neither you nor Mr Cormit knowing?' This came from a surprised Miss Thompson.

'To make a duplicate, or even a quick impression?' said Treasure.

'Yes,' Megan answered. 'I don't know why Ernie never thought of that.'

Treasure got up. 'All right, Megan. I'm going to leave you both and see what I can dig up elsewhere. I need a word with Miss Thompson outside before I go. You won't mind?'

The girl shook her head: there was a look of deep resignation on her face. 'Thanks for what you're doing.'

A few moments later the banker was holding open the door of the police station for the attractive lawyer. As they emerged onto sunlit St Aldate's he was saying, 'And Olwyn Struthers, her sister, wants all legal costs billed to her. I'll guarantee them till she gets here tomorrow.'

'Someone like Megan Rees is entitled to free legal aid, Mr Treasure. That's how I come to be here.'

'And she's lucky to have got such an evidently competent solicitor from such a reputable firm. If I may say so.' He gave an embarrassed smile. 'Mrs Struthers doesn't want you to feel any cost constraint over the time you give to the case. And if it comes to a trial for murder, she wants the best barrister for the job, not just someone who's available for the indigent. She's able to pay. Understood?'

'I think so,' Miss Thompson answered, flattered, and mildly amused at his tycoonish way of ordering legal talent. 'I'm afraid a murder charge is still likely.' As the two strolled slowly up the sloping pavement in the direction of Christ Church, the lawyer continued, 'Mrs Struthers is very concerned for her sister, except they seem to have been out of touch till now. It's none of my business, but why d'you suppose she allowed Megan to sink so low without doing something?'

'I asked the same question. Olwyn simply didn't know where Megan was, or what had happened to her. Megan had literally chosen to drop out. It started when she lost her place at a Welsh university, for failing an exam. In fact she'd had some kind of breakdown that no one knew about at the time. Her widower father was furious at the failure and kicked her out of the house. He's done worse since. Olwyn was already in America.'

'And Megan was too ashamed to contact her?'

'Or too proud. Meantime, she's led a hell of a life, according to Mrs Midden who seems to be her only confidant. It's all doubly perplexing because apparently Megan is intellectually as bright as Olwyn. Incidentally, I think her telling me yesterday that she was Olwyn's sister was a disguised cry for help.'

Miss Thompson nodded. 'I wondered about that. Well, I think I'd better get back to my client. Right now the police aren't looking far beyond Megan for a murderer, you know? And you can't really blame them.' She hesitated. 'They may still get bail stopped on a drugs charge because of more serious charges pending.'

The two now came to a halt, facing each other.

'I'm sure you'll do your best,' said Treasure. 'So will you telephone me at All Saints, after you're done with the Magistrates' Court? If I've gone over to the Moneybuckle they'll tell you.'

'Fine.' She pushed her hair from her eyes. 'Look, there's something else I ought to say. Right now I think you and her sister are Megan's best hope of not being charged with murder. Of course, if she is charged and tried, on balance she could very likely be acquitted.'

'You mean the evidence is so obvious as to be questionable for that reason?'

'Yes. If she'd done it, you'd have expected a confession, and the plea that he was a pervert who'd driven her to it. It's probably why they haven't charged her already. But a trial of that kind, if it happened, could finish someone in her state. Even if she did get off.' She paused, looking steadily into his eyes as she added, 'So if you feel there's anything you could tell the police now – anything that lit up another suspect, I think you should do it.'

Treasure held her gaze, also unblinking, as he replied, 'Point taken. You realise nearly all the people we were talking about in there are friends of mine?' Then he glanced across the road at Pembroke Street, and back

146

again, while formulating his next words. 'But yes, I do now have questions to put to several people. But no, I'm not ready even to *show* any of them to the lions yet. Not quite yet. But on what we've gleaned in the last few minutes, I can tell you, I'm totally certain Megan Rees is innocent.'

Chapter Fourteen

'Good morning, Miss Chance. You look well today.' He hesitated to say that the lady also looked recovered.

'Thank you, Mr Treasure, I'm quite recovered.' So Miss Chance had said it for him. 'I don't mean to interrupt. I came to apologise again for my conduct last night.'

'No apologies necessary. Could have happened to any-one. Antihistamines and drink really don't seem to mix. Do sit down. That chair's quite comfy. Would you like some coffee? There's plenty.'

They were in Treasure's sitting room. The banker had returned from the police station a few minutes before. He had been between telephone calls when Miss Chance had appeared. The coffee had been provided by Midden a minute earlier, promptly on request, and with enough spare cups for a small party.

'No coffee, thank you. And I really mustn't detain you.' Even so, Miss Chance took the armchair indicated. She sat bolt upright, facing the deep window onto New Quad. She seemed to be in the clothes she had worn on the previous afternoon – only the ankle socks were a distinguishing shade of purple instead of white. 'I've heard about Mr Cormit's murder. It must have come as a shock to all of you who went there after dinner.'

'It was. Did you know him?' Treasure settled himself on the window seat.

'By sight only. I'd been to the shop once. Some weeks

ago. The circumstances of the death sound bizarre as well as horrid. Are we to accept that the Welsh girl living with him did it?'

'No, we certainly aren't. Her name's Megan Rees. The police are keeping her for questioning. I'm trying to help her.'

'Good for you. I remember her quite clearly from my visit. A sad young woman. Not attractive in the physical way, but intelligent. I should have said capable of suicide but not murder.'

'Is that a philosopher's considered judgement?'

'Not at all.' She smoothed the skirt over her knees. 'More out of my experience as Moral Tutor to generations of young women at St Agnes. Is there anything I can do? I understand the Constable sketches were involved. Were they taken?'

'No, but they were moved. By the murderer, according to Miss Rees.' He went on to explain the circumstances.

'Curious,' observed Miss Chance at the end. 'Do you suppose the criminal meant to take them and was disturbed? Or did he or she expect to return for them?'

'There's a third possibility,' said Treasure, rising to cross to the telephone which had started ringing. 'Ah good. Put her through, please,' he said into the instrument, then looked toward his visitor. 'It's my secretary,' he explained, dropping into the chair behind the desk. 'Good morning, Miss Gaunt.'

The conversation that followed was brief, and fairly one-sided. From Treasure's short comments on what he was being told, the news was evidently bad. 'Exactly what I expected, I'm afraid,' was his most ominous interjection toward the end.

'Sorry about that,' he said to Miss Chance later, as he was returning to the window seat.

'Your secretary works on Saturdays?'

'Miss Gaunt is a paragon who'd work on Christmas Day if necessary. Provided she'd been to Mass first.' He smiled.

'She's dug up some information I needed. Nothing to do with Cormit's death.'

'I trust the following may not be either,' rejoined Miss Chance, with a worried look. 'But I think it proper to mention. You know my bicycle was borrowed for a period last evening?'

'I gathered from Steven Bickworthy it was there the second time you looked.'

'But not the first time. I was not mistaken in that. When I returned with Mr Bickworthy, the machine was being brought in from the street by Mr Gavon.'

'Was it he who'd borrowed it?'

'He said not. He found it leaning against the wall of the college. In St Giles.'

'Any damage?'

'A little. Not to the machine. The light gaberdine cloak I keep in the wicker basket had been torn. And my silk headscarf had been knotted so tightly I've yet to get it undone.'

'So they'd both been used?'

'Without doubt. But that's only half the story, Mr Treasure. The college porter has just told me he saw me leave twice last night.'

'Did you leave twice?'

'Certainly not. I left once. Just after eleven-thirty. The porter had a note of that. He also believes he saw me leave with my bicycle twenty minutes earlier. He says he saw me both times on the television screen in the lodge.'

'Isn't their camera switched off when they close the old iron gates below the car park?'

'I think not. But the gates aren't closed until midnight in any case. These events were some time before that.'

'Perhaps the porter only recognised the bike first time?'

'On the contrary. He recognised me, he says. By my cloak and headscarf. They are objects nearly as familiar as my machine. It follows he didn't see the face under the scarf. On what he calls my second departure, the real one,

150

I hadn't donned the cloak and scarf. You remember it was a very close evening?'

'Which is why you didn't discover the damage till this morning? Did the porter see Bryan Gavon bring the bike in?'

'He says he didn't. The duty porter can't be watching the screen the whole time, of course. In this instance, he says it's likely he was engaged outside the lodge, locking the main door to the college. That one is normally locked at eleven-thirty.'

'The time fits, certainly.'

'That's what I believe. Nevertheless, the porter naturally construed that I had re-entered the college myself. It's probably of no consequence,' Miss Chance concluded, but in a tone suggesting she really thought otherwise. 'If it were, Mr Gavon would no doubt affirm the true facts.'

'Anything to oblige a lady,' said Gavon himself, loudly. He had entered the room with only a peremptory knock, and in time to hear the last sentence. 'Morning both. Is that coffee hot, Mark? Good. Ghastly news about Cormit. Midden just told me.' He poured himself coffee.

'Bryan, you didn't see who left Miss Chance's bicycle in St Giles last night?' asked Treasure.

'Afraid not.' Balancing his cup, he joined the banker on the window seat. 'It was there when I happened along. It looked lonely and vulnerable, so I brought it in. Anything wrong about it?'

'Not really, Mr Gavon. And I'm grateful to you,' said Miss Chance, rising from her seat. 'Now I must be going. I shall see you both at the meeting this afternoon.'

After the lady had left, Treasure briefly described his involvement in the aftermath of the murder, from his interview with Detective Inspector Holmes up to the present. 'I think the police may want your confirmation on some points, Bryan,' he said in conclusion.

151

'And welcome to it,' said the publisher. 'Anything in particular?'

'I told them you left Cormit's place with Edith Norn at about ten forty-five.'

'Quite right.'

'They may want to know what you did between then and the time you brought in the bike.'

'That's easy. I walked Edith home. She has a flat in Summertown. About a mile up the road. We weren't hurrying. I went in for a minute.' He gave Treasure a sudden quizzical look. 'Are you suggesting we may all of us need alibis for the time of the murder?'

'If the police look beyond Megan Rees for a murderer, they're bound to question people who knew about the Constable sketches.'

'But there are droves who did,' the other replied defensively. 'Mind if I have more coffee? I'm avoiding going in for breakfast proper. Trying to cut down on food. And the early-morning sermon from Bertram Bodd. I got one of those last year.'

'Help yourself. I don't believe there are many people outside the Moneybuckle group who knew about the sketches. It seems to me Cormit had Ostracher targeted to buy them, and Radout and Julian Barners as unknowing collaborators. In those circumstances, it's unlikely Cormit would have done much about interesting other buyers.'

'That's possible, I suppose. Of course, he'd shown the sketches to the Bond Street dealer who made the offer.'

'According to Megan Rees, he'd done nothing of the sort. When he went to London last week he didn't take the Constables with him. But she thinks he was going to see someone to talk about them.' Treasure paused before adding, 'She's also saying you were a regular customer of Cormit's.'

'Hardly regular. I dropped in from time to time. Over the British canals project. The book I've been writing. He unearthed a copy of a privately published contemporary work on the Oxford and Banbury canal.' Gavon chuckled. 'So that was cunning. Having us all convinced about the Bond Street offer.'

'It wasn't you he saw in London, Bryan?'

'Good God no. Look, if you're taking all this so seriously, Edith will vouch for where I was. I mean at what you've said was the critical time.'

'I just think it'll be easier if the police can eliminate Moneybuckle people from any inquiry. Can you remember exactly what time you left Edith?'

'Well not exactly. It was around eleven. Or a bit after, probably. Then I came back here.'

'Straight back?'

'Nearly. It was such a pleasant night, at the end I took Parks Road past Keble, then back up Museum Road to St Giles. Come to think of it, it must have been after eleven when I left Edith, because I didn't get here till nearly half past.'

'Possibly Edith knows what time you left her.'

'And then we'll alibi each other, won't we? If a woman murdered Cormit, surely it has to be the Rees girl?' He looked down at a lapel of the dark, double-breasted blazer he was wearing, then gave it a casual flick with his fingers. 'On second thoughts, I hope Edith won't be bothered by the police. She has a very sensitive nature.'

'According to Miss Rees, Edith was also a customer of Cormit's.'

'And of every other second-hand bookseller in Oxford, I should think. Books are that girl's life. Her flat is knee deep in tattered tomes, taken in like so many stray dogs. She re-binds them. Competently too.'

Treasure nodded. 'I meant to ask you, d'you know what was upsetting her on the staircase last evening?'

'Oh that? I wondered too, at the time. All mended later.' He smoothed a hand across his chin. 'Actually, she burst in to cry on my shoulder. Felt thwarted because Charlotte Lundle was with me. That was why she ran out again.'

153

'She looked pretty desperate.' Except Treasure remembered she had appeared quite normal only moments before in the quadrangle.

'There was good reason for the desperation, Mark. At the time. Keep it to yourself, but poor Edith thought she was preggers. It was a false alarm. Resolved almost immediately afterwards. All that running up and down our staircase probably.'

'She seemed a good deal more composed after dinner, certainly.'

'Well that was why. I've since counselled her on how to get her love-making better organised.'

'Does she usually come to you with her troubles?'

'If I'm about.' He parted his hands in a gesture of resignation. 'Scourge of my later life, dear boy. I'm always attracting young women, but only for the most exemplary, moral reasons. And innocent moral purposes too. It's very disheartening, not to say frustrating, for a natural lecher like me.'

In the ordinary way, Treasure might have matched the levity, and challenged the contention. As it was, he had more serious things on his mind.

'You start work commendably early,' Treasure said to Steven Bickworthy, five minutes later: Steven had just opened the door of the Moneybuckle in response to the other's ring.

'I'm not expected to come in on Saturdays at all. But I'm getting Monday off instead. It's because of the governors' meeting. Thanks again for the drinks last night, sir. And the advice.'

'Pleasure. If you do decide on merchant banking as a career, why don't you write to me before the Easter vacation?'

'I've decided already. But won't it depend on the results of my finals?'

'To an extent, I suppose. And your capacity to work

154

outrageous hours. That nice girl Clair says you're going to get a first. That should be good enough academically, even for Grenwood, Phipps.'

'Pity Clair isn't an examiner.'

'I'd trust her judgement even so.' Treasure grinned. 'You parry her political views very well.'

'That unrepentant, old-style socialism is a pose.'

'But she does seem to have an informed social conscience,' said Treasure. 'Of a quite practical kind. It suggests that with experience her politics will move to the right a bit. But I may be prejudiced,' he added, without actually meaning it. 'Is Westerly about?'

They had come through the carved oak double doors and were standing outside Steven's office in the main library.

'Mr Westerly's upstairs in his room. Edith's here too. Working in the basement. I heard about the murder. You had a detective around after we'd all left?'

'Yes. The people in our party were the last to see Cormit before he got the chop. Nasty business. Anyway, it needn't concern you. I hope we didn't keep you up too late.'

'Not at all. Mr Westerly was up pretty late too, but he was first in today. That was after being here last thing.

'You mean he left after everyone else yesterday?' Treasure put the question casually.

'Probably. But he came back later, too. After he was with you. At the bookshop.'

'You saw him?'

'Coming out. I was across at All Saints. It was when I was seeing Miss Chance off on her famous yellow bike.'

'At eleven-thirty?' The banker waited for the confirming nod from Steven, then mounted the wide, bulbously balustraded oak stairs with the shining brass outer treads.

Westerly was seated at his desk, and half rose as Treasure entered his room on the upper floor.

'I'm afraid we have to have another word about this insurance business,' Treasure began, after closing the door firmly, and taking a seat in front of the desk. He had offered no apology for his unheralded appearance.

'The Hawksmoor drawing is safe,' said Westerly. 'It wasn't burned. There was a call from the Chinese Embassy early this morning.' He spoke hollowly and without the exuberance the news should have evinced. He looked tired and drawn. He was without coat or tie, and the white shirt he was wearing needed washing.

'Well that really is good news. You must be highly relieved.' Treasure waited for a response, but, getting none, he continued, 'It also reduces the immediate impact of what I have to ask you, though not, I'm afraid, its potential gravity. That address you gave me for the insurance broker in Reading. It's a corner newsagents. An accommodation address I imagine. Is that right?'

'Yes. You sent someone to check it.' This came as an assertion, not a question.

'My office did. So does this AQC outfit exist at all?'

Westerly exhaled a long breath, it seemed possibly in relief – though such an impression or reaction was difficult to credit. 'It existed in a way,' he said. 'It's me. I mean, I invented the name. As to the address, there was hardly any correspondence. At least, I never needed to post any. I . . . I had to have an address though, to open a bank account, you see? And in case anyone else wrote. I had some letterheads printed, too. It wasn't expensive. I used to check by telephone with the shop, in case there were letters.' He was pulling methodically on his beard as he spoke, and staring vacantly over Treasure's shoulder. His account had been a lucid, and only slightly nervous, dull recital of fact, with no emotion in the voice.

'And the cheques for the insurance premiums?'

'I paid them into a bank account in Reading. In the name of Broker. A Q C Broker. It was quite a simple ruse. Alan Quentin Charles Broker.' Without warning, he gave a sudden short, nearly maniacal shriek of laughter. 'Sorry. So, sorry. Not myself.' His face made embarrassed contortions.

'How long had you been using this ruse?'

'Two years.'

'So every time the Moneybuckle has needed to insure anything, you've been signing and sending cheques to yourself? There's been no actual insurance cover?'

Moneybuckle's Custodian showed momentary surprise, or it might even have been righteous shock. 'Oh, it was only to do with items we sent out on loan. The main insurance, for the building and the contents, that's always been done direct with an insurance company.'

'You hadn't taken that over too?'

'I'd thought of it, but the auditors might have asked to see the policies. They never bother with the occasional bits of temporary cover. I supplied receipts for those, and typed out simple cover notes. On the letterhead. It's all in the AQC file here.' He paused, shaking his head from side to side. 'I had to have the money, you see?'

'But the risk you took? Good Lord, man, the first suggestion of loss, like yesterday, and the whole scheme blows up in your face.'

'Not really, Mr Treasure. You see, loan exhibitions are always so well looked after. As a rule, the works are far safer than they'd normally be. The Peking fire is the only time I've ever had a scare, and that's been groundless. There was a fire, but the exhibits were rescued unharmed. The first news reports weren't correct. It was my bad luck you happened to be here to make enquiries. I could have brazened it out still.'

'I don't see how.'

'By pretending AQC had disappeared. Flitted without trace.'

'But the bank account?'

'I closed it yesterday. The newsagent wouldn't recognise me. I've only been there twice, ages ago.'

'So why decide to come clean now?'

'I'm not dishonest, except by necessity,' was the extent of Westerly's unsatisfactory response. Then he lowered his gaze so that it centred on the file in front of him, the one he had taken such pains to secrete away the night before.

'How much money did you take?' Treasure tried again.

Slowly Westerly lifted a hand and opened the cover of the file, leaning over it. 'Five thousand, eight hundred and thirty pounds.' He was reading from the exposed top sheet. 'A large sum. Not enough though. Not nearly enough. Of course, it wasn't a loss to the Moneybuckle.'

'Because you claimed back the premiums from the exhibition organisers?'

'In every case, Mr Treasure. Even so, I'm still prepared to make up the sum if you say so. I can. Easily. I shan't need money now.'

The plop of a heavy tear dropping onto the file cover had an unexpectedly shattering effect on the short silence that followed.

'You want to tell me about last night? What you did after you left me?' Treasure asked quietly.

Westerly remained still for a moment, then lifted his head. 'I came in here.'

'For how long?'

'Ten minutes or so.'

'You were seen leaving at eleven–thirty. If you were here only ten minutes, where had you been between coming here and when you left me?'

The Custodian's face clouded in perplexity. He took out his handkerchief. 'I don't know. Killing . . . ' He blew his nose loudly. 'Killing time. I hung about a bit. Out of sight. Till I was sure you'd all be indoors. I didn't want to be seen coming here.'

'Did you go back to Cormit's?'

'To Cormit's? No, why should I?'

'He died last night. Did you know?'

158

'No, I didn't know? I'm sorry. But more for myself. You could say I died last night too.'

'I don't understand. You'd better explain.'

The tick of a clock seemed to grow bolder in its intrusiveness until Westerly was ready to speak again. 'When I got home,' he said, 'I found Rebecca gone. Rebecca, my wife. She's left me. For someone else. She won't be coming back. Ever.'

Westerly's inane, unfocused smile suffused his face while, paradoxically, huge tears rolled down to make rivulets through his beard.

Chapter Fifteen

'Sorry I missed you. I took off for Woodstock early, but I gathered it was after you'd left. Pretty town,' said Ostracher to Treasure. 'Your message was waiting when I got back just now. Mr Midden said you'd be over here. This is Westerly's room isn't it? Is he joining us?'

'Westerly's been taken ill,' the banker answered with what he considered reasonable accuracy. He was in Westerly's chair and motioned the American to take the seat he, Treasure, had been occupying earlier. 'I've sent him home. I don't think he'll be at the meeting.'

'Bad as that?'

Worse than anything Ostracher would have in mind, thought Treasure, while not proposing to go into details yet. He had decided what ought to be done about Moneybuckle's Custodian, though not exactly how it should be handled. Getting the man out of the place had seemed a sensible first step.

'What took you to Woodstock?' It was just after nine-thirty. If Ostracher had driven the eight miles to view the place as a tourist and come back already, he couldn't have been very impressed.

'It wasn't to see Blenheim Palace. I've been over that before. Winston Churchill's birthplace.' He paused to give the fact, or his knowing it, full exposure. 'I did have the cab driver go up to the palace on the way back. Just to catch sight of it again. Flawed building, of course, but it still has great presence.' The American nodded over his own judgement. 'There's a jeweller in the town Mr Midden put me on to. Has a lot of Victorian silver miniatures, though he doesn't know much about them. My wife Kate collects them. Not the modern stuff. That's mostly junk. See here.'

The speaker had removed a flat box from the capacious side pocket of his elegant grey silk jacket. He removed the box top and a covering of tissue paper to reveal more than a dozen miniature replicas.

'You bought wholesale?' Treasure observed dryly.

'But for slow onward distribution,' said Ostracher, beaming. 'Great Christmas stocking fillers. Anniversary and birthday markers. Never my principal present to Kate, you understand, but it'll bring her untold joy to add these to her collection. At between two hundred and two hundred and fifty dollars apiece they're great value, too. In the States they'd be twice the price, and pretty hard to locate nowadays. That's true even in this country. For the real McCoy that is. These are all hallmarked London or Birmingham. Made mostly in the eighteen–eighties and nineties. That's when miniatures were all the rage.'

He was setting out the little collection on the desk top.

'Artefacts for expensive doll's-houses,' said Treasure, fingering a delicately fashioned, inch-high replica of a farmhouse rocking chair.

'But never made to a standard scale. Couldn't be, of course. And maybe that's part of the charm. This French horn with valves that move, it's way out of proportion with the rocker, say, or this ornate little Victorian bedstead.'

'Or the hinged handcuffs. Very nice, all of them.' Except metal bedsteads and manacles carried uncomfortable associations at the moment.

'To a collector the scale doesn't matter,' Ostracher explained. 'It's the variety. I called Kate last night, after I'd been in touch with the jeweller. She knows I'm bringing the cuffs and the bedstead. They're her compensation for not making the trip over this time. The rest can be surprises at other times.' He began gathering up the items. 'But I'm sorry, I've deflected you with my new finds. There was something you wanted to talk about? Is it Mr Cormit's murder? I heard about that. Shocking thing. They say the Constable sketches weren't taken or harmed.'

'I wanted a word about the murder, yes. To warn you the police will probably want to speak to you this morning. I had to give them your name as someone who'd been with Cormit last evening.'

'Of course. Always glad to help the police.' Ostracher pulled a face. 'Now why did I say always? Don't ever remember having to help them before.'

'You could also help me by answering some of the questions the police are likely to put. I'll tell you why later.'

'Surely. Go ahead.'

'You and Julian Barners stayed on at the dinner table after the rest of us went down to Cormit's place?'

'That's right, Mark. Till Mr Midden politely turned us out. He needed to straighten up the room for today. The rest of the help had gone by then.'

'What time was that, do you remember?'

'Exactly eleven. Julian and I took a slow turn around the garden afterwards. We talked pictures. Then Julian proposed a serious walk around the town. Too energetic for me. It was hot still and, tell you the truth, I'd taken too much of that vintage Dow.'

'What time did you part?'

'It was a little before eleven-fifteen. In the lodge. I stayed on, talking to the porter. I went in there with Julian. He needed to check there'd still be someone on duty to let him in. That's if he came back after midnight. All the gates are locked by that time. In the end, the porter lent him a key.'

'Then you went back to your rooms?'

'Yes. I'm not sure of the time. Around eleven-twenty, I guess. I nearly dropped in on you next door. Saw you

162

through the window. But then I was sure I could hear my telephone ringing. It wasn't when I got inside. Could have been yours I suppose. I gather we have the only phones on the staircase.'

'It was probably mine. I'd called Midden in his pantry about then, but didn't get through. The line was faulty all evening. He called me back though, straight away. Guessed it was me trying to reach him. He's really very efficient. Anyway, you should have joined us.'

'I was pretty bushed by then, Mark. Not so much tired as unsociable. And I had some calls of my own to make. The bank was fixing an extra line of credit. In case I needed money in a hurry. To buy the Constables. That's what the call during dinner was about.'

'Did you happen to call Cormit himself when you reached your rooms?'

Ostracher shook his head. 'No. I'd fixed to see him again with Julian Barners later this morning. I needed to sleep on the decision whether to buy the sketches. Now I guess I'll need to wait for an authorised seller. An executor or an heir.'

'May I ask if you'd decided to buy?'

'Yes I had. Provided my offer was accepted.' Ostracher had answered absently, his mind still on the previous point. 'I gather the young woman I saw there wasn't Mr Cormit's wife?'

'No, they weren't married. She's probably about to be accused of his murder.'

'You don't say? I haven't heard any of the details.'

'I'm sure the girl's innocent, and I'm trying to help her. Hence the questions. She was living with him. He was divorced from his wife. If you're wondering who will inherit, it looks as though it could be Mrs Midden.'

'Our Mr Midden's wife? That's another surprise. Say, she hadn't been living with Cormit too?'

'She's Cormit's half-sister. It seems he has no other relatives.'

163

'You know it was Mr Midden who put me on to the sketches in the first place?' Ostracher ran a big hand over a furrowed brow and the shining bald area above. 'He never said Mr Cormit was his brother-in-law.' He paused. 'Seems to me he should have done.'

'You must understand, Detective Inspector, we can't take account of charges not being put before the court. No matter how serious. Is that quite clear?' As she spoke, the lady chairman of the three magistrates was looking over her rimless glasses at Holmes.

'Yes, Your Worship.' The Detective Inspector was standing in the witness box to the left, below the bench. He had resented the mild admonition, though he had expected it. He was mentally cursing what he considered wringing wet magistrates as well as his own weak-spirited superior.

The chairman of the court was a well-preserved matron, sixtyish, and grey haired, with a soft clear voice. She had understanding eyes and a naturally kind expression. Both these features were sources of temporary hope to felons and scant solace to policemen. The magistrates on either side of her, one male, the other female, were both much younger than herself.

The court did not normally sit on Saturdays. It was doing so now to diminish a backlog of cases.

'Thank you, Detective Inspector. You may step down.' The chairman's gaze momentarily followed Holmes' progress back toward the police bench, then switched to the young woman in the dock before her. 'Megan Rees, this court will not be trying your case either this morning or later. That will be done by a higher court. Do you understand?'

'Yes, Your Worship.' Megan's answer was just audible, and followed a backward nod from Miss Thompson who was sitting just below her.

'Since you've pleaded not guilty to the charges of possessing and supplying illegal drugs, and elected for trial by jury,

164

we have to decide whether it's proper to allow you bail till that can happen,' the magistrate went on. 'We also have to take into account that the police oppose bail, as you've just heard.'

'May it please Your Worship?'

'Yes, Miss Thompson?'

'About the two admitted previous convictions, my client pleaded guilty both times,' said Miss Thompson, standing.

'You've told me that already.' But the kindly expression was enduring.

'I should have said too that she was given maximum remission from the short prison sentence the second time, with no complaints at all from her parole officer.'

'When was her parole over?'

'Two months ago, Your Worship.'

'Did you say she'd have somewhere to live if . . . ?' The speaker paused, looking at her notes. 'Yes you did. With Mrs Valerie Midden in St John Street. Is Mrs Midden in court?'

'Yes. Here, Your Worship,' Val Midden said in an embarrassed voice that no one heard. She had only half risen from her seat in the body of the court, but was waving her right arm about strenuously, more as if she were making a reluctant farewell than merely identifying herself.

'Mrs Midden, you confirm that you'd take in Miss Rees until the time of her trial?'

'Yes, Your Worship. It's the least I . . . ' Mrs Midden, only slightly emboldened at being personally addressed, allowed her words to peter out. She remained half standing, uncomfortable, and casting about nervously at officials who might indicate whether she should sit down again.

The magistrate had turned away with a nod, returning her attention to the young woman in the dock.

'Miss Rees, if you are given bail, will you promise to stay with Mrs Midden and do everything else the court requires?'

'Yes, Your Worship. I'll do anything.'

The Clerk to the Court, a very short man in a black gown, got up suddenly from his desk immediately below the bench. He turned about, stood on his chair, and began a whispered conference with the three magistrates who were leaning forward, heads converging for the same purpose.

The vexed Holmes scowled even more deeply at this regular court ritual.

'Very well,' said the older magistrate eventually, when the Clerk had resumed his place. 'Bail is granted on a surety of two thousand pounds. Is that likely to be forthcoming, Miss Thompson?'

'Yes, Your Worship,' the lawyer answered, standing quickly.

'So don't let us down, Miss Rees. Or the friends who are standing by you.'

'No, Your Worship. Thank you.'

Detective Inspector Holmes sucked his teeth. He also trod on the foot of the uniformed usher. This was in his haste to leave the court before the magistrates, who had decided to take a break. The swift exit was the policeman's way of registering disapproval – except no one save the usher had reason to notice.

'And you say you left Mr Cormit's at ten forty-five, sir?' said Detective Sergeant Piper to the Reverend Professor Bertram Bodd.

It was just after ten o'clock. They were in Bodd's room which was on the middle landing of the staircase next to Treasure's, in New Quad.

'I believe that's right,' murmured Bodd, shifting uncomfortably in the single armchair that was altogether too small for his bulk; it also had an obscene sag in its well-worn seat.

It was an undergraduate room with no embellishment. Considering his status, Bodd thought he deserved better, but he hadn't complained.

He was dressed in a clerical collar, black stock and a black suit of unseasonable weight. It was his 'meeting' suit, and less ill-fitting and grubby than he made it appear by burdening the pockets with papers and peppering the shoulders with scurf. When Piper had arrived he had been reading the ecclesiastical appointments vacant column of *The Times*.

'Did you come away with other members of the party, sir?' The tall young policeman was seated on the edge of the unmade bed.

'I caught up with Miss Lundle and Doctor Radout. In Little Clarendon Street. We walked up together.'

'Did you notice other members of the group leave the shop, sir? There were seven of you altogether.'

'You mean physically leave through the door? No, I don't believe I did. I saw two of them behind us in the street a little later. Mr Gavon and Miss Norn.'

'That'll do, sir. Thank you.' The Sergeant made a note in his book. 'You didn't see Mr Treasure with er . . . Mr Westerly was it?'

'No. Not then. I saw Treasure soon after I got back here. So he must have been close behind us.'

'And when you reached the college, did you separate from the other two?'

'Yes. After we'd carried on through to the college garden. I'd already begun to feel like the third wheel of the chariot.'

'I'm sorry, sir?'

'That my presence made one too many. Doctor Radout obviously wanted Miss Lundle's company to himself. And why not? They're both single, though I must say he's a bit old for . . . ' Bodd's accelerating delivery halted in mid-sentence, but his eyebrows continued to twitch.

'Bit old for what, sir?'

'For skittish behaviour. Altogether too old, probably. That'd be the trouble.' At this point Bodd appeared more to be addressing himself than the policeman.

167

'So where did you go then, sir?'

'Go?' Bodd blinked, shook his head, and started brushing hard with his sleeve at the fairly clean middle of his jacket. 'I didn't go anywhere. I met the college chaplain in Old Quad. He invited me to his rooms.'

'And that's where you went?'

'No, I had another engagement. We stayed in the quad for a little. He's very opposed to the ordination of women. So am I. Miss Chance had been trying to persuade him to a contrary view. Her arguments are largely fallacious. I know them well. Gravely undoctrinal. I was doing my best to make him see that.'

'Did the two of you talk for long, sir? You and the chaplain?'

'I fear he hardly talked at all,' said Bodd vigorously, and looking dispirited. 'Oh, I see. For a quarter of an hour, perhaps. Time flies when the subject engrosses,' he ended, with remarkable insensitivity.

'So you parted at what time, sir?'

'About ten-past eleven.' He paused. 'I'd left a note to say I'd be calling on someone at eleven-thirty. In St Ebbes. It was two or three minutes before that by the Carfax clock when I passed there later.'

'You walked to Carfax, sir? After you left the chaplain?'

'That's right. Some of the way with Julian Barners. We happened to meet outside the lodge. We parted when he turned left into the Broad. He walks rather quickly.'

'He went down Broad Street, sir?'

'That's right.'

Piper scribbled as he spoke. 'And you saw this person in St Ebbes quite soon after you left Carfax?'

'A minute or two later, yes.'

'Let's say at eleven-thirty.' The policeman made another note. 'Would you mind giving me the name and address of the person, sir?'

Bodd stiffened. 'A Mrs La Toque.' He added the address after consulting a worn pocket book. 'She won't be there now. She's travelling. International clientele.' He had repeated the lady's own words.

'That's interesting, sir. What profession is she in?'

The professor twisted in the armchair which responded with an ominous creak. 'Mrs La Toque is . . . ' He cleared his throat loudly. 'She's a noted chiropodist. Retained by many of the leading ballet companies. International ballet companies.'

'And ordinary people too, I expect, sir.' Detective Sergeant Piper gave an involuntary glance at Bodd's extremely large feet – objects encased in cracking black patent leather shoes intended to be worn only with his evening suit.

Bodd leaned forward slightly to follow the other's gaze, and thus became the second to notice that he was wearing odd socks.

'I believe she has individual private clients too. A few.' Bodd, still staring at his socks, was remembering the doorstep encounter with the Professor of Moral Philosophy. 'That's not why I went to see her.' He waited to see if the Sergeant would press for the reason. When he didn't, Bodd suddenly felt a compunction to offer it anyway. 'I'm a collector,' he vouchsafed in the manner of someone passing a state secret to an emissary of a friendly foreign power. It was high time, he told himself, to come out of the closet.

'A collector of ballerinas' shoes, sir?'

Bodd looked deflated. 'That's right. How did you know?'

'The worn-out pink pair in the box look a bit small for you, sir.'

Bodd turned his head in the direction of the Sergeant's gaze. He had forgotten the open box on the table. 'Those belonged to Pavlova. I traded some Danilovas and some de Valoises for them.' He straightened in the chair. 'It's not a fetish, you understand?'

Piper made to dispel any suggestion to the contrary with an energetic nod of agreement. 'Very interesting hobby I should think, sir. Got a large collection, have you?'

'Not large, but select.' Bodd had pulled himself out of the chair and gone over to the table where he lifted the shoes from the box. He presented them resting on tissue paper for the Sergeant's inspection, but without letting them out of his hands. 'It's possible to build up one's holding with exchanges. Or part-exchanges. Mrs La Toque is a recognised dealer. Well placed, of course,' he observed earnestly.

'Very nice, sir. I expect ballet dancers get through a lot of shoes.'

'An immense number. Which should make things easy for collectors. The difficulty is in establishing total authenticity. That's essential, of course. Such beautiful creatures.' He was regarding the shoes with a mixture of reverence and awe, moving his fingers sensitively over the toe-pieces. Then, as if waking from a reverie, he moved to put them back in the box. 'People misunderstand one's interest in such things. They easily misconstrue, you know?' He paused, blinked at the Detective Sergeant, then closed the box before returning to his seat.

'Quite so, sir. Well I think that'll be all. No doubt Mrs La Toque could confirm you joined her at the time you say.' And even if she was a minute or so out, it seemed impossible that the ponderous professor could have done the murder in Walton Street ten minutes before being received in St Ebbes.

Professor Bodd's account seemed also to eliminate Mr Julian Barners from the list of possible suspects – and from the need for Detective Sergeant Piper to interview him.

Chapter Sixteen

'This is more a cold sepulchral crypt than a library extension,' said Treasure to Edith Norn. He was regarding the
Assistant Custodian from where he was standing on the
last step of the staircase down to the Moneybuckle basement.

'It's a dungeon. But nice and cool.' She had looked
up from her work at the sound of his voice.

She was seated at the knee-hole of a twin pedestal
wooden chest of heroic proportions. There were three
of these table-height monsters arranged down the
centre aisle of the basement. Edith was at the middle
one, immediately opposite the stairs. The pedestals
housed banks of wide drawers with twin brass handles.
They were very slim drawers, of the kind used to store
plans or drawings.

The basement was groin-vaulted in the Norman manner,
only very flattened. This was in sharp contrast to the
'gothicised' upstairs. The vaulting sprang from stunted
stone pillars. Two rows of pillars divided the space into
three aisles. The staircase pierced the nearside aisle in
the middle, between two pillars. The remainder of this
aisle and the farther side aisle were filled with rows of
free-standing bookcases that touched the ceiling at the
sides. The mediaeval-style, hinged reading racks attached
to the bookcases looked more ornamental than usable.

The only lighting was from single lamps dangling absurdly
from the bosses of the 'twelfth-century' vaulting. These were

filtering illumination through to barely half the bookstacks in the side aisles. The artificial lighting down the centre aisle was unobstructed, but there was no natural light at all.

Treasure was examining the area seriously for the first time. He judged its design as pretentious and impracticable – a pity, since its perpetrator had probably started with the worthy belief that the place was good for something better than a coal cellar.

'You're busy?' he said, moving toward Edith.

The girl lowered her glasses down her nose, leaned back, and waved her hands over the uneven stacks of mounted and unmounted pictures arranged on the big worktop before her. Close to her right hand was an open, loose-leaf ledger, a thick and battered exercise book, and sheets of large sticky labels. 'Everything has to be catalogued before it can be indexed. Would you believe, the only catalogue that existed was this?' She tapped the exercise book. 'It dates from the last century. And it doesn't include half the items. Trouble is, nobody's wanted to look at the things since before the First World War. And I mean nobody. Not so far as we can tell.'

'I suppose because the Moneybuckle is an architectural library, not an art gallery,' said Treasure, now near enough to be eyeing the exhibits.

'That's right. People don't come here to see the work of obscure watercolourists. Scale drawings and architectural concepts are different. But we keep all those sort of goodies on the upper floors.'

'And the books that are down here?' He wandered over into the far aisle.

'Foreign language, duplicates, and peripheral reference,' she announced, in a tone that assumed the hearer would understand the utter dispensability of such categories. 'Very few of our students ever need anything from those stacks,' she added, for fear her assumption was unjustified – which it had been.

'I see,' said Treasure, aware she was a good deal more relaxed than at any time the night before. She was also showing more confidence in her own work environment than she did outside it. 'And this stuff's been living in the drawers of these chests?' he asked, returning to stand beside her chair.

'Mmm. A lot of it ought to be thrown away, but I can't take the responsibility for that. Just recommending.' She pulled a face.

Treasure picked up a pencilled landscape. 'This is dreadfully amateur.'

'A relic of the Oxford Sunday Art Club. Miss Chance's great-grandfather ran that when he was Custodian. I have the membership list right here.' She produced another battered notebook. 'Some very notable Victorian academics were members. I'm afraid none of them was much of an artist. That particular drawing's hideous, I agree. But it's still above average.'

'Well it hardly rates a place in this establishment.'

'We really shall get rid of a lot eventually. But Mr Westerly wants it done his way. In case anything outstanding turns up.'

'And has it?'

'Yes. A watercolour which we've classified as pre-Raphaelite School. It just could be a Holman-Hunt. Oh, and there's a wash-drawing that may be by Turner of Oxford. Not J M W Turner. The other one. They're both upstairs, with some others, for Mr Barners to look at this afternoon.'

'So you can't afford to take chances,' said Treasure, but doubtfully.

'For the time being, I'm cataloguing absolutely everything, so Steven Bickworthy can get on with the indexing.'

'Wouldn't it be more practical— ?'

'To weed out first? Yes,' she interrupted with a grin, 'but we're three-quarters there, now. I'm giving them all titles and attributions where possible, and drawer numbers.'

'Some of them could have rarity value, I suppose?'

'Exactly. There's a drawing somewhere of a little girl, signed and dated by the Oxford Professor of Jurisprudence in eighteen ninety-three. Not great art, but jolly interesting. And it'll all be easy enough to rearrange when we thin out later.'

Treasure turned over several more pieces. 'Is this what Bryan Gavon was helping with?'

'Yes.' She looked down as she spoke, but not before Treasure had seen her expression cloud.

'I didn't mean to interrupt your work, but I want to know whether you'd mind standing in for the Custodian this afternoon? For the part of the meeting you both usually attend. He's gone home sick.'

She looked up again. 'I wrote nearly all his annual report, so I expect I can deliver it. He looked terrible earlier on. I thought he might have been affected by the murder. I know I was.' She shuddered.

'In his case I don't think it was the murder.' The banker didn't feel entitled to enlarge on the point. 'Incidentally, I told the police you left Cormit's shop with Bryan Gavon last night. They may want you to confirm that. I believe he walked you home?'

She hesitated. 'Is that what he said?'

'Yes. Isn't it true?'

'It's true. I'm just surprised . . . ' She shook her head. 'Oh, never mind.'

'Can you remember what time you parted?'

'I'm not sure. Just before eleven, I should think. My flat's not far.'

'The police may ask you the same question, that's all.' He paused, hoping for a response, but when there was none he asked, 'Had you been to the bookshop before?'

'A couple of times with Bryan. Once or twice by myself. Are they arresting the girl for the murder?' She put the wash-drawing she had been studying to one side and picked up another.

'No. And I've just heard she's been given bail.' He was moving around the chest as he spoke, idly examining more works of art and near art. 'The charge isn't that serious. Over drugs. Well, not serious when compared to murder.'

'I'm glad. I don't believe she could have done it. Though I think he probably used her.' This had come with especial feeling.

It was the second time Treasure had heard that particular opinion. 'She's going to stay with the Middens for the moment.'

'Mrs Midden was Mr Cormit's sister.'

'Yes. You knew that? Did Bryan Gavon know I wonder? I meant to ask him.' That was broadly true, but he was fishing now for an unprejudiced answer all the same.

'I think so. Who stood bail?'

'I did. Through her solicitor. I wasn't in court.'

'Was the bail high?'

'For what she's formally accused of so far, yes. Let's say it was weighted by other considerations. Anyway, she's not likely to skip.' He smiled.

There was a pause, then the girl said, 'You're very generous. And understanding.'

'Megan Rees has no one else handy.'

'Perhaps she's not the only one,' Edith blurted, then bit her lip. 'Sorry, I didn't mean . . . Bryan says that about you too. About your being good with people.' She hesitated, fingering the edge of a drawing. 'You've known him a long time.'

'Since university days, yes.'

'Do you know his wife?'

'Yes. Quite well. She's a doctor.'

'I know. Are they happily married?' The forced casualness in the question was given away by the blush now rising in her cheeks.

Treasure was immediately opposite her now. 'I'm afraid so,' he answered with a rueful smile. He felt he hadn't been the only one fishing for unprejudiced comments, just as he was now becoming uncomfortably sure it hadn't been

175

fatherly advice Edith had been getting from Gavon.

'It's none of my business, and please don't tell Bryan I asked you, but . . . but someone told me they might be divorcing.'

'I don't believe that's true. But I could be wrong,' he offered diplomatically. He folded his arms. 'You know, Bryan's so effusive, I imagine he sometimes gives women the impression— '

'That he's crazy about them?' she interrupted, looking up at him squarely, really for the first time. She put down the drawing she was holding because they were both aware her hand was trembling. 'I think so, too. Not me, of course. I was smitten for a while. Perhaps he told you?'

'No. Why should he?'

'I thought men . . .' She shook her head without completing the sentence, then said, 'Anyway, I'm afraid I was awfully rude to him last night.'

'Turned him out into the night?'

'No, we were in the street. Outside my flat. I didn't invite him in.' She pushed her glasses back up along her nose. 'Anyway, I think I've now become immune to Bryan's charms. Effusions, as you'd say. It's Miss Lundle who ought to watch out, don't you think?'

She was doing her naïve best to look defiant at having said anything so outrageous, but the result was pathetically contrived – just like the basement architecture.

'Told you the view was better up here,' announced Clair Witherton, slightly breathless and flopping onto the window seat of her top-floor room. 'You can see across St John's College and Trinity to the Broad. Sorry about the mess in here. Sit here in the window. It'll improve my image no end.'

'The view's delightful. So's the room. The climb's a bit harrowing,' said Treasure coming across to join her.

He had just walked over from the Moneybuckle. He had met Clair outside his rooms, and accepted an invitation to join her briefly for iced coffee.

The room was untidy, in a comfortable way, and had been made much more attractive than the one Bodd was in. Here the college fitments had been upstaged by a liberal scatter of cushions, some colourful pictures, and a billowing Liberty print duvet on the bed, with matching pillows put sofa-style along the wall. There was a flouncing display of pretty clothes on the uncovered rail at the back of the room, with pieces of expensive-looking luggage stacked to one side of it. A collection of scents and cosmetics took up more space on the desk top than the unorganised pile of books, notes and old essays in front of them.

The only witness to the occupier's political allegiance was a mailed copy of *Tribune* still in its wrapper – lying on top of the latest issue of *Harpers*.

'Coffee's in the kitchen fridge outside. I'll just get it,' said Clair, rising energetically and running both hands through her auburn hair. 'Oh, and I wanted to say thanks again for pep-talking Steven last night. He's got a marvellous mind, but he's not assertive enough yet. He is with me, but not where it matters.'

'I imagine it matters with you too.'

'OK. And I adore him. I meant he doesn't push himself career-wise.'

'That's just caution, I expect.' As he spoke, he was aware of a door being closed nearby.

'You think he'll make a banker?'

'You approve of merchant bankers?'

'I approve of you. But you're the only one I know,' she answered with a dazzling smile.

'Well "there's nothing in banking but what you ought to be able to learn in a week or two".'

'It's easy for you to say that.'

'I didn't. I was quoting. Judge Thomas Mellon. Around eighteen sixty-nine. He founded a pretty enduring bank in Pittsburgh, Pennsylvania.'

'Don't you need more than intuition these days?'

'You always did. But having some still helps.'

'I expect . . . Oh God, there's my Aunt Barbara.' Clair, still standing by the window, pointed at a scurrying figure approaching the end of the quadrangle. 'She lives in Wallingford. She'll be parked on a double-yellow line in St Giles, and she'll be bringing me home-made strawberry jam and Tory Party pamphlets. Except she's going the wrong way. No sense of direction in anything.'

Misguided Aunt Barbara had already disappeared through the arch leading to Old Quad.

'Hadn't you better go after her?'

'I'm sorry. D'you mind? Won't take a second. She won't be stopping. I'll come right back. If you want to help yourself to coffee, there are glasses in there.' Pointing toward a cupboard, she left in some confusion.

A moment later the banker followed Clair out to the landing, armed with two glasses. The first door he tried led to a shower room. He had more luck with the second which opened onto a minute inside kitchen. He had to close the kitchen door behind him before he could open the small refrigerator which stood on the floor, under a two-hob electric cooker plate. As he bent down he was astonished suddenly to hear the sound of a familiar voice.

'I still think you should have told Mark Treasure. You did have the chance this morning.'

The speaker was unmistakably Charlotte Lundle.

'And blown the whole marvellous idea when it's just about to end in a flourish?' This was equally unmistakably Bryan Gavon, sounding relaxed and in his usual high spirits.

'You think Mark won't approve?'

'At this stage I think he'd be stiff-necked about it. He'd have to be. Different when it's all over.'

It was as if the two were standing just outside the kitchen. Treasure had already opened the door to check, but the landing was empty. He went on getting the coffee, determined to pillory his friend at the first opportunity for calling him stiff-necked.

'But if the sketches really are at the centre of Cormit's murder,' came Charlotte's voice again.

'Which I don't believe they are.'

'What if the police think they are?'

'I'm sure they don't. And there's really no reason why they should. Not if you analyse it. The sketches weren't pinched, or anything.'

'Which is just as well. They were moved, you said.'

'The girl says, apparently. By this phantom figure she claims broke in and locked her up.'

'You don't believe her?'

'I think he died through some kind of ghastly accident, while they were having fun and games on the bed.'

'Nothing to do with the sketches?'

'Shouldn't think so.' But Gavon had answered with less certainty.

'But what about his heir? Won't whoever's going to inherit from him be living in a fool's paradise already?'

'I thought about that. It's Midden's wife probably. Can't be helped. Anyway, the thing'll be over later today. We really don't want it spoiled at this stage.'

'So as soon as the offer's made you'll— '

'Take the worthy Ostracher quietly aside and tell him the name of the true owner of the sketches, and how the provenance was faked. After that you can go to town with the exclusive story. If you still want.'

'Honestly, I'm not sure I do now.'

'Suits me. There's another way, of course.'

To this point Treasure could hardly have avoided overhearing the conversation. He knew it must be taking place in Gavon's room, and then relayed to the kitchen through a ventilator. It was embarrassing, but he had been here legitimately, fetching iced coffee, and purposely making a great deal of noise about it.

But the last statement from Gavon had the banker momentarily rooted – as much by incredulity as by the compulsion to know more.

179

Chapter Seventeen

'I wasn't eavesdropping. I've explained exactly how I came to be in the kitchen,' Treasure insisted stiffly.

'And stayed there,' Bryan Gavon replied with a stolid glare.

'But I didn't stay there. I'll admit I was tempted.'

'Well I feel I've been called to the headmaster's study for an expellable offence,' complained Charlotte Lundle. 'Can you both cool it? It's not the end of the world. Or the end of your friendship. At least I hope not. If it were, I should feel terribly responsible.'

All three were standing in Treasure's sitting room. They had trooped down there on his insistence in the interest of privacy. That was after he had brusquely broken in on the conversation upstairs.

On the way down they had encountered a hurrying Clair Witherton coming up, and balancing six pots of strawberry jam in her arms. Treasure had apologised to her for having to cut short their tête-à-tête, and left her longing to know the reason – also why there was such an obvious coolness between himself and his companions.

'This has really very little to do with Charlotte,' said Gavon, thrusting his hands deep into the side pockets of his blazer.

'Well I'm glad to hear that.'

'It has quite a lot to do with me, actually,' Charlotte contradicted, 'But if it's all the same to you two, I prefer to sit before sentence.'

180

'Sorry.'

'Sorry.'

The men had uttered the same word simultaneously. Both stood aside, in an overly mannered way, to let Charlotte reach an armchair.

'You spoke of an exclusive story,' said Treasure, still with firmness, but with less rancour than before. He had moved to stand in front of the desk, to the right of the window.

'A story for the *Bloomsbury Review*,' Charlotte explained. 'Showing how easy it is to provide doubtful works of art with impeccable bogus backgrounds. Could have been a good circulation builder. Still could.' She glanced at Gavon.

'Is that really your style?' asked Treasure.

'Bit gutter press you think? Don't you believe it. You should read us. Investigative journalism on our special subjects is largely the secret of our success. Our readers are all for a bit of indecent exposure in the prissy art world. Analytically presented, of course. By experts, not hacks. And at three pounds a copy, it pays to titillate the readers. So, you see, I am involved.'

'But it wasn't Charlotte's idea,' said Gavon.

'Good, because it may have cost Cormit his life.'

'That's unnecessarily savage, Mark. The girl killed him. Probably by accident. That's obviously what the police think.'

'They've seen you?'

'Both of us. A red-headed young Irishman, in plain-clothes,' Charlotte put in.

'Who really wasn't very interested in the sketches,' Gavon added.

'Well I am. And I wish you'd both indulge me, ahead of Charlotte's readers. I can't promise not to be stiff-necked about it, of course. But then that's no more than you expected.' He moved some papers and sat on the desk, arms folded in front of him.

181

'Sorry about that, Mark.' Gavon looked genuinely contrite. He sank into the other armchair beside Charlotte, which meant they were both facing Treasure.

'Do I assume the sketches didn't come from the Smith family Bible?' The banker was addressing Gavon.

'They didn't come from there, no.'

'And they didn't belong to Cormit?'

'That's right. I gave them to him. It all started when he told me about the Bible– '

'You gave them to him?' Treasure interrupted.

'Yes.' Gavon, unperturbed, was discarding a cushion from behind his back. 'He mentioned the Bible when I was in the shop after Christmas,' he said.

'When Selina Smith was still alive?'

'That's right. One of her ancestors had worked on the cutting of the Grand Union Canal. It was recorded in the Bible. Cormit thought I might be interested. I wasn't specially, not for that reason. Then he mentioned the Smith family connection with Lucas the engraver.'

'Which gave Bryan the idea,' put in Charlotte. 'It was brilliant. To offer some rather good School of Constable sketches as if they were real Constables. On the basis of their traceable descent through the family servants of David Lucas. Then see what happened.'

'Provided you could have the lie embroidered a bit more along the way?' commented Treasure dryly.

'Accepted,' Gavon responded. 'But what else? I wanted to see how far one could get with authentification by simply tarting up origins. Which wouldn't make a blind bit of difference to whether the works were real Constables or not. That being something that ought to be decided solely on their merits as art.'

'Isn't that a somewhat naïve premise?'

'Yes,' Charlotte acknowledged promptly. 'But it shouldn't be. And that's the whole point. Some commercial art galleries are too ready to trade suspect work on the strength of where it comes from, not on genuine proof of who did it. As though the word of, say, some impoverished Italian Count, that a painting's been in his family for generations, gives it total authenticity. Except it then turns out to be something faked last year in a Kennington garret.'

'Isn't that kind of thing well enough known already?'

'Not at all. Not with chapter and verse,' said Gavon. 'The dealers who do get caught never cough up any details. And that also applies to a lot of so-called independent art connoisseurs who are financially involved with the dealers. When there's trouble, the art world's always ready to close ranks to protect its own.'

'But here was a chance to demonstrate an art con from scratch.' Charlotte fingered the big topaz ring she was wearing as she spoke.

'The Bible was key, of course,' put in Gavon. 'Cormit tried to get it for me after Christmas, but the old girl wasn't selling. He picked it up straight after she died though.'

'And you made Cormit party to the whole plan?'

'Certainly not. He thought he was into a real bit of high-toned art manipulation. And he couldn't wait to collect his part of the spoils,' said Gavon with relish.

'You mean he thought you were passing off fakes as Constables?'

'Not fakes. Just works with an undecided attribution.'

'But why did you need him? Why didn't you handle the whole thing yourself, once you'd got hold of the Bible?'

'I needed him for colour.' Gavon smirked before continuing. 'He was a dealer, after all. Not the sort that experts should have accepted on trust, perhaps. They did though.' He leaned forward, rubbing his hands. 'Yes, I engaged him to sell the work as his own property, with a commission of fifty per cent of whatever price he could get.'

'Fifty?'

'To keep him eager. Less any commission he agreed to pay anyone else over the sale.'

'The size of his commission didn't really matter,' put in Charlotte. 'The sale wasn't to go through. He couldn't sell without Bryan's permission.'

'And if I refused to sell, which is what I intended all along, he was to get an additional handling fee of a thousand pounds,' said Gavon. 'I'd paid him five hundred already. He was earning it, too.'

'All courtesy of the *Bloomsbury Review*?' Treasure questioned, looking from one to the other.

Gavon chuckled. 'No. I met all advance payments. I've been humouring a private whim, after all. Charlotte wasn't obliged to publish the story.'

'So Cormit did go to London to see you last week? You told me he didn't.'

'Wrong again, Mark. And fancy thinking I'd lie to you,' said Gavon in mock outrage. 'He went to London on quite other business, but I told him to put it about he'd seen a dealer who'd offered him twenty grand for the sketches. That was the bit that really got Julian Barners going.'

Treasure frowned. 'Is it part of your idea to wreck Julian's reputation.'

'Certainly not. He's going to come out as a blameless innocent. So will Radout. Quite blameless.'

Treasure wondered if the over-assurance was advertising an unease. 'I don't follow,' he said.

'They've both good as said the works are genuine. Later today we're sure one or both of them would have told Ostracher how much to offer. Each had the chance to ask Cormit for a hidden commission, and neither did. Cormit would have told me. But they've both swallowed the bogus background story. Same applies to Professor Bodd, come to that.'

'I see,' said Treasure, but sounding unconvinced. 'Midden may not come out of it so well.'

'I know nothing about his part,' said Gavon dismissively. 'If Cormit promised him a sweetener to tee up Ostracher, that's his business. Of course, Midden may have done something of the sort out of family loyalty.' He shook his head. 'I'd no idea even that they were related.'

Treasure opened his mouth to say something in reply, then closed it again without uttering. A moment later, when he did speak, he was looking directly at Charlotte. 'You're not happy about some of this?'

She shifted in her chair. 'No. Not any more.' She glanced at Gavon, then her eyes dropped again to focus on her ring.

'Because of the murder?'

'Partly.' She let out a sigh. 'I'm not really as comfortable as Bryan about Julian Barners and darling Doctor Radout. About how they'll look. If we've succeeded. I just wish now it hadn't been them we'd involved. Or the professor.'

'But I've explained— ' Gavon began.

'Charlotte,' Treasure interrupted, getting up from the desk. 'Would you think me very rude if I asked you to leave us?'

She looked from one man to the other. 'I suppose not,' she said. 'Not if you can resolve things better without me. I've got plenty else to do.'

Both men were standing as she got to her feet. Treasure opened the door for her. After she had gone he asked, 'Were you seriously expecting Charlotte to go along with the consequences at the end?'

'I don't see why not. You evidently don't think I was?'

'I can imagine her enthusing over the idea at the start. But when it came to the crunch, didn't you expect she'd baulk completely over shopping Radout and the other two?'

'They won't be shopped. We've explained that.' Gavon resumed his seat. 'It's only the murder that's spoiled it for Charlotte. Otherwise, she's as hard-boiled as anyone in Fleet Street. As she said, you really ought to read her magazine.'

Treasure pouted. 'Sorry, I can't go along with that.' He walked over to the window, then stood staring out. 'The arrangement with Cormit led everyone to assume the sketches were his. Whatever happened, that left you absolutely clean, of course.'

'So what? It had no significance once a firm offer was made.'

'When you say you meant to call the whole thing off? But what if Charlotte went predictably cool on everybody being exposed as easy dupes? I repeat, predictably? In other words, if she came to feel as she did today. Even without there being a murder.'

'I still don't understand what you're getting at.'

'Oh, it's quite simple.' He turned to face Gavon. 'It'd be easy to believe you had another plan all along. That you meant to go through with having Ostracher buy the sketches. Without exposing anyone. That you were quite ready to split the quarter of a million, or whatever they fetched, with Cormit.'

Gavon let his hands drop loosely over the arms of his chair, and moved his head from side to side in a de-restricting movement. 'I assume you're romancing. Not aiming a brutal insult at an old and trusted mate.' He spoke without acrimony, smiling disarmingly.

'I'm postulating, Bryan. In your own interests. Postulating as the police may do.'

The other man leaned forward. 'So why would I have brought Charlotte into it? Or Cormit? And what would have been the purpose?'

'Charlotte was to egg on Radout and the other experts. Cormit you've explained already. The purpose would obviously have been to make money.'

'I have money.'

'How fortunate if you have more than enough. Most people don't. There was a rumour some months back that your company was in financial trouble.'

'Really, Mark, this is grotesque. Sure, the company had cash-flow problems at the beginning of the year. To be frank, we're not out of that wood yet, but that has absolutely nothing to do with any of this.'

Treasure responded with raised eyebrows only. Then he said, 'Coming back to Charlotte, at this point, did you perhaps count on her suddenly going cold on making public fools of several respected friends? Other Moneybuckle governors? Even though she'd helped a lot by enthusing over the sketches. For that reason, I doubt you'd have expected problems bringing her round to a different solution. Including one that involved letting the sale go through.'

'Letting Ostracher buy the sketches? But why— ?'

'Especially if you pleaded your corporate cash-flow problem to Charlotte,' Treasure had broken in firmly. 'You see Bryan, I think you've been romancing more than I have, and much more effectively. Which goes for your relationship with Edith Norn, too.'

Gavon fell back in his chair with a roar of laughter. 'What an imagination. But what the devil has Edith to do with it? All right, she probably fancies me. So does Charlotte, as it happens. I can't help it, for God's sake.' He held up his hands, palms outwards, in mock surrender. 'So are you jealous, or something? You used not to be so bloody Puritan.' Now he waved one arm in a dismissive way. 'OK, on mature consideration, I accept you're trying to warn me. To protect me. Because I've done something that could be embarrassing since the murder. Slightly embarrassing. Thank you very much. So is that the end of it?'

'Not quite. There's one glaring omission still, which possibly involves Edith. You see you haven't yet mentioned where the sketches came from, although I believe I've guessed.'

Gavon was suddenly no longer smiling or relaxed. 'I'm sorry, Mark, but the source of the sketches is my business. Highly confidential. I couldn't tell you without your jumping to wrong conclusions. You can guess as much as you like, and welcome. I'm not going to tell you.'

'All right, let that lie. For the moment,' said Treasure, to the other's evident relief. 'Let's go back to Cormit instead. Although you needed him to front for you, at the end of the day – to be precise, the end of yesterday – did his fifty per cent suddenly loom as a really unnecessary expense? And extravagance? That's if the sale went through?'

'Mark, I've told you, there was no question of a sale going through.'

'If that's really the case, didn't you expect him to be miffed, very miffed indeed, when you came to announce there'd be no sale?'

'He had fifteen hundred quid to make up for the loss of his commission.'

'Oh, come on. On your own admission, he stood to make better than a hundred thousand if there was a sale.'

Gavon glowered. 'All right, I expected him to be a bit upset. But he knew from the start the whole thing was problematical.'

Treasure shook his head slowly. 'In the circumstances, don't you think you may need a better answer than that?'

'For whom? In what circumstance?' But the belligerence in the tone was unconvincing.

'The circumstance that a sale *was* to go through. That you *could* have persuaded Charlotte not to oppose it. That you'd contracted to pay half the proceeds to Cormit, and regretted it. And, finally, that Cormit was then conveniently murdered. In all those circumstances Bryan, I really think there's quite a pressing need for you at least to find a witness.'

'To what?'

'To where you were at eleven-fifteen last night.'

Chapter Eighteen

Detective Sergeant Piper turned a page in his notebook. 'So far Gavon looks like the one who could have got there and back without effort. That's assuming Professor Bodd and Doctor Radout wouldn't have had the energy or the stomach for murder.' He took a sip of coffee, looking across his cup at Detective Constable O'Donnell. 'Don't know how you cope with all those calories.'

'Exercise, Skipper.' O'Donnell scooped the last piece of coffee cake from his plate. 'What about motive, though? He's a ladies' man, of course,' he ended speculatively.

They were sitting at an isolated corner table in the coffee bar off Little Clarendon Street, and talking in subdued voices – not that there was any risk of their being overheard. The place was empty except for the counter staff. It was too late for 'elevenses', and too early for the light lunch trade. They had met here at O'Donnell's suggestion: he liked the home-made cakes that were served. Piper had taken nothing to eat.

'You could send up half the blokes in Oxford for being ladies' men,' said the Detective Sergeant.

'Sure there's not many can work at it as hard as him, though.' O'Donnell moved his plate looking for unconsumed crumbs. 'He walks Miss Norn home from Cormit's at ten forty-five. Then he's back in Treasure's room at the college, to join Miss Lundle, at eleven thirty-two. He leaves with her when the party breaks up. Their rooms are on the same staircase. Very cosy.' Ginger eyebrows raised, he leaned across the narrow table, before completing in an even softer tone, 'And would you know, that college porter says the same two women were in and out of Gavon's room all afternoon?' He drew back with a confidential sort of nod.

'Together or separate?'

'Separate I suppose. He'd have said otherwise.' O'Donnell's face clouded: he was a strict Catholic, and not sympathetic toward permissiveness. 'You're not supposing the three of them might have been having— ?'

'An orgy? Or just business meetings?' He enjoyed watching the Irishman preparing to shock himself.

'Ah. Of course, they're all involved with the Moneybuckle. No, I'd say the porter meant they went to Gavon's room separately.'

'How does the porter know all this?'

'They know everything, college porters.' O'Donnell rubbed his freckled, button nose with the flat of one hand. 'Mind if I get a bit of cake?'

'Another bit?'

'Different sort. Lemon.' He was to and from the counter in seconds. 'Gavon's married. To a doctor,' he offered on his return, wetting his lips as he looked down at the pristine yellow icing on the generous wedge of confection. 'Want a bit?'

'No thanks. And Miss Norn says he left her about eleven?'

'They both said that. Both vague about the exact time though. He said he went in for a minute. She said he didn't. Only into the porch. For a second. It's a big house. Converted into flats. Quite firm she was about it, anyway.'

'Like it was otherwise some kind of insult to her virtue?'

'P'raps. It's more likely they weren't on friendly terms.'

'Could they have had a row?'

'That's what I thought.' O'Donnell forked a large piece of cake into his mouth.

'So who was right? About whether he went in?'

'She was,' said the Detective Constable, still chewing. He swallowed quickly with an effort. 'I went back to see him again. After I'd been to her at the Moneybuckle. He still couldn't be sure about the time he'd left her.'

'Let's say "around eleven" means it was between five-to and five-past. He could still have made it to Cormit's. Easily, if he left her at five-to. Easier still if he slipped down into the college, dressed up in Miss Chance's things, then used her bike to get to the shop and back.'

'And we've now got a reliable eye witness who saw someone answering the description of Miss Chance cycling the wrong way up Little Clarendon Street. That was at eleven twenty-five.'

'Someone impersonating Miss Chance, according to the lady herself of course,' the Detective Sergeant corrected while consulting the notebook. 'Yes, the witness is the householder at number thirty-eight B. From an upstairs window. Happens to be a very vigilant citizen. Who has it in for anyone who doesn't respect this street is one way. According to the copper who interviewed him, he couldn't swear he'd seen Miss Chance's face, but he was sure of the time, the yellow bike, and the clothing. That's the scarf and the cloak.'

'And we're accepting it couldn't have been Miss Chance, Skipper?'

Piper nodded. 'Which means it's someone with a lot of explaining to do. In the circumstances.'

'And if Forensic find hairs in that scarf?'

'They have. Except so far they all belong to Miss Chance.'

'And the cloak?'

'There are some black serge fibres. They don't seem to match anything in Miss Chance's wardrobe.'

'Are you thinking they could be off a dinner jacket?' asked the Irishman eagerly.

The other man grimaced. 'You mean Gavon's dinner jacket? If he did go into the college for the bike, wouldn't your eagle-eyed porter have seen him?'

191

'Not if Gavon used the main door in the lodge. That's not under electronic surveillance. Only the vehicle gate further along.'

'And Gavon isn't too tall to have passed for Miss Chance?' Piper asked. 'I mean when he went out again?'

'Not hunched over a bike. Seen from the back in the scarf and cloak. That way almost anybody could have passed as her. It's the yellow bike you'd notice.' O'Donnell took another mouthful of cake. 'Terrible nerve, wheeling the bike back in later, wouldn't you say? As if he'd just found it? And this cake is like me mother made it. You sure you don't want some?' There wasn't much left.

Piper shook his head. 'No insult to your mother.' He smiled. 'And the porter definitely hadn't seen him come in before that?'

'No. But he can't be watching everything. Not the TV picture of the far gate, and the lodge gate from a little window in his office. Not with the lodge itself to run as well. With the telephone too. There's plenty doing in that job at night. Sure, there were a lot of people in and out of the lodge between eleven and eleven-fifteen. Gavon could have nipped past it easy without ever being seen. The porter didn't see him bringing in the bike just before eleven-thirty, either.'

Piper played with the crumpled, empty sugar package in front of him. 'And if Gavon left Miss Norn around eleven, and really walked straight back to the college, why did it take so long?'

'There's no law against walking slow, Skipper.'

The Detective Sergeant flattened the sugar package on the table. It had a sepia image of Magdalen College printed on it. 'And he only begins to qualify as a murder suspect if those sketches are a big enough motive,' he said flatly.

'Which they are, according to the experts.'

'So if the murderer wasn't Megan Rees, and if Cormit was done in for the sketches, why are the sketches still there?'

'Depends on who gets them next, would you say?'

'Mrs Midden gets them. Or she thinks so.' Piper had just been to see her at the house in St John Street. 'And she's accounted for at the critical time,' he added, in response to O'Donnell's querrulous look.

'Same as her husband then?'

Piper nodded. 'There was a phone call to the house at eleven-fifteen from a man called Haycock. Friend of Midden's. Checking on a tentative arrangement they had to go fishing tomorrow, Sunday.'

'Now would that be a strange time for such a call?' the Irishman asked, suspiciously.

'It was by arrangement. Haycock had rung before. Earlier in the evening. He was going to be away today. He rang again at eleven-fifteen because Midden had told him he'd definitely be home, and certain by then if he'd be free for the fishing.'

'But he wasn't home. Because of pressure of work. Like us, Skipper.' O'Donnell beamed. 'And Haycock confirms the call? That he spoke to Mrs Midden?'

'Mrs Haycock does. As I said, he's away today, but she was with him when he made the call. She had a word with Mrs Midden after. Quite a long word.' Piper looked at the time. 'So Mrs Midden's out of it. But so's Gavon most likely, unless there's tangible evidence and a motive. Sherlock's not going to wear a suspect who doesn't have a clear motive. Not when we've got one already with motive and opportunity as long as your arm.'

O'Donnell was looking down at his arm in a reflex kind of way when the radio transmitter in this top pocket started to emit electronic chords. 'Talk of the Devil,' he said. 'Oh, no disrespect intended to the DI, Skipper,' he added quickly, before pressing the receive button.

The Oxford Ashmolean, the oldest museum in Britain, was founded in 1683 by Elias Ashmole. It contains one of the most important collections of paintings in Europe. The building in which the museum has been housed since 1845 is arguably the finest example of Greek Revival architecture to be found anywhere. It dominates the corner of Beaumont Street and St Giles.

Naturally, Julian Barners would never have taken such an artistic gem for granted. But now, as he mounted the steps to the Ashmolean's east wing in St Giles, his mind had not consciously turned to savouring C R Cockerell's Ionic masterpiece. He was much too preoccupied with the coming opportunity to impress a visitor with the Constable paintings recently put on view inside the building. They were pictures that hadn't been shown for some time. It was debatable whether it was Constable who was to impress, or Barners dispensing knowledge of Constable – though perhaps not debatable to Barners.

Lost in anticipation, he nearly knocked into Treasure who had come hurrying down the steps and stopped before him.

'Ah. I'm meeting Ostracher inside,' said Barners, taken aback. But there was already the strong implication that Treasure was not expected to join the party.

'He told me as much. He's going to be late.'

'How tiresome.' Barners took a slim, gold half-hunter from a pocket of the pale pink, silk waistcoat. He glanced at the time, closed the watch again, then slipped it back into the pocket, while continuing to finger the gold chain attached to it.

He was, as always, most elegantly turned out. The off-white, light-weight suit was flawless in its tailoring, and quite uncreased. The jacket was long, single-breasted, and tightly waisted. The trousers were unfashionably slim, but right for the wearer, like the white silk shirt and the red tie with the immense knot. In one hand he was carrying gloves and a panama hat.

'Did Ostracher happen to mention who or what was detaining him?'

194

'He didn't have to. I'm afraid I'm responsible.' Treasure turned about, drawing the other to the top of the steps, and then on to an open area at the side. 'He'll meet you inside in half an hour. In the room with the re-hung Constables.'

'I don't understand?'

'I have some things to tell you. And to ask. That won't take half an hour, but you might have been late, and it was imperative we speak. Ostracher and I then have another urgent appointment before he joins you. He's gone ahead.' The banker cleared his throat. 'The Constable sketches didn't come from Selina Smith's Bible.'

Barners blinked sharply. 'Indeed? So where did they come from?'

'I'm not sure yet. I believe probably from a less promising source.'

'That may be. I find it difficult to doubt they're authentic even so.'

'I'm glad to hear you say that. Ostracher tells me you'd advised him to offer two hundred thousand pounds for the three.'

'If he thought it appropriate to tell you.' The speaker shrugged, implying the sense of appropriateness was something he was failing to share.

'I didn't ask if he knew Cormit had agreed to pay you a twenty-five per cent commission on the sale.'

This time there was the merest flicker of surprise. 'He wouldn't have known for the simplest of reasons: because such a statement would have been untrue. Also, I imagine, highly slanderous.' Barners slid a silk handkerchief from his sleeve, and touched it to his temple, pausing as he brought it down again to enquire, 'Cormit is dead, isn't he?'

'Yes. But he did tell someone else about the commission.'

The handkerchief went back to the sleeve, and the hand rose again, a crooked middle forefinger directed gently to smooth an arched eyebrow. 'There's nothing in writing. I shall deny any such arrangement.'

'It doesn't matter now whether you do or not. There'll be no sale. Cormit didn't own the sketches. Even though they probably cost him his life.'

'But I've just been told he died in the course of some . . . hm . . . sordid sexual excess.' The savoured, near alliteration was followed by a pained expression.

'That's not true. His girl friend didn't do it. He was murdered by someone who broke in on them.' Treasure watched the other's reaction before continuing. 'The call you made from my room just before dinner last night. It was to Cormit?'

'I can't recall.'

'It probably won't matter eventually what you recall. The porter logged the number. Except his log sheet's been mislaid. No doubt it'll turn up again, with the number you asked for on it.'

'There's no need to be so brusque. I was going to say I couldn't recall the exact time of the event. Yes, I telephoned Cormit.'

'And you do remember what the call was about? To agree the size of the commission. Something you hadn't had a chance to do earlier. When you were at Cormit's with Ostracher. You'd only had time then to establish the principle. That a commission would be paid.'

'I've told you, that's something I shall deny utterly.'

'And, in the circumstances, I don't blame you. Just so long as for this particular privileged conversation you keep the sequence of events clear in your mind. So let's just say the call was to Cormit. You intended denying it to me, but if the police ask you the same question— '

'The police? Why should the police want to know if I rang Cormit then?'

'Because only two calls were received at the shop after six last night. The police are very anxious to know who made them.'

The imperious brow furrowed. 'And if they ask me?'

'It's in your own best interests that you tell them the truth. Which is why I needed to find you first. To warn you. The police are investigating a murder. Statements are being taken. The sort likely to be quoted later, in open court. Reputations may be at stake. The reputations of organisations and individuals. Like the Moneybuckle. Like you.' The banker's speech had been clipped, and his phrases pointed. 'The police will want to know if you called Cormit, not what you said to him. If you admit you made the call, I think that'll be the end of it. If you deny it, they'll have to go on looking for the caller, tracing him by what they can get on what was said. The girl heard one side of the call. She may not be the most desirable sort of witness. But what she'll say about commissions won't sound like invention.'

There was silence between the two after Treasure's soliloquy. Then Barners' concentrated gaze returned from what might have seemed a critical study of the Randolph Hotel opposite. 'Thank you, Mark,' he said quietly. 'I'll do as you say. I accept you've been to some trouble on my account.'

'In fairness, I had another consideration.'

'How uncompromising you are with yourself. You have more questions?'

'Three more. Did you telephone Cormit earlier last evening? Before the call you made from my room? Probably at around six-twenty?'

'No. At that time Ostracher and I were still together.'

'That's what he says. I needed to be sure. Next, can you remember where you were between eleven-fifteen and eleven twenty-five last night?'

Barners' eyes cast about him while he took a series of deep breaths through the aquiline nose, the almost transparent walls of that delicate feature pulsing visibly as he did so. 'I assume the exact minutes are important, or you wouldn't press me to be so precise.' He took one more deep breath. 'At eleven-fifteen I *believe* I was walking down the Turl and into the High, by myself. Ten minutes later I was almost certainly standing on Magdalen Bridge, or beginning my walk back to . . . in this direction. However, one doesn't schedule an evening walk like a railway company.'

'You passed a number of public telephone boxes in that ten minutes. Did you make a phone call?'

'Certainly not.'

'You're quite sure?'

'Quite sure.'

'That you didn't ring Cormit again? Didn't ring him, and have the call answered, but not by Cormit? It's important.'

'I swear to God I did no such thing.'

'I didn't think you could have done. But I'm glad to hear it all the same,' said Treasure, meaning it.

Chapter Nineteen

'We've finished with the place,' said Detective Inspector Holmes.

But the admission had seemed to pain the policeman – mostly because he was a bad actor. He continued standing in the centre of Cormit's shop, glowering at the muddle of books, and treating the other four people present to purposely un-appraising, almost shifty glances.

It was exactly midday.

Treasure had just arrived, accompanied by Megan Rees. Ostracher had been waiting for them at the door. A uniformed policeman had been on duty outside.

Midden, in formal black jacket and striped trousers, had come ahead of the others, directly from the college. He had placed himself a little removed from the rest, with head bent. This was a pose calculated both unctuously to portray proper deference in the presence of two affluent Moneybuckle governors, as well as to indicate respect for his dead brother-in-law. With eyes lowered too, he had so far avoided meeting the gaze of Megan Rees.

Altogether in the circumstances, from his appearance and demeanour, Midden would have passed for an expectant undertaker.

Megan seemed less fraught than she had been in court two hours earlier.

When Treasure had called for the girl at Midden's house in St John Street, Val Midden had offered to come with them to the shop. Treasure had said Mrs Midden's presence there wouldn't be necessary, since her husband had already been invited by the police. He had explained that Detective Inspector Holmes wanted formally to hand over the premises to one of the Middens – an act which it was assumed would be less painful for Mr Midden than for his wife.

The banker had pressed Megan to go along with him, but without offering her any very specific reason. In a general way he had said he wanted her to show him the upstairs layout in Walton Street, and that she could pick up her things from there at the same time. But this had been chiefly to allay concern on the part of the wary Mrs Midden that Megan was being needlessly involved again with the police.

To her credit, Val Midden had shown no great surprise or disappointment when Treasure had revealed that the Constable sketches had not belonged to her dead half-brother after all.

'Pity. I'd hoped they'd raise a pound or two for Megan here. Mr Midden will be disappointed,' were her first comments. Then she had turned to the girl. 'Too good to be true it was, love. That's what I thought when my hubby said they might be valuable. I told him things like that don't happen to the likes of us. Never mind, we're not that poor. Ernie's business could fetch a bit all the same. You shall have some of that, and welcome.'

They had left her on that unselfish note.

Treasure hadn't mentioned that it was he and not Holmes who had instigated the noon meeting.

In truth, the police were nowhere near through with their examination of the Walton Street property. As Senior Investigating Officer, Holmes had arranged to make it seem that they were – and on special conditions. He had been persuaded to co-operate, but he was heavily sceptical about the outcome.

The Detective Inspector had simply accepted Treasure's half-intuitive conviction that an important revelation would result from the meeting.

He had also accepted an invitation to a drink afterwards.

'So if Mr Midden likes to take charge of the keys,' Holmes now offered, holding up two keys on a ring, one Chubb and one Yale.

'Thank you.' Midden moved forward quietly to take them. 'My wife has a front-door key already. Ernie, her brother, he gave it to her some time back. I didn't know till last night. Till after the . . . er . . . tragedy.'

'She still has the key, Mr Midden?' Holmes demanded, over-casually, and nodding his head as if he knew the answer. 'It hasn't been lost or stolen?'

'No, it's quite safe. I've brought it with me. In case I needed it to get in. Or lock up after.' Midden produced a single Chubb key from his pocket, laying it beside the other two keys in his open palm. The single key looked identical to the Chubb, except it was a lot less worn. 'My wife kept it in a box. A wooden box,' Midden ended earnestly, as though the composition of the box had some obvious importance.

'In a box, Mr Midden. And it was there last night?'

'So far as I know. It was this morning. As I said, I didn't know till— '

'Sorry to be late, Inspector. After I left you, I was diverted by the cheese shop in Little Clarendon Street.' Bryan Gavon had entered, interrupting breezily. He nodded to the others while holding up a coloured shop bag. 'Nice hunk of ripe gorgonzola in here, so don't come too close. It may be biting. Morning Miss Rees. Glad to hear you've had your liberty restored. Quite right too.'

The speaker beamed approvingly at Holmes, whose emotionless expression hardly altered: only the policeman's eyes registered, with the merest flicker, his likely disagreement with the last comment.

'I've got those three drawings back from Forensic, Mr Gavon,' said Holmes now, opening a black, battered leather briefcase.

'All our fingerprints were on them, of course,' offered Gavon promptly. 'We all handled them at some point last evening. At least I assume you did too, Armin? When you were here before dinner.'

Ostracher nodded. 'Does that mean you'll want specimens of our fingerprints for comparison, Inspector? Just for elimination purposes,' he added, to dispel any notions to the contrary.

Holmes caught Treasure's eye as he replied. 'That won't be necessary, sir. It's the sealed envelope they were in that interested us.' He removed this from the case. 'It has some smudged prints of Mr Cormit's on it. Otherwise, it seems the last person to handle it was wearing gloves.'

'Only the immaculate Julian Barners wears gloves,' Gavon observed, with what was beginning to sound a bit like forced cheerfulness. 'And I gather he's got an alibi. Lucky Julian.'

'Since you've opened the envelope, can we see the sketches?' This was Ostracher again, in a voice redolent with concern.

'Once I've handed them to Mr Midden, and got a receipt, he can show them to anyone he likes, sir,' answered Holmes. He offered the envelope to Midden, who took it gingerly. 'If you'd like to check they're there, Mr Midden?'

'This is a great responsibility,' said Midden heavily, like someone receiving a vote of thanks and who, for convention's sake, is going to deny deserving it. He removed the three sketches from the cover and balanced them across the tightly packed rows of books on the small centre table. It was the place where Cormit had displayed them the previous evening.

'It's a responsibility you won't have to exercise for very long, Mr Midden,' Ostracher volunteered gruffly, while poring over the sketches. 'Not now we know they really belong to Mr Gavon.'

To that point, Midden's face had been a picture of sober and constrained contentment. Now it registered spontaneous disbelief as he looked from Ostracher to Gavon. 'I don't understand, sir?'

'Cormit was only acting as Mr Gavon's agent,' said Treasure. 'He was on commission.'

Midden blinked several times, then rallied a little. 'With respect, we'll need proof of that, won't we,' he responded, boldly for him. 'I mean, I'm only speaking on behalf of my wife's family, sir,' followed half apologetically.

'Quite right, Mr Midden,' Gavon responded, withdrawing a folded sheet of notepaper from his inside pocket. 'If you'd like to look at this. It's our signed letter of agreement. Ernie Cormit's and mine.'

Treasure glanced at his watch. 'While you're sorting that out, would you all excuse Miss Rees and me for a minute? I want to look around upstairs, if that's all right, Inspector?'

'All right with me, sir.' But the policeman seemed to be more interested in studying Gavon's reaction to the proposal.

'And for Miss Rees to collect some of her things?' Treasure added.

'It's up to Mr Midden, really, sir,' said Holmes, momentarily shifting his gaze.

'Is that all right with you, Mr Midden?' Treasure asked.

'Oh . . . Oh yes, of course, sir.' Midden looked up from reading the paper in his hand.

'I'll only take what's mine,' said the girl in a hardly audible voice. It was the first time she had spoken since her arrival.

Holmes looked at her now and nodded. Midden, for his part, was still too absorbed to pay attention to a remark that had obviously been addressed to him.

'If you'll forgive my saying so, Bryan, I think you've been less than straightforward in all of this,' Ostracher began, as Treasure and Megan started threading their way toward the narrow stairs at the rear, the banker sensing that there was more suppressed pique in the American's tone than was evident from his mild choice of words.

Treasure looked at the time again, as Megan paused before the first step, then clumsily began the ascent. At one point she appeared to overbalance. The banker took her elbow from behind and steadied her to the top. She stopped there, hands clasped tightly together over her breasts. Then she shuddered, and turned around, her slim body bent forward like a penitent's.

'I can't go on,' she whispered.

The conversation in the shop below was from here undecipherable, but had evidently grown more heated than it had been earlier. Gavon's voice was predominating.

'I can't go any further,' Megan insisted again to Treasure.

'I want to look at that bathroom,' he said.

'It's along there. The closed door.'

'You'll have to come with me. It's important.'

'Please don't make me. I can't face it.'

'Only the bathroom. Not the bedroom. And you don't have to collect your things today. Not if you don't want.'

'But you said . . . ' She looked up at him slowly. 'I can come back some other time?'

Now he sensed she was on the brink of tears. He reached for one of her hands, pulling it gently but firmly from the other. 'Trust me. The bathroom's important. Quickly. We won't need to stay long. I promise.'

Reluctantly she allowed him to guide her forward.

They passed the open kitchen door. The bedroom door ahead at the end was open too. The unmade bed was clearly visible, but the coats had been removed from the corridor floor. There was a light burning in the alcove on the left.

Treasure opened the bathroom door into the corridor.

Megan gulped as she stepped inside. She pulled on the light, but turned about before she could look at the lit interior.

The cheap fitments in the narrow room were all white. The chrome on the taps was peeling, like the paint on the scored, black hardboard cover fixed to the side of the bath. The walls were painted a bilious yellow. There was green mottled lino on the floor that clashed with a crumpled red towel hanging from a rail, its bottom trailing to the floor. The washbasin was opposite the bath with a half-opened medicine cabinet above. The black covered loo was against the far wall. A topless plastic bottle of glutinous shampoo had been tipped into the bath, its blood-red contents disgorged and solidified.

'I don't want to look,' the girl said.

'I don't blame you,' Treasure answered. 'It must have been very frightening to be locked in here. With no window. Not knowing what was to happen next.' Again he looked at the time.

The two were standing just inside the room, against the bath. Treasure still had hold of Megan's hand. Despite her intention, her eyes opened with a start when she heard the door close. After that her whole body began to tremble.

'Just bear up for another few seconds,' said Treasure, putting his arms around her. He was willing the plan would work, but conscious that it might already have failed.

Then they heard it. They both heard it. An electronic wail that penetrated clearly from somewhere in the house.

The girl gasped and clutched at his jacket.

'You hear that?' he demanded. 'What is it? Quick.'

'The telephone. Just like last night. It—'

'No it isn't.' And as he spoke the noise stopped. Then, almost immediately, a distinctly different, more warbling tone replaced the first.

'That's the telephone,' he said, hugging her. 'And that's the answer,' he added confidently.

'I don't know what you mean,' Midden insisted defensively a minute later. There was no deference now in tone or manner.

'I think you do know, Mr Midden. And Mr Treasure thinks the same,' said Holmes, giving an uncertain glance at the banker who was standing beside him again, with Megan Rees.

'I was never here last night. I couldn't have been.'

'On the contrary, you had lots of opportunity to get here and back quite easily,' said Treasure. 'On Miss Chance's bike. After you'd emptied the SCR of guests and helpers. At eleven. You had nearly half an hour at your disposal then, till you reappeared with that coffee tray.'

Midden reddened. 'I was about my business in college.'

'I telephoned you in your pantry at eleven-nineteen. You didn't answer. The call automatically switched to your pager. You were in Cormit's bedroom at the time. Megan Rees heard the bleep from the bathroom, from where we both heard it just now.'

'She heard it from the SCR cellar, you mean?' Midden insisted. 'Because that's where I was. Well, on my way from there to my pantry. I remember it clear. And I called you back straight away on the pantry phone.'

'Without checking with the porter to find out who was paging you?'

'Wasn't worth troubling him when I could guess. There was only you could have been wanting to reach me.'

'Only me and Mr Ostracher, to be more exact. The only guests with telephones, and both connected to numbered night lines plugged in at eleven. Regular numbers that you knew well enough. But you guessed wrong first time. You rang Mr Ostracher. He wasn't in his room. He was approaching it at the time, but he wasn't in it. So then you rang me. It would have been more efficient to call the porter in the first place. Why didn't you?'

'I told you, because I guessed it'd be you.' Midden paused, confused. 'Well, you or Mr Ostracher.'

'It wasn't because you could only call the porter on an outside phone? A call that would be indicated on his outside switchboard? Because you were a long way from the college at the time? It wouldn't have done for the porter to know that, would it? To know you weren't in college? That you were right here?'

'He couldn't have known I was . . . That's not true.' Midden pulled out a handkerchief and wiped his face. 'I can sue you for saying that. In front of witnesses. You all heard it?' He looked at Ostracher, then at Gavon, but got back only stony stares. 'Police witnesses,' he added, more angrily this time, in Holmes' direction.

'A call from here to Mr Treasure's number at the college. That'd be a matter of record, Mr Midden,' said the Detective Inspector diffidently. 'British Telecom will have it on automatic log.'

'But not that I made it?'

'I received only one call last night, Mr Midden.' This was Treasure. 'At eleven-twenty precisely. It was from you. That's certainly a matter of record. And witness. There were three people with me. The record alone will prove you couldn't have been in the college, so you might as well admit it.'

Midden twice opened his mouth to speak, but no words came. He made a series of short grunts, then he said, 'OK. I nipped home for a bit. There's no crime in that. I was bloody tired. Expected to go on working till well after midnight. So I took a break. At eleven. Slipped down home. Doesn't take two minutes.'

'The porter didn't see you leave?'

'I didn't mean him to.' His face twitched at the admission. 'When my pager went, I called you back from the phone in my house.'

'Ah, you couldn't have done that, Mr Midden. Not at eleven-twenty you couldn't,' said Holmes, in a matter-of-fact tone. 'Your wife has already told us she was on the telephone continuously from eleven-fifteen till after eleven-thirty. With a Mr Haycock, then his wife.'

'She's wrong.'

'You mean all three of them were wrong, Mr Midden?' There was silence for a moment, then Midden barked,

'It's a conspiracy, that's what it is. You're all out to get me. To save this slut.' He pointed at Megan, his arm shaking with rage. 'She killed Ernie. Everybody knows that. She's a whore. A jail bird. A frigging drug addict. That's what she is. It's diabolical, saying I killed Ernie.'

'No one's said that, Mr Midden,' said Holmes quickly for the record – and by way of self-protection in the event of a later enquiry.

'No one's said it yet, but I'm about to,' put in Treasure. 'You killed Cormit after you'd learned the value of the sketches at dinner. He'd already tried to cut back on what he'd promised to pay you. For using your position to help set up the sale to one of us. That was ungrateful of him, but it hardly justified murder.'

'I never— '

'You thought your brother-in-law owned the sketches, of course. And you were scared he'd marry Megan. Meaning your wife would never share or inherit anything of his. If he died, though, that'd be different. So you took your wife's key to this place, which you knew she had all the time. You cycled down here in disguise, waited your opportunity, then killed him. I must say you were pretty cool about it all. The phone calls— '

'It's lies! Lies! I'll sue you, you rotten, rich bastard,' Midden broke in at last, shaking with anger, his face apoplectic, his fists raised and clenched. 'There's no proof of any of it. No bloody proof.'

'Except for several of your hairs found in Miss Chance's scarf,' said Treasure coolly. 'And a whole clutch of fibres from that jacket you're wearing inside her cloak. With those and the rest of the evidence, there's not a chance you'll get away with it now. Much better to admit you killed him. Better for yourself in the end. You know that?'

Midden had clutched his sleeve at the mention of the jacket, then released it. He looked almost pleadingly at

Holmes who responded by starting to move around toward him.

The policeman, Megan, Treasure, and Ostracher were standing with their backs to the street door, making a half-circle around the centre table. Gavon was behind Ostracher.

Midden had been alone on the other side of the table. Now, as if on impulse, he stooped and clutched at the table-top. With a roar he up-ended it, heaving the table and its considerable load of books at the others whose reaction was to fall back in a body – Ostracher with a howl of pain because the table had caught his shin. Quickly Midden had turned about and was making for the rear of the shop, pulling down sets of shelves as he went, creating havoc behind him.

Before any of the others had started serious pursuit through the dust and clutter, Midden had unbolted the back door. Head down, he charged across the little backyard, wrenched open a wooden gate, then wheeled left into the back alley, and to the left again when he reached the side road onto Walton Street.

'Stop him,' yelled Holmes, who had plunged over the débris in hot pursuit – reacting more quickly than any-one else.

'Stop him. Police,' he roared again when he reached the side road, alerting the Constable in the shop doorway around the corner.

'Stop him,' Holmes hollered once more at Detective Constable O'Donnell who had appeared from the right in Walton Street, and who now broke into a sprint.

'Got you, me boyo!'

But O'Donnell had spoken too soon.

Seeing there were police on three sides of him, all virtually on top of him, the panicked fugitive took the only remaining route. He dived heedlessly across the busy street.

By a near miracle he got in front of the hurtling

furniture van unscathed: it blocked all three of his pursuers. But his luck over this was too brief to enjoy.

Midden was hit by an accelerating yellow bus in the opposite lane.

He died later on the way to the hospital.

Chapter Twenty

'It was Miss Chance who pointed me at the truth of it. When we talked this morning,' said Treasure, elbows on the arms of his chair, hands together and pointing upwards in a prayerful sort of way.

'Me?' put in Miss Chance. 'I'm not sure I follow you, Mr Treasure.' Her tone was enquiring but far from regretful: it wasn't every day one was credited with helping to unmask a murderer. Further, anything that helped to cloud the memory of her unworthy performance at dinner the previous evening was to be firmly encouraged.

It was approaching two-thirty in the afternoon. Despite the drama earlier, the governors of the Moneybuckle Endowment were preparing to begin their annual meeting. They were seated at the oblong table outside the Custodian's room on the upper floor of their building. In the absence of Westerly, Edith Norn was on Treasure's right on one long side of the table, the minute book open before her. Bodd was on Treasure's left, with Ostracher on Edith's other side. Bryan Gavon, Charlotte Lundle and Doctor Radout were on the opposite side of the table, with Charlotte in the middle.

'Well I wish you'd made it plainer you weren't gunning for me,' said Gavon.

'I also felt I was under suspicion,' said Bodd gravely. 'By the police.'

'Oh come off it, Bertie,' put in Doctor Radout, who was drawn up very close to Charlotte. He was on a chair with sagging upholstery which made it lower than the others, deepening the impression that he was filling the role of Charlotte's dutiful vassal.

'You were going to say, Mr Treasure?' pressed Miss Chance, anxious not to be done out of the promised complimentary disclosure. She was seated alone at one short side of the table; Julian Barners was similarly placed at the opposite end.

The banker smiled. 'Because I told you the killer moved the sketches to a different hiding place, Miss Chance, you said he might have been about to take them and was disturbed— '

'Or else that he was intending to return for them. I remember,' the lady cut in briskly. 'However, I don't see— ?'

'Well, to me that had to suggest a third alternative. It seemed he wasn't disturbed. And in the circumstances, for him to plan coming back again would have been crazy. So was he simply encouraging the police and everyone else to adopt one of those obvious explanations?'

'Oh,' uttered Miss Chance, crestfallen.

'Sorry, logical explanations. And if that was so, wasn't it plain he really intended the sketches should remain at Cormit's? Only he moved them about to imply the opposite, knowing they'd be found.'

'He wanted them found, you mean? Kept safe for the person he was certain would inherit them. His wife,' said Charlotte.

'Who couldn't be suspect since her husband had set her up with a carefully contrived alibi. The telephone call from the Haycocks,' Treasure enlarged.

'While Midden himself considered he was adequately covered,' said Ostracher.

'Certainly Midden thought he was safe,' the banker answered. 'In the sense the police and everyone else accepted that he was gainfully employed during that critical half hour.'

'In and around the SCR,' Ostracher added. 'In the company of other servants and guests.'

'Which wasn't really the case at all,' said Treasure. 'He'd purposely got rid of everybody by eleven. But what kept his story credible was the fact he'd returned my call at eleven-twenty.'

'It must have taken some nerve to use the phone in the shop after he'd committed the murder.' Charlotte shuddered by way of emphasis.

'Not nearly as much nerve as fastening the bag over squirming Cormit's head, and leaving him to die,' said Gavon, ignoring a sharp admonitory look of severe displeasure from Ostracher who was seated diagonally opposite to him.

Ostracher's coolness toward Gavon had been clear since the American's arrival.

'I don't think he came determined to kill Cormit,' said Treasure. 'Only to steal the sketches. Before it was too late. He knew where they were kept. Megan conveniently going into the bathroom when she did simply played into his hands. Almost invited him to do in the helpless Cormit, knowing she'd be blamed.'

'And he used the plastic bag he'd brought for the sketches to suffocate Cormit?' Gavon surmised.

'Very likely. It didn't come from Cormit's.'

'Mark, it was brilliant of you to figure what Miss Rees thought was the phone bell was really Midden's pager.' This was Charlotte.

'Not brilliant at all. A matter of slow deduction. If anyone had called Ernie Cormit so late last night it almost had to be one of us, about the sketches. I checked. None of us did call him. I'd happened to hear Midden's pager bleeping when I was at his house, early today. It sounded very like one of the new telephones until you actually compared the two noises.'

'And you arranged for Megan Rees to do just that?' Charlotte asked.

213

'Courtesy of Steven Bickworthy and Clair Witherton, his girl friend. They stage-managed that carefully timed exercise. From the telephone in my rooms.'

'Stupid question probably, but why d'you suppose Midden hadn't turned off his pager?' asked Radout.

'Because, to protect his alibi, he couldn't possibly afford not to know if anyone was trying to reach him,' Treasure answered.

'It *was* a stupid question,' said Radout meekly.

'And although he got into Cormit's using his wife's key, he didn't want anyone to suspect that,' continued the banker. 'So he chose not to lock the door again when he left, giving the impression it had been open all the time.'

'Even though locking it would have made Megan look even more guilty? As if no one else could have got into the place?' Charlotte asked.

'The choice he took meant he could volunteer his wife had a key he didn't know about,' Treasure replied. 'It was safer, probably, than telling her not to let on she had it. That would almost certainly have made her suspicious of him, and he really couldn't afford to let that happen. Cormit was her half-brother after all.'

'The police knew about your telephone ruse, of course, Mark,' said Professor Bodd, in a slightly hurt tone.

'Knew, and agreed to co-operate. Only as observers though. Detective Inspector Holmes was decidedly unhopeful about my theory, and touchy about being present if I openly accused Midden of murder. In the end, though, he was very supportive. A sound policeman, if a trifle eccentric.'

'I suppose you couldn't blame him for not wanting to pass up a wholly convincing murderer in Megan Rees,' observed Gavon.

'Nonsense,' protested Charlotte.

'And it really hung on what happened after Miss Rees recognised the bleeper noise?' said Ostracher.

'How Midden reacted to my bluster.' Treasure smiled grimly. 'The hairs in the headscarf and the fibres in the cloak were part invention and part supposition. But it really was necessary to weigh in hard while he was off balance, as it were. It worked, anyway. Too well, in a way. I'm deeply sorry for Mrs Midden.' There was an awkward pause, then Treasure looked at the time. 'Well, perhaps we should begin the meeting,' he said.

A minute later, with the formal opening business over, Treasure asked Edith Norn if she would withdraw and wait in her office downstairs until summoned. She nodded, gave a shy smile, and left immediately.

'Some of you must be wondering why the Custodian isn't here,' said Treasure. 'He was very upset about something, so I sent him home. Before he went, he gave me his resignation to put before the meeting. I suggest we accept it. Since the Moneybuckle has just closed for the long vacation, I suggest also that we waive any question of notice. We'd normally have been entitled to three months. In other words, I suggest we accept he's left, as from today.'

Radout cleared his throat. 'Mr Chairman, may I formally propose we accept the Custodian's notice with regret, but with immediate effect,' he announced loudly and earnestly.

'I'd like to second that proposal,' Ostracher came in afterwards quickly.

'Those in favour?' Treasure watched every head nod in assent – though there was bewilderment showing on a few faces.

'That was well rehearsed,' said Gavon irreverently. 'Something nasty in the woodshed, is there?'

Julian Barners winced but said nothing. He had remained mute from the start.

'There *is* a bit more to the matter than we need minute officially,' said Treasure, but without looking at Gavon. 'I've taken the opportunity ahead of the meeting to discuss it with Radout, Ostracher and Miss Chance, the three most senior governors. We're of one mind in the matter.' He paused so that others might recollect that the four governors involved would effectively make a majority of five of the eight, he, as chairman, having an extra casting vote.

'Norman Westerly, our ex-Custodian, has left us owing the Endowment five thousand, eight hundred and thirty pounds,' Treasure continued. 'The money was not secured in any way, and you could say he helped himself to it.' He paused, frowning. 'Yes, you could definitely say that. In any event, he's satisfied me that that's the exact figure owing, and he's contracted to repay the whole sum, in a different guise, before the beginning of the next academic year. I'm quite sure he'll cough up. Our having to sue him for the money would be highly embarrassing for him, apart from making it necessary to disclose the er . . . unconventional method he used to borrow it in the first place. I should add that, to ensure the Endowment isn't in any sense at risk, Armin Ostracher has kindly agreed to underwrite the debt in the interim.'

There followed general murmurs of approval at this.

Treasure leaned forward. 'May I take it then that the governors formally accept, with thanks, the pledged donation of five thousand, eight hundred and thirty pounds to the general fund from the ex-Custodian? I think the matter is best minuted in that way.'

'Donation?' questioned Charlotte Lundle opposite, her perfect eyebrows arching in equally perfect perplexity.

Ostracher coughed. 'What the chairman's getting at is there isn't any way of accounting for the loan in the first place, nor, it follows, for repaying it. Not without creating a scandal at worst, as well as a problem for our auditors. I'm sure we should agree a donation covers the point well enough,' he concluded heavily, staring around the table.

Since such practical imperatives were invariably accepted in Ostracher's office on Wall Street, especially when he was personally guaranteeing any losses, he was sure as hell it should end the discussion on St Giles. It did. There were more murmurs of agreement.

So the exit of the wretched Westerly went without fuss, discomforting record, or real regret – and especially without besmirching the good name of the Moneybuckle Endowment.

'I asked Miss Norn to withdraw because I want to propose we offer her the post of Custodian. Immediately. On a trial basis,' Treasure announced next. 'Her permanent appointment to be confirmed a year from now, if we're satisfied with her performance. I've sounded her out already. She's happy to accept on that basis.' He stared pointedly at Decimus Radout who seemed to have forgotten his further pre-arranged role and was whispering something to Charlotte.

'Oh . . . sorry. Didn't quite hear,' said the doctor, sitting up straight. 'Er . . . I second the proposal.'

'What a good idea,' put in Charlotte with great enthusiasm. 'Saves us having to waste time interviewing strings of far less worthy candidates. Edith seems very competent. But can we improve on the salary?'

'On that, Miss Chance has come up with an ingenious solution,' said Treasure. 'It seems there's nothing in our constitution to stop the Custodian and the Assistant Custodian being one and the same person.'

'Taking both salaries, you mean?' This was Professor Bodd, not in an opposing way, but somewhat wistfully because nothing so convenient had ever happened to him.

'I've spoken to our accountant on the telephone this morning,' said Miss Chance. 'He sees no objection. And he's promised to consult our lawyer straightaway. Victorian legal-trust draughtsmen were notoriously sloppy in guarding against *determined* circumvention. So we should be all right.'

'And is Miss Norn to run the place single-handed? What about her academic work?' asked Bodd, with genuine concern.

'There's nothing to stop the governors authorising the appointment of an assistant archivist at a reasonable salary.

217

That's all that's needed,' Miss Chance supplied promptly. 'Mr Westerly could have asked for that at any time. Except he was so obsessed with keeping costs down. I suppose in the hope that that would help us find a way to improve his own stipend.'

'Then the new Custodian should be told to hire such an assistant,' said Treasure. 'Agreed? Thank you. Decimus, would you care to . . . ?'

But the doctor was already making for the stairs to summon Edith.

When the new Custodian had rejoined the meeting, and accepted the congratulations of all present, Treasure called the governors to order once again with: 'There's one other extra item I'd like to table now. It concerns a subject that's been on all our minds. The three John Constable sketches.' He looked around the table before continuing. 'For reasons of his own, Bryan Gavon didn't disclose until this morning that he's the real owner of the sketches. How this happened is his business, like the somewhat unusual way he chose to go about establishing a provenance for them.'

The last carefully phrased remark earned a highly audible snort from Ostracher.

Treasure had paused, looking across at Gavon as though expecting him to speak, but, since there was no word from that quarter, he resumed, 'I understand from Bryan that settling the attribution of the sketches is now to be left in the capable hands of Julian Barners and Decimus Radout.'

The brief silence that followed was broken by Barners, speaking for the first time. 'Doctor Radout and I are well enough convinced the works are by Constable.' The tapered, long-fingered hands were lifted together, then made a movement like a blossom opening. 'Our belief is to be augmented by scientific tests.' He stressed the last two words, wrinkling his nose in evident disdain after pronouncing them. 'The tests will be made at the direction of Mr Gavon.'

'And at his expense,' put in Radout. 'A particularly noble gesture,' he added, with few present yet understanding quite why the gesture was so special.

'Which brings us to the point. To the good news,' said Treasure. 'Whatever the outcome of the tests, and as you've heard, our experts are fairly confident, Bryan Gavon is donating the sketches to the Moneybuckle Endowment absolutely and in perpetuity. That had been his intention from the beginning.'

'Bravo!' called Miss Chance, slapping the table vigorously with an open palm.

'That's an astonishingly generous action,' said Ostracher. 'Astonishingly generous,' he repeated. Slowly he rose from his seat, then walked around to Gavon and formally shook him by the hand. 'I'd no idea you had that in mind.' Then, looking the other straight in the eye, he added, 'You'll forgive me if I seemed to have misjudged your motives.'

'Not at all. Not at all,' responded an embarrassed Gavon, above the general hub-bub.

Charlotte smiled her own approval – less rapturously, perhaps, than most of the others, though not because she had been deprived of a notable article for her magazine. Simply, she had a presentiment that Bryan Gavon's benevolence might have been given an irresistible shove from somewhere.

Edith Norn had an exactly similar feeling.

And both women were right.

'Was it really just an inspired guess on your part, darling? Knowing those sketches came from the Moneybuckle dungeon?' Molly Treasure asked her husband. It was Saturday, a week later. The two were breakfasting in the sunshine, on the terrace of their Chelsea home.

Treasure looked up from the letter he was reading. 'I suppose it was. Not inspired, exactly. It stands to reason, things of that kind could easily have got into the original art collection unidentified. Probably picked

219

up by Theodore Moneybuckle himself as part of a job lot at auction. Then donated to the Endowment when he set up the place. When he needed to add general artistic bulk. It seems the architectural collection was quite slim at the start.'

'But you said this Edith Norn thought the stuff she was cataloguing was pretty worthless.'

'Not entirely. She told me she'd unearthed a possible Holman Hunt, and a Turner of Oxford. It turns out she was right about the first.'

'I see. And Bryan Gavon confessed to you in the end he'd lifted the Constables from the Moneybuckle? When she wasn't looking?'

Treasure swallowed some coffee before replying. 'Borrowed, he said. But no one else is to know that. Ever. He confessed, as you put it, soon after Midden went under the bus. Bryan was very shaken because the sketches had caused two deaths. At the time he was also scared stiff. He might not have come clean otherwise. And I'm ashamed to say I bullied him a bit into the bargain.'

'But, surely, he'd begun with the intention of telling all in the end? Of handing back the sketches when he'd done with them? After the *exposé* he and Charlotte Lundle were planning? Of course, that was all before the murder.'

'I hope that's what he really intended.' Treasure had put down the letter. 'Bryan insists neither Charlotte nor Edith knew where he really got the sketches,' he said.

'So was he scared about what could come out at a trial?' Molly's tone was concerned: she was fond of Bryan Gavon and his wife, especially Bryan.

'Early on, yes. But he needn't have been. Neither of the deaths have led to criminal proceedings. Only to hearings this week in the relative obscurity of the Oxford Coroner's Court.'

'Because the police know Midden was the murderer?'

'And because they don't prosecute dead men. Of course, Midden's own death was an accident witnessed by three

220

policemen. None of it's made the front page anywhere. The problem for Bryan has been to avoid stirring the ashes.'

'By having to admit he purloined the sketches in the first place?'

'And caused the deaths.'

'Only indirectly,' Molly protested.

Treasure shrugged. 'Whichever way, it would have made quite a news item. With all kinds of embarrassing ramifications. On the other hand, he couldn't go on claiming the sketches were his.'

'Well not after he'd told you they weren't. I suppose if you hadn't made him . . . ' Molly hesitated, then decided not to complete the hypothesis. 'So it was your idea he should donate the sketches to the Moneybuckle?' she ended.

'As the least . . . complicated solution. Incidentally, it seems to have increased Bryan's social status no end. *The Times*' Art Editor described him yesterday as a noted public benefactor. And I hear his company's credit rating has been uplifted at a particularly appropriate time.' He gave a wry chuckle.

'But in the end, they're not Constables after all?'

Treasure picked up the letter again. 'Decimus Radout writes that the tests neither proved nor disproved the authenticity of any of the three works. Though he and Barners still think they're the real thing.'

'So is that all right?'

'Not quite. It shouldn't spoil their being appreciated for what they are. Fine works of art. I'm sure they'll be much admired in Oxford, and when we loan them elsewhere. Properly insured.' He frowned over the last point. 'No, to say the least, it'd be more satisfying to know whether they really are from Constable's Oxford Sketchbooks. Or that they're inspired copies, or just deliberate fakes.'

'With the originals still lying in someone's dusty attic,' said Molly.

'Or in some other undisturbed archive. I mean it's beyond dispute that at least one Constable sketch of what he called Oxford Bridge did once exist.' He shook his head. 'It's inconceivable that anyone should knowingly have destroyed it.'

And so it still remains.